BOUNTY

A MOCKLORE COLLECTION

TANSY RAYNER ROBERTS

Bounty
Tansy Rayner Roberts
ISBN: 978-0-6481741-4-1 (ebook)
ISBN: 978-0-6481741-8-9 (print)

Collection first published in Australia in 2016
by FableCroft Publishing

This edition © 2018 published by the author
Cover design by Tania Walker © 2016

Hobgoblin Boots © 2004
Previously published: Scrybe Press

Queen of Courtesans © 2016

Delta Void & the Unicorn Soup © 2002
Previously published: AustrAlien Absurdities

Delta Void's Day Off © 2016

Delta Void & the Clockwork Man © 2002
Previously published: Agog! Fantastic Fiction

Delta Void & the Stray God © 2005
Previously published: Andromeda Spaceways Inflight Magazine 2005

The moral right of the author has been asserted.
All rights reserved. Without limiting the rights under copyright above, no part of this publication may be reproduced, stored in or introduced into a retrieval system, or transmitted in any form, or by any means (electronic, mechanical, photocopying, recording or otherwise), without the prior written permission of both the copyright owner and the above publisher of this book.

Created with Vellum

CONTENTS

I

BOUNTY FENETRE IS NOT A BOUNTY HUNTER

HOBGOBLIN BOOTS

HEROES

When I was thirteen years old, my mother ran away from home. No one was surprised. She had always been the flighty type. I was old enough to take care of myself anyway, always running off somewhere on an adventure or a scrape. Truth is, I was hardly home at all and when she left our village it is entirely possible that she just forgot about me.

Or maybe it was me she was running away from.

In any case, I was prepared to go it alone. I'd been planning to Seek My Fortune at some stage, so why not now? There was this cute little chainmail number at the smithy's which would suit me perfectly—well, it would once I figured out how to fix it so it bared my midriff. And boots, I was going to need some serious boots if I was going to make my way in the world. Yeah, I had it all sorted out.

Ma Fortuna had other ideas.

Everyone knows Ma Fortuna and no one ever argues with her. She wasn't born in our village: she just turned up one day, married old 'Ticker' Triclover and started producing kids by the bucketful. In the year my mother left, Ma Fortuna was a recent widow and just about the most respectable person in the cosmos. There was no way she was going to let a thirteen year old girl make her own way in the world—not without a good hot supper inside her, anyway. Minutes after the news of my mother's departure spread through the village, Ma Fortuna was standing on my doorstep with a hot kettle, a handful of dusters and a look of extreme determination.

Before the tea was cold, I had somehow agreed to come and live with her family. Don't ask me how it happened. I remember trying to explain what my plans were, but she just kept dusting things. The subject was closed.

So I was hustled with my few worldly belongings into the big, rambling house on the hill. I found myself in a kitchen teeming with the Triclover kids, ranging in ages from twelve to three years old. The one I was most wary of was Luco (Luc to his friends), Ma's firstborn and the Triclover with the most right to protest me being dragged into his family.

We had always been on opposite sides of the playground, Luc and I. While I was causing havoc with the Void twins among the girls, he was kinging it over the boys. I had never been able to figure out what they saw in him, a skinny little nobody like that. What had he done to make himself leader of the pack?

That evening, with the Triclover kids crowding around to set the table, most of them jostling into me as if I was already one of the clan, I caught Luc looking at me. He had a funny little face, a long nose and very serious eyes. When he saw me staring, he smiled. Not the slow, strange smile of a boy discovering girls for the first time—I'd seen enough of those that year.

No, it was nice. He looked like he was considering the possibility of liking me—and suddenly I liked him right back.

~

My name is Bounty Fenetre—proof, if anything, of how flighty my mother was. Truthfully, it's only a shortened version of the true horror she landed me with. The main benefit of losing my mother at the age of thirteen is that she isn't around to blab my full name to anyone.

I was born in the Year of the Vampyre Aelves. A lot of kids were born that year. The Market Faire was cancelled due to union problems, and it became necessary to remind mortals why Mocklore held a Market Faire every year. It's a tribute to the faerie folk of the OtherRealm—you know, the moonlight dimension, the unknown orchard, land of the fey —and when the Market Faire didn't happen, all hell broke loose. The Faerie Quene sent a horde of vampyre aelves to punish the thoughtless mortals with their wild magic, their intense sexual charisma, and their powerful commitment to pretentious spelling choices. The aelves tore across the land, seducing maidens (hence the population explosion), biting and brooding on rooftops and being really pedantic about grammar. Most of the kids born nine months later had extra sharp teeth, or the trendy pale-skin, black hair look. A few actually came out as pure vampyres, which caused some fun and games. Bet you didn't know it was hereditary.

Not me, though. My mum wouldn't settle for any old common or garden pixie. She batted her eyelashes at the Lord of the Hobgoblins, who was supervising the raid. So I'm half-hobgoblin, which means I have a genetic predisposition towards big eyes, narrow hips, rock-hard abdominal muscles and hair that can't settle to any style other than 'chaotic tangle'.

My father died. No, not died exactly. He faded away. You see, the Faerie Quene captured this princess, and these heroes went to rescue her, as heroes do—one thing led to another, and they ended up sealing the Faerie Quene and her son up in ice forever. The Quene's absence meant the vampyre aelves couldn't return to the OtherRealm, so they just went on seducing and brooding and breeding and composing a whole school of angsty epic poetry that the mortal world would be so much better without. The heroes managed to banish most of the aelves through a magic door, so the story goes, but they never found my father.

Fullblood fey folk can't spend more than a few days in the mortal world before they start to fade. That's what happened to Lord Nanneke of the Hobgoblins. Trapped here, he faded away. And I never knew him. So, there I was, not even born, already stuck with a flighty mother, a non-existent father and hobgoblin hips.

I spent the remainder of my childhood with the Triclovers and loved them dearly, but by the age of seventeen I had to get away on my own. Luc was sixteen by then and his case was even more urgent than mine. Ma Fortuna wanted him to go into the family business—chasing rogue clockwork through the Skullcap Mountains. If he didn't want to end up like his father, he had to find himself another career option—and fast.

~

There's a pond outside our village: a large murky puddle, adorned with lilies of an unfashionable colour and inhabited by the worst gang of second-rate water nymphs in the known world.

Mocklore Survival Guide #1: Water nymphs.
Worse than dryads, worse than ice sprites—hell, they're worse than graduates from Mistress Minx's Finishing School for Terminally Silly Damsels. If you ever have an

urge to ask a serious question of a water nymph, don't bother. You'll sacrifice three hours of your life for no good reason. She'll giggle for two of those hours, and she'll spend the rest of the time pulling your hair. For some reason, most straight mortal men find them incredibly attractive.

Not ours, though. Our pond nymphs don't attract the local boys, or any boys. I wouldn't want to be bitchy (gods forbid), but the sight of one of our nymphs would curdle wine. They go through all the traditional motions—they comb their hair with shells, and pout and giggle. But for some reason the poor lasses crawled out of the pond muck with the worst case of 'murder face' that the Empire has ever seen. They've been known to send full-grown men screaming into the night.

Anyway, there's a secluded patch of water separated from the main pond by a big clump of spiky reeds. We call it the Lagoon, and this is where the locals swim—mostly to avoid the nymphs, since they stick to the main pond (although their giggles are shrill enough to carry for leagues in every direction), but also because every now and then, a stranger passes by and decides to go for a dip. When you live in a tiny village, you have to get your entertainment where you can.

That's where Luc and I were that afternoon, floating lazily in the Lagoon (two swimming strokes wide and two swimming strokes long, three if there's been heavy rain) and contemplating our future. Ma Fortuna had not given up on Luc joining the family business, though she was temporarily placated when his younger brother Franc volunteered himself for clockwork duty.

Luc and I had been reluctantly granted permission to Seek Our Fortunes, as long as we vowed that if we didn't succeed at something within a year, we would come home, get married (either to each other or to equally suitable partners, we knew she had a list somewhere but didn't dare ask) and start producing Ma's first wave of grandchildren.

Needless to say, we were both pretty anxious that the whole Fortune Seeking thing would work out.

Luc ducked his head under the water, wetting his hair—he hated the way it curled up in every direction, even when cut as short as humanly possible. "What are you going to do, Bounty?" he asked me. "What do you want to do with your life?"

I pretended to think about it. "There's always my name-sake to consider." He looked at me in that familiar, half-puzzled way. I grinned and mouthed the words 'bounty hunter' at him.

"You wouldn't really." He sounded offended by the idea.

I splashed him. "Why not? I can't sing, I can't swoon, I hate dressmaking, I'm lousy at blacksmithing and the job of Emperor is already taken. What else am I qualified for?"

"You could be a hero," he suggested, and something in those thoughtful, dark eyes of his almost made me believe him.

I laughed it off. "Are you kidding? That's too unselfish for my style. Bounty-hunting will suit me down to the ground. Fewer overheads than piracy, less career pressure than the Profithood..." I mostly said it to wind him up. The whole point of Seeking my Fortune was to put off making any decisions about my future as long as possible. I was used to improvising.

Luc, though, I worried about Luc. What skills did he have that would keep him alive in the big bad world out there?

"Is that what *you* want to be?" I asked lightly. "A hero?"

He didn't answer, which made me nervous. He wasn't seriously considering it, was he? Suddenly he held up a hand. "We've got company."

I splashed the single stroke it took to reach the reeds and peered through to the main pond. "Speaking of heroes!"

Mocklore Survival Guide #2: Heroes.

You can see them coming a mile off. In Zibria they wear lion skins and sandals. In Axgaard they wear leather and beards (everyone wears leather and beards in Axgaard). Everywhere else, they dress like overblown actors with a fairy tale fixation. There are always a few common factors. A sword—heroes have to have a sword. It's the law. And a smug, self-righteous expression. But it's the horse that really gives them away.

Despite my tender age of seventeen, I had done my fair share of travelling. I'd even climbed the Skullcaps and lived to tell the tale. That particular round trip takes anywhere from a week to six months, depending on how many magical catastrophes, alternate dimensions and mutant goats you run across—and this was in the days before the Glimmer made everything a hundred times worse.

Anyway, I had been around enough to know that if you've got yourself a good pair of boots, the only places in Mocklore you can't get to on foot are not the kind of places where you take a horse—ravines, swamps, sentient jungles, that sort of thing. Apart from spring ploughing (if you can't afford oxen) and the occasional carriage going up and down the Great Mocklore Road, there isn't a lot of use for horsepower.

If you see a man sitting on the back of a horse: chances are he's in the hero business.

The fellow visiting our pond on that particular day was dressed like Prince Charming gone bad. Very, very bad. I peeked through the rushes at his ruffled whiter-than-white shirt, his shiny black leather trews (leather should never be shiny), his long dove grey boots, his shoulder-length curly tresses, his hat with a feather in it. I whispered to Luc, "So this is your future, boyo?" I swallowed back the words, 'are you sure?' because Luc was a lot like me—the quickest way to talk him into something was to suggest it was a bad idea.

Luc didn't laugh. He was too busy staring at Prince Charming. "He looks it," he whispered to me, quite seriously. "He looks the part. That's got to be the first step."

When Luc puts his brain in gear, it's amazing the things he can come up with. On that particular balmy afternoon, he came up with a doozy of a plan. He tore his eyes away from Hero Boy and flashed me that sudden cheerful grin, the one that was starting to have a serious swoony effect on the other girls in the village. "Let's steal his clothes."

~

Separating a hero from his clothes is easier than you'd think. Don't forget, I have these big, long-lashed hobgoblin eyes going for me. Plus a handy pond. To be honest, the pond did most of the work for me. It was warm, and Hero Boy had already decided to go for a swim. He swung a leg over the back of his horse and jumped down to the bank, pulling off his dove grey boots. I could conquer the world with boots like those.

The whiter-than-white ruffled shirt and the feathered hat followed the boots, then Hero Boy eased himself out of his shiny black leather trews, which took quite a long time. I could have averted my eyes modestly, but I didn't.

Mind you, I had to stifle a shout of laughter when Hero Boy's curly black wig joined the rest of the clothes pile.

Once he was stripped (apart from an oversized pair of long-johns which didn't match the hero aesthetic but provided vital protection from leather chafing), Hero Boy plunged with a meaty splash into the middle of our village pond.

Under usual circumstances, three things would happen at this point:

1) The water nymphs would appear, as if from nowhere.

2) They would pounce on the hapless stranger and attempt to seduce him.

3) The hapless stranger's response would be to run screaming from the pond, taking his clothes with him.

To prevent this from happening, I whistled softly beneath my breath, my mouth half in and half out of the water at the point where the pond meets the beginning of the Lagoon. It was a tune my mother used to sing to me and I think it has some magic in it because it's worked a few times.

It was working now. Instead of terrifying our visitor with their murder faces, the pond nymphs drifted towards the Lagoon. They raised their aggressive eyebrows up out of the water and stared at me. Even at a distance they gave me the chills, their writhing watery veins trapped under see-through skin, and their chins sharper than pick-axes. "Whass you doing?" hissed Globula, the bluest of them.

"We goss a hero ssoo pounce on," complained the greenish one (I can never remember her name) in a wet whisper.

"I know," I said. "But just this once, could you let me do the pouncing? I fancy a go at it."

The watery pond nymphs all looked at me suspiciously.

"Whass for?" said Gremmla finally. She's the one that's almost yellowish, but not quite.

I knew what she was asking. Fair trade. Like most fey folk, water nymphs use promises as their currency. "What do you want?" I asked her.

"Whass you willing ssoo promise?" she belted back, looking pleased with herself for her stellar negotiation skills.

I tried to think of something they might like. "I'm going out into the big wide world this week. I promise that on my first visit home, I'll bring you some water lilies in a decent colour."

This had the desired effect. The poor things had been living with beige lilies for far too long. Their eyes lit up—a scary sight, since their eyes look like angry swirls of muddy water on a good day.

"Purple?" choked Globula as if she could hardly believe it.

"Blue, pink!" clamored the greenish one.

"Crimsssssson," said Gremmla in a firm voice.

"All colours," I said extravagantly, then stopped myself. "Wait, I don't want to be held to that one. How about if I promise at least three reasonably exciting colours of lily?"

They hesitated, but agreed to it. We kissed each other's noses to seal the deal (not something I recommend anyone do with nymphs who belong to a stagnant body of water). I pulled off my bathing chemise. "Okay, ladies. Watch and learn."

Hero Boy was splashing around in the water with his back to me. Unfortunately, he was facing his pile of clothes. I could see Luc hovering in the trees to my left, unwilling to make a move until Hero Boy was suitably distracted.

I've always been good at causing distractions.

I rolled silently on to my back and began to stroke lazily towards Hero Boy. He made such a noise with his splashing that he didn't see me until I crashed into him. I dove under the water and emerged with a squeal. "Oh, *sir*! What are you doing?"

My outraged tone and obvious nakedness did the trick. He apologised so many times that I thought his tongue might fall out (not that he wasn't getting a good eyeful at the same time).

I squealed a bit more, mostly about what my father and

six older brothers would do when they found out about this scandal. Hero Boy paled at the thought of seven burly farmers coming after him, and prepared to make a hasty exit. He turned just in time to see Luc making away with his clothes. He roared and ran after him, but didn't get very far because a) he was naked and barefoot and b) among other things, Luc had stolen his horse.

~

By the time Luc and I met up, deep in the woods around our village, we were both laughing so hysterically that neither of us could talk. Even the horse was amused—I don't think he'd been too impressed by his previous owner.

In case you're wondering, yes I *had* taken the time to snatch up my own clothes, and I was now respectably dressed.

It was time to examine the loot. Along with the clothes and the horse, there were a couple of well-stuffed saddlebags. Not too shabby for our first efforts at Seeking our Fortune. As long as Ma never found out about this, we'd be right.

While Luc tried to figure out how to button up a white ruffled shirt, I tried on the dove-grey boots. They were very good boots. They went all the way up to my knees, which you couldn't see under my modest village dress (hand-stitched by Ma Fortuna) but I was already planning a new outfit around the boots.

"Hey, hand them over," Luc protested when he noticed I had staked my claim.

I tossed the black curly wig at him. "Consider them my commission. Just be glad I didn't take a fancy to the leather trews. What's the sword like?"

Luc looked embarrassed. "I didn't take his sword."

I paused halfway in the act of unbuckling the first saddlebag. Of all the necessary props for a hero, a sword is right up there. "*Why not?*"

Luc shuffled his feet. "Well, it might have been an heirloom."

"No," I said, gingerly removing my arm from inside the saddlebag and flipping it open so he could see the contents. "I think *this* is the heirloom."

Inside the saddlebag was a huge, oozing, rotting troll head. Turned out our Hero Boy was more impressive than your average show-pony. He'd bagged a troll.

"I feel sick," said Luc. He did look pretty green.

"No time for that," I said brightly. "It's time to say our goodbyes and hit the open road. This gives me *such* a brilliant idea."

TAVERNS

The first step to becoming a hero is to look like one. The second step is to be recognised as a hero, by other heroes as well as by the world at large. As far as I could see, short of actually spending a few years performing good deeds and buttering up news minstrels, there was only one way to achieve hero recognition.

Sure, this was tossing Luc in at the deep end. But even if he sank without a trace, he'd at least get a glimpse of what real heroes looked and acted like. Maybe it would put him off the idea.

Mocklore Survival Guide #3: Taverns.

There are a lot of these in Mocklore. Inns, hostelries, watering holes, ale houses, wine bars, beer bars, home-brewed cider bars. When a community is stuck on a small island, they want to be sure they can get a drink around every corner. As well as the ordinary taverns, there are the trade bars. There's a profit-scoundrel bar in Dreadnought, an assassin bar at the top of the Teatime Mountain, a woodcutter bar behind every other oak tree and about fourteen exotic dancer/spy bars in Zibria. There's even an ex-Emperor bar somewhere in Skullcap now, though that wasn't around in our youth.

Unless you're an exotic dancer (they're welcome everywhere except the Sparkling Nuns' Beer Hut), you don't set foot into a trade tavern without belonging to the trade. Everyone still remembers that nasty incident when two blacksmiths accidentally walked into the Braidmakers' Community Cabaret Club. Braidmakers are scary.

There's a hero bar, obviously. It's smack bang in the middle of the city of Axgaard, which is such a hero thing to do—you have to be brave to walk through Axgaard in daylight, let alone during traditional drinking hours. Getting as far as the Twelve Labours Saloon is a heroic quest all on its own. The streets are filled with sword-wielding maniacs and prematurely-bearded children playing target games with knives and each other's braids.

Luc and I had thought out our plan carefully. Well, I had thought it out carefully and then spent a lot of time talking him into it. I was in costume as an exotic dancer, which involved a lacy white two-piece dress and lots of jingling beads. Luc was dressed in the Hero Boy costume, with his old brown boots blacked up for the occasion. Naturally, I was hanging on to the lovely long grey boots we'd stolen.

The horse was far too sensible to allow itself to be dragged within the city walls, so we tethered it to a tree before going in.

The Twelve Labours Saloon stood in the city square, bright white from roof to welcome mat. It was built from shiny white stone, surrounded by pillars. It would look perfect in Zibria, where every building is either a temple or just looks like one, but in the shambling, lopsided city of Axgaard (built from splintering timber and rusty nails from old orange boxes) it stood out like a naked male troll in a convent. Still, at least it stayed up whenever the rest of the city burned down around it, which happened every other week.

"What now?" Luc whispered.

"Relax," I hissed back. "Whatever happens, go along with me and act *cool*. You're a hero now. Confidence is your middle name."

"Right," he said uncertainly. My hero.

The noise from inside the Twelve Labours Saloon was deafening. Clashing tankards harmonised with raucous laughter, loud belching, bad piano music and the sound of fists smashing into furniture. It was quite restrained compared to the goings on in the street around us, so I didn't hesitate to march through the door. Luc waited in the street for his cue.

I should explain that in Mocklore the hero business is mostly a male profession. There are a few women who do it, but they are the kind of girls who are far too pragmatic to hang out in bars. The first time I realised this with any degree of clarity was while standing in that doorway.

All eyes looked at me. Male eyes. I've never felt so outnumbered in my life. Somewhere, a bloke playing a piano struck a few false notes and then lapsed into silence. I know this is an often-used psychological trick to intimidate people, but it was working.

Still, I had a job to do. I had a bosom to heave and I was damn well going to heave it. I took a deep breath and the bosom started heaving all on its own. I clasped my hands together in a traditional distressed maiden pose and let them have it. "Trolls! On the Great Road, swarming all over me!"

Now I was properly categorised as a damsel in distress with news of a potential adventure, the heroes dropped their hostility. One of them, a giant of a bloke wearing a black leather jerkin over a shirt even whiter and frillier than Luc's, leaped to his feet and pounded a fist against the wall, causing a thin shower of marble dust to fall down from the high ceiling. "A troll, you say?" he roared in delight. "What you need is a HERO!"

"Augghhyeah!!" chorused the others, smashing their tankards over each other's heads.

One hero, smaller than the rest, sighed and pulled his twirly moustache. "I don't believe you used that line *again*," he complained.

"It's a classic," protested the giant in ruffles, pouting.

"There's a chasm between classic and cliché," groaned the hero with the moustache. "And not one of you morons can tell the difference."

I felt myself losing control of the conversation. "There's already a hero facing those monsters," I gasped, swooning against a pillar and hanging on to it for dear life. "Luco the Magnificent, the greatest hero I have ever known. But he's outnumbered four to one, I fear he is lost forever!"

"Right, Thimbleknees," bellowed the giant hero, dragging the thin moustached hero up out of his chair and setting him on his feet. "Let's go. And if you say one more word about my dramatic monologues, I'll bloody thump you!"

Right on cue, the tavern door flew open. The piano player, caught flatfooted, started playing jauntily again for a few seconds before striking the traditional false notes and lapsing into silence.

Luc stood there in the doorway: some of my best work, even if I do say so myself. With a few stitches here and there (lucky Ma Fortuna taught him to use a needle), the hero costume fit him perfectly. The black curls of the wig were perfectly slightly askew, and a touch of face powder (Corpse White No. 8) gave him the dramatic vampyre aesthetic that was so fashionable with our generation.

He gripped the huge, dripping troll head in one hand, allowing the blood to pool on the floor. We'd bought a bag of blood and mutton chunks from a butcher's stall to freshen up the head after so many days mouldering in a saddlebag.

When Luc spoke, his voice bounced off the marble walls. Living with younger siblings really teaches you to project. "I told you there was no need to go for help, fair maiden. Four trolls is hardly enough to build up a sweat!" He dropped the head on the floor with a heavy squelch, stepped casually over it and headed for the bar. "Is anyone going to buy me a drink?"

There was a long pause.

In a sane universe, he would have been beaten up. They would have seen through him in an instant and smashed his face in or hung him upside down from the roof gutters. Luc knew this, which is why it took me so long to talk him into my brilliant plan. But I was counting on something he didn't even know he had: a strange, unexplainable charisma that had transformed the most average boy in the school into a king of the playground. Luc had something that made everyone like him and look up to him. Even me, and I don't look up to anyone. Maybe it was a genetic thing from Ma Fortuna—who rocked the ability to make everyone follow even the most unreasonable of demands (hence me wearing a respectable dress for the past four years).

But Luc wasn't like that. He didn't *make* people do anything. They did it because they genuinely liked him and they wanted him to like them. I was careful to only take advantage of this sparingly, because if he ever realised the truth about his talent, he had the potential to become the most insufferable (and dangerous) person in the Mocklore Empire.

I held my breath for a full minute, but it was worth the wait. It worked. One minute they were staring at Luc like they couldn't figure out whether to kill him or just rip his arms off, and the next they were slapping him on the back and buying him drinks. Lots of drinks.

Soon, they were all rowdily settled around a table swapping troll stories. Luc was among them, swept up in an ocean of ruffled white shirts, tight leather trousers and foaming beer tankards.

It was a good half an hour before anyone noticed me again, and that was when the trouble started. I was dangling my legs on one of the rickety bar stools, sipping something sweet. I'm a sucker for drinks that come out of pretty bottles. This one tasted like a cross between cherry cordial and salt-whisky. I was bored, keeping half an ear on the conversation of the heroes—they had moved on from trolls to giants and were all lying their arses off.

A hand slapped me on the shoulder, spinning me around. Luckily, the stool wasn't up to much, or the force of that blow might have had me whizzing around for hours. Instead, the stool rotated once and cracked hard, leaving me jammed lopsidedly against the bar. I twisted my neck up to see who was responsible. Uh-oh.

She was scary. Half a foot taller than me and far more intimidating in the bust region. She was squeezed into a bronze corset that made her look like a tiny-waisted giantess. Metal bangles lined her muscular arms. Her copper-red hair jangled in thousands of tiny braids, each holding either a bell or a blade. Her skirt was a short curtain of metal coins. Her bare thighs were toned slabs of lethal weapon. Even her boots were shinier than mine.

She was a real exotic dancer, and I was in trouble.

The dancer sneered at me, leaned her bosom forward and shoved her nose about an inch from mine. "What the hell do you think you are?"

I didn't have the nerve to claim that I shared status with her—it was laughable. This woman was a professional. "Damsel in distress," I squeaked.

She raised an eyebrow in such a scorching expression of disdain that I'm surprised my fringe didn't catch fire. "Distress?"

Well, I was in distress now. I pointed at Luc amid the gang of boasting heroes, none of whom had noticed my predicament. "He rescued me. From a troll."

The scary bronze woman didn't back off. Instead, she pointed her muscular finger at the tawdry line of bells I had made Luc stitch to my damsel-in-distress frock. "Looks to me like you fancy yourself as a bit of a *dancer*."

Shit, I was going to die.

The heroes finally sniffed out a brewing fight. This wasn't helpful. Chairs scraped back as they all tried to get a better view, and some weasel-nosed skeezebucket scratched odds on the menu blackboard. Luc looked worried.

I'd like to say that what I did next was to prevent him getting his head pulled off by the scary bronze lady when he inevitably tried to rescue me, but it was nothing so rational. The combination of an audience of leather-clad men, an unbeatable female opponent and odds of 100-1 against my survival brought out the worst in me.

I pushed myself off the broken bar stool. Fortunately, her nose was no longer pressed into my face. Unfortunately, this was because she was now a whole foot taller than me. I gave her the hobgoblin stare—it's an ability that anyone with a smidgen of fey folk blood is born with, an ability to look at someone as if you are the mistress of the universe and they are the dirt under your fingernails.

Usually it forces my opponent to step back a bit and check they don't have crumbs in their teeth. The scary bronze lady didn't even flinch. Instead, her mouth twitched into a purr of a smile, and she stuck out her hand. "Lilya."

Cautiously, I clasped my hand to hers. "Bounty."

As soon as I touched her hand, I realised my mistake. Her grip changed, and I was suddenly airborne. The ceiling twisted up to meet me, and THUD. I lay on my back, the wind knocked out of me. Lilya grinned in triumph and brought her hands together a few times in a slow clap. The heroes joined in.

The dratted piano started up again with a boppy tune that matched the beat. Lilya began to dance. Given that I wasn't sure I would ever walk again, I had no choice but to watch her. And damn, she was good. She stomped and spun and turned her body inside out with rippling stomach action. Her body was steel one minute; water the next. She flowed and oozed and rattled and shimmied. She was sexy as hell.

I crawled painfully to the door, my back screaming in a hundred different ways. Lilya's meaty hand grasped the back of my skimpy outfit and dragged me to my feet by my breast-band. I hung from her hand, a few inches off the floor. She still moved in perfect time to the music. Then she dropped me, clapped her hands and slapped them once against her thighs.

Everyone looked expectantly at me. Waiting for me to join the dance. Now, I'd seen combat dancing before. It's a nasty business—someone always ends up maimed. In the crowd, I found Luc's steady gaze, and remembered that I'd talked him into striding into a hero bar with a giant troll's head bleeding from his hand. The least I could do was do a bit of dancing.

My back screamed out in a hundred new and interesting ways as I clapped my hands, slapped my thighs and accepted the invitation to dance. Even now, years later, most of that night is a foggy blur of painful, sweaty memories. Lilya and I danced and jumped and shimmied our butts off in a stomping, sweating duel. After an hour or so, the heroes stopped watching and wandered back to swap stories and play cards. We barely noticed. We weren't dancing for them.

Finally, somewhere near midnight, my hobgoblin stamina deserted me. I slumped over a bar stool, my legs trembling in a paralysed, jelly custard kind of way. "I give up. You win."

Lilya hoisted me up so I was sitting properly on the bar stool. "Well, yeah," she said with a toothsome grin. "Buy me a drink, sweetheart?"

I nodded hazily, signaling to the barman. "You bet, babe."

A few minutes later, one of the larger bearded heroes came up beside us to order a huge round of beer. "That new bloke's not bad," he said with an impressed kind of leer. "Eight trolls in one day. Can't do better than that."

"Oh, he's a champ," I managed through a haze of cherry cordial and salt-whisky with extra gin for good measure.

When the sun rose the next morning, Lilya and I staggered arm in arm out of the tavern, barely able to stand without each other's help. We found Luc tied to a flagpole in the middle of the square, draped in women's underwear and garlands of flowers. Various axes were stuck in the pole from where they had been drunkenly thrown at him.

"They called your bluff?" I asked sympathetically.

"No," he said in a stunned, croaky voice. "This is what they do when they *like* you. They think I'm one of them!"

I let go of Lilya and she crashed to the cobblestones with a booming thump. I squinted up at Luc, trying to gauge how easily it would be to get him down in my current inebriated state. "Fancy a drink?"

PRINCESSES

Okay, so Luc had been accepted into the hero community. He even had an official licence scrawled in crayon on the back of a beer mat. Now it was time to introduce him to the world in general—after all, heroes don't go around advertising each other. My own portrayal of a damsel in distress was less than convincing, so what we needed to do was find a blushing maiden and make her think Luc had saved her life.

You might think it would be easier to find a damsel in distress and *actually* save her life. Maybe so, but my mind doesn't work that way.

We'd been walking for several days since Axgaard, dragging the reluctant horse behind us. We were near Zibria when we saw the carriage.

Remember what I said about horses, and how no one in their right mind would ride one across the messy landscape of Mocklore? That goes double for carriages. Triple, quadruple—if I could think of a word that meant more times than quadruple, I'd use it. Away from the cities or the Great Mocklore Road, no one would even consider travelling in a horse-drawn carriage.

Nevertheless, there it was. A carriage bumped its way along the lower Zibrian moorland, occasionally lodging a spindly wheel in an oversized rabbit-hole. As carriages go, it was as impractical as humanly possible. It was round and pumpkin-shaped, which means the occupants would have to curl up inside like hunchbacked slugs. It was also gilded, which made it prey for any passing thug or profit-scoundrel —at least, it would if the constant jolting of the journey hadn't scraped off half the gilt work.

The profit-scoundrels were probably following behind at a safe distance, picking the golden flakes off the trees and rocks. The wheels of the carriage were high and thin. They kept getting snagged on branches, tall blades of grass and the aforementioned rabbit holes. The two horses pulling the damn thing were covered from head to toe in silver bells, cockle-shells and other atrocities of beadwork. The contraption lurched from side to side despite the desperate flailings of a queasy coachman. By the looks of it, a gust of wind from the wrong direction would collapse coach, horses and all into a pile of very attractive rubble.

Inside the carriage, there was a princess. There would have to be, really.

Mocklore Survival Guide #4: Princesses.

Technically, there aren't any in Mocklore any more, given that a princess should be the daughter of a king, a queen or an emperor. Kings and queens were abolished sometime in the last century, and Emperor Timregis (this was in the days before he was horribly assassinated) had been on the throne nearly fifty years without producing an heir. However, because people like having princes and princesses around (for the sake of fairy tales if nothing else), the rules of etiquette were rewritten so that the children of Lordlings were given the honorary status of prince/esses.

The summer I turned seventeen and went to Seek Fortune, there were exactly two princesses in Mocklore, both daughters of the Jarl of Axgaard. One of them was crowned Jarl herself a few years later, and the other took herself off to join the Sparkling Nuns. I knew instantly that this was not one of the Axgaard girls. No braids, no rosy cheeks, no battle-axes cunningly disguised as jewellery. This was a foreign princess, a different kettle of fish altogether.

Mocklore Survival Guide #5: Foreign Princesses.

Foreign princesses visiting the Mocklore Empire follow a

certain pattern. They wear floaty dresses, pointy hats and wistful expressions. Occasionally a few of them come here looking for husbands (preferably princes or heroes) but they tend to get scared off by the various magical explosions, mysterious events and dangerous creatures that most native Mocklorns take for granted. Occasionally, they get eaten by dragons. But that only happened twice.

This girl was the foreign princess to end all foreign princesses. Her hat had not one, but two pointy bits. Instead of going straight up, the pointy bits curled around in an elaborate headdress from which tiny silver beads dangled prettily. A mesh of jeweled netting held the rest of the princess's blonde hair in place. Her gown was velvet, attached to a fluffy cape that trailed out of both windows of the carriage. Both the gown and the cape were pink. Why anyone would deliberately create pink velvet is beyond me. But there you are. There she was. A painted doll crying out to be rescued from something.

I couldn't hold myself back.

In order to put my latest devilishly cunning plan into action, Luc and I had to go fishing. Luckily, it's something we're both rather good at. Within two hours we had a hoard of a dozen large trout and several handfuls of tiddlers.

"It's a waste of good fish," Luc warned me.

I grinned at him, stuffing my bodice with tiddlers. "You're saying that because you didn't think of it first."

We left the stream and made our way across the uneven ground. There was no road, of course, so the stupid carriage had only rattled along about half a mile during the time we had taken to gather our fish. "Up, I think," I said to Luc. He smiled back at me, liking this part. We're both champion tree-climbers from way back—truth be told, he's a smidge better at it than I am, even taking skirts into account.

We swarmed up separate trees, jumping from branch to branch until we were right over the carriage, which was stuck in yet another rabbit hole. I pulled a trout out of Luc's sack, aimed carefully and struck the coachman in the left ear. He jumped wildly and stared at the fish as it flopped on the ground. Luc threw two fish in quick succession, one hitting the coach and the other slapping the coachman on the back of his head. The coachman looked up in alarm, but the foliage was thick enough to hide us from sight. I let a handful of tiddlers dribble through my fingers. They plopped against the coach and pattered around the poor idiot's feet.

With a strangled yelp, the coachman threw himself at the carriage door and scrambled inside. "Your highness!" we heard. "It's a rain of fish! We must shelter, I've heard *terrible* stories!"

I grinned. Good to see traditions surviving, such as the grand old tavern tradition that all servants of foreign aristocrats must be told horror stories about Mocklore's environmental hazards until they are quivering wrecks.

A princessly voice reached us from within the carriage. "Do something about it!" she commanded.

Luc leaned out of his branch and lobbed a large trout so perfectly that it bounced inside the window of the carriage. I could have kissed him. The princess and the coachman both screamed in unison.

I left Luc in charge of fish-hurling, and scampered down from the branches. Time to make my entrance. I threw myself at the carriage, beating on the door. "Please, please help me! Give me shelter from the rain of fish!"

"Don't let it in!" cried the princess, miserable cow.

I looked pitiful, clawing gently at the door, trying to get the coachman's sympathy.

"It's only a girl, your highness," he said.

Luc lobbed a medium-sized trout at the carriage, which bounced off and slapped me in the bosom. I'm not sure how deliberate it was, but I screamed loudly enough to be convincing, and the coachman swung the door open to drag me inside.

The curvy insides of the carriage were well padded but desperately uncomfortable, particularly with three of us packed in. Not that I was busy gawping at the décor. I had a job to do. It involved hysterical sobbing, plus dialogue. "Oh, thank you, kind sir, my lady. The storm came up so suddenly, and I was afeared! I've heard of people drowning in fish season."

"Yes, I've heard that," the coachman agreed. Bless those precious tavern stories.

The princess wrinkled her nose and was about to say something, but Luc had the great timing to smack more trout down on the roof of the carriage, along with a couple of rocks to shake us up.

"Ohhh!!" screamed the princess, grabbing at the coachman.

"Oh-ohhhh!!" screamed the coachman, grabbing my knee.

I managed not to grab anyone, but I bounced a few times to make the carriage rattle, and joined in the screaming. "What will we do?" I wailed. "This could go on for days and the carriage will break under the weight of all the fish!"

Since the princess and the coachman both had their eyes tightly shut, I grabbed the last handful of tiddlers from my bodice and threw them at the pointy headdress. Some of them stuck there. The rest tumbled down into her highness's royal lap.

"Ooooooh," she squealed.

Then, bless him, I heard Luc's hero voice. He was getting awfully good at dramatic timing. "Don't worry!" he bellowed from outside. "I'll save you!"

And he did.

What we pretended later was that he had thrown a giant fishhook at the carriage, secured it, and pulled the weight of the carriage, occupants and horses at great speed for several miles across the countryside. It made a great story, and Luc looked suitably modest while he told it.

The truth, of course, was that he hitched our horse up to their horses and let them do the work until we were in a suitably different-looking bit of Zibrian countryside. The coachman and the princess were both so shaken that they had no problem believing our version, particularly as they didn't know Luc and I were in league together.

We ate rabbit for supper—barbecued over the campfire, half-charred and delicious. I managed to drip a few hints to Princess Desirée (can you believe someone seriously gave that name to a princess? Why not just call her 'Marry-me-quick') about how Luco the Magnificent was a Baron in disguise, and half these lands belonged to him. Her eyes sparkled.

Luc got wind of what I was doing and dragged me away from the others under the pretext of showing me 'the way to that village you mentioned, young lady.'

"What the hell do you think you're doing, Bounty?" he hissed.

I acted innocent. Big hobgoblin eyes are good for that. "I'm helping."

"*How* are you helping?"

"Well, now she thinks you're a Baron, she's definitely interested. And once we show her the castle—"

"I don't have a castle!"

"What I thought was, I'd go ahead and tip a few peasants

some coin to say these lands belong to Baron Luco, and clear the way for you to the castle."

"What castle, Bounty?"

"When we were kids, the Void twins told me about the old witch city of Shadowe, and how their Uncle Imago turned it into a giant castle. It's not far from here."

"I can only think of one reason why someone would want a giant castle, and it doesn't sound good," said Luc suspiciously.

"Technically he's not a giant, apart from being forty feet tall—but that's not important. What I thought was, I could talk him into lying low for a bit. We only need a teeny bit of giant castle to impress the princess over there, and we can always promise old Uncle Imago a cut of the dowry if she…"

"If she what?" Luc demanded. "If she marries me? Is that the plan here, Bounty? Because I thought we were Seeking our Fortune as an *alternative* to settling down and getting married!"

"Marriage to a foreign princess is a Fortune," I argued. "You'll be made for life."

I've never seen Luc so angry and so cold at the same time. "Some simpering little rich wife to keep me in velvet shoes and roast peacock? Is that what you think I want? Or do you want me married off so you can strut away and start your brand new life with a clear conscience?"

That last guess was uncomfortably accurate, apart from the strutting bit. "Luc, you're overreacting. I wanted to give you a good start in life before I start my adventures. It's not like we were planning to hang out together forever!"

He stared at me with ice in his eyes. Hurt, wounded ice. He turned on his heel and went back to the campfire.

I sat down suddenly. My legs didn't feel like standing upright. Had he thought we were a life partnership? That didn't make sense. He *knew* me. He knew I was fickle, and shallow, and heartless… and despite all that, I had a horrible feeling that he might be in love with me.

Ouch.

~

I didn't go back to the campfire for a long time. When I did, the princess was fast asleep, curled up in her ornate carriage like a particularly bendy kitten. The coachman sprawled out on the grass, snoring noisily. Luc was still awake.

"I don't want to talk," he muttered.

I hesitated. "I don't suppose you want to go on with the giant castle plan, either?"

"No."

"So what do we do?"

He looked at me, finally, and the ice was still there. "I think you should follow your other plan, Bounty. The one about us going our separate ways."

"But you're not—" I swallowed what I was going to say, but Luc caught it anyway.

"Not ready? Not set for life? I can take care of myself, Bounty. It *is* possible. I don't need to marry a princess and I don't need you."

I had been going about this wrong. Protecting him, making all these plans on his behalf—he would never really grow up and stand on his own two legs until I was gone. The best thing I could do for him was leave. I should have done it from the start. It was going to hurt more, this way.

Luc was there suddenly, standing close to me. He took the bag off me and let it fall to the grass. "Not right now," he said softly. "You might break your leg in the dark."

"I can see in the dark," I whispered back. "And it's a full moon." The sky was black around us, no moon in sight. "I mean, it will be. When it pops up. Which could be any minute now."

Luc hesitated, and his fingertips touched mine. "I thought," he muttered. "If we're splitting up for good, if that's it, then—"

If I was leaving, then I could do the thing that I'd been wondering about for half my life. It wasn't like I had to worry about making things more complicated, not if I wasn't going to see him again for months, or years.

So, yes. I shoved my mouth in his general direction, and kissed him square on the mouth. Neither of us had much practice at this, but we figured it out pretty fast.

To my surprise—or maybe not—Luc slid his arms around my waist, pressed his hand into my hair, and sneakily turned the kiss into something more sweet and gentle than I had intended. "I love you, Bounty," he mumbled into my mouth.

"Still want me to leave?" I had to check.

"Yes," he said without hesitation.

"Good." I slipped my fingers into his belt, started untucking his white shirt. "Those are the only circumstances under which I would do this."

"I know," he said, and pulled me down on to the grass.

I had been keeping tabs on him via the village girls (no particular reason, I'm nosy, that's all), and I knew for a fact that this was his first time, but his fingers and his mouth felt pretty expert to me. We kissed and we touched and we rolled a little way away from the dying campfire, for the sake of modesty.

His skin was silver in the darkness and I suppose mine must have been too. When the moment came, of total naked togetherness, he held me tight and wouldn't let me go.

Finally, he slept. When he woke up, I wouldn't be there. It was the beginning of a pattern that would last a lifetime, and I was okay with that.

CHAINMAIL

There was a Memorable Moon that night. Our moon-cycles in Mocklore are as unpredictable as rainfall—the moon can wax and wane over a day and half if she feels so inclined, or she can stretch it over weeks and weeks and weeks. One year we had the same crescent moon for four months. You don't want to know what that sort of thing does to the tides—but it explains our lack of seaside towns, and why the fishing trade is considered the most dangerous of professions.

Once in a while, the erratic cycles catch up with the moon and she gives everyone a treat for putting up with her frivolous behaviour. She swells into extra-fat fullness and hangs in the sky like a huge, beautiful teardrop. She becomes so wonderful, so powerful that people fall in and out of love without even noticing. Children are conceived, nightflowers bloom and the barriers between this world and the next open up a little wider than usual. We call it a Memorable Moon. It changes lives.

That night, lying on the grass in the middle of nowhere, I watched the moon rise and I knew what kind of moon it was. I watched it while I found my clothes and tugged on my boots. I kept watching it as I walked out of the castle and into the castle, heading toward my next adventure, leaving Luc behind.

If I'd thought to watch where I was going instead of staring at the damned moon all night, things might have turned out differently. But, no. My eyes were full of moon and my head was full of thoughts, so I didn't even realise when my feet first crossed from one world to the next.

The first thing I noticed was the voices. Whispering, teasing voices. I thought it was the trees or the wind or the wind in the trees. It's a logical assumption. You hear a hollow howling, a gentle whispering, a chitter-chattering of nothing in particular and you think—wind, trees. Even if your blood is of the fey, you think that. But then you catch words in the wind, questions in the trees and you realise it's something else altogether.

Invisible fingers tugged at the tiny hairs on my skin. They scampered across the back of my neck, traced the line of my spine, rattled in my ears. Tiny voices pricked and poked at me.

Whoareyouwhodoyouthinkyouarewhyareyouhere?

I retraced my steps and flung myself around in circles. I walked quickly and I ran and I rolled around in the dirt, but nothing would shake them off. I pinched and I slapped, but the scampering fingers and the grabbing little voices hung on for dear life.

Whoareyouwhodoyouthinkyouarewhyareyouhere?

Louder and louder they questioned me, tugged at me, grazed their teeth across my skin.

Whoareyouwhodoyouthinkyouarewhyareyouhere?

Eventually, I broke. I screamed out my true name—I whispered it, yelled it, chattered it, sang it, shrieked it over and over, but it wasn't enough to satisfy them. I could see faces now, bursting out of tree trunks and the night sky and the ground at my feet.

Whoareyouwhodoyouthinkyouarewhyareyouhere?

Their voices pressed against me, rough and demanding, with such intensity that I thought I would fly apart into a million tumbling pieces. I stared pleadingly at the moon that had got me into this mess, but she was having none of helping the likes of me. My insides went very calm as I realised the answer, the one that would satisfy all three questions at the same time. I knew where I was, and I knew what they wanted.

I dropped to one knee. The clawing, prying fingers fell away from my skin. I spoke in as steady a voice as I could manage under the circumstances. Somehow, it turned into a scream. "I am Bountiful Julietta Esmereldina Fenetre, daughter of Lord Nanneke of the Hobgoblins! *I belong here.*"

The trees crashed together and a figure climbed out from under them. He was small and gnarled, with nut-brown skin. As he shambled along, he trailed wispy ropes of hair and braided grass behind him. He wore a ragged robe of berry beads and oozing weeds. His face was peaceful and ugly. His eyes were sharp and beautiful.

"Well," he grumbled. "Why did you not say so in the first place?"

> Mocklore Survival Guide #6: The OtherRealm.
>
> *Also known as the unknown orchard, the moonlight dimension, the land of the fey. The beginning of the end and the end of the beginning. Scary stuff. Scary, beautiful stuff. I can't describe what it's like there, not with any degree of accuracy. Sorry. If you survive it too, good luck to you. If you don't—nothing I could possibly say would have helped you.*

A feeling of deep green peace overtook me as the Other-Realm drew me in. It settled in my stomach and grounded me. It was nothing like that, not really, because I have no words to describe it. I can't explain how soft the trailing vines were as they brushed my face, or how the grass felt cold and clear and perfect under my feet.

Let me just say, as an example of why this world was paradise, that the first thing that the gnarled, nut-brown chieftain did was take me shopping.

Oh, yes.

~

They call it the Sparkle Market. This is where the faeries and the goblins and the aelves and the other magical, unreal folk bring their magical wares. Occasionally, when I'm walking through the mortal world, I'll hear their bells and scramble off to find them because I'm dying for a cup of acorn coffee and a chance to browse the second-hand wings stall. Their visits to the mortal world are rare, and they always seem a little more subdued than they do at home. Here in the Other-Realm, the Sparkle Market is always and forever and colour and light, and they never ever *ever* run out of acorn coffee.

That first visit was extraordinary. I wandered past stalls and banners and winged, multi-coloured people, feeling at home for the first time in my life. It was only then that I acknowledged to myself how out-of-place I had always felt, in the village, at Ma Fortuna's place, in the big bad world. This was my home.

There were frocks everywhere, as far as the eye could see. Sunset frocks, glass frocks, frocks made of forgotten promises and good intentions and grass and leaves and tomorrows and fairy tales. "Pick one," said the nut-brown chieftain, stomping along beside me.

I couldn't possibly choose from that wealth of beauty. "Are you sure?"

He ran his dark eyes over the torn remains of my fish-stained white lace dancer disguise. "You're one of us, lass. Should you not dress the part?"

I stopped to admire a delicate rose bodice and bluebell skirt. "I can't choose." It all seemed far better than I deserved.

"You should," he muttered ominously. I knew without him having to tell me that this was far more important than a costume change. It was about accepting these people, this world, their bounty as my heritage.

I scanned the stalls, ignoring the dancing creatures and happy music. I let my eyes roam up and down the rows of colour and beauty and natural magic. Something caught my gaze. I moved towards it, and the rest of the Sparkle Market melted away. There was just the one stall and the gleaming two-piece hanging on display.

It was chainmail, finer and more elegantly linked than any of those pieces I drooled over at the village blacksmith's. Silver-steel chainmail, forming a short bodice and low-slung hip skirt. It was armour and seduction all in one, and I loved it instantly. I pointed, and several flower faeries leaped forward to unpeel my ragged white garments. They bathed my skin with dock leaves and soft mountain grasses, then fitted the chainmail to my body.

It fit like a glove—like a silken lingerie glove with full underwire support. The magical chainmail draped over my breasts and hips, baring my midriff, glittering and shimmering. The flower maidens cooed and chattered, braiding my hair with clover and forget-me-nots.

No one would ever take me seriously in an outfit like this. It was perfect.

"Fine," agreed the nut-brown chieftain. "Granfiddich," he grunted, pointing at himself. "Grandfather," he added.

I hesitated. "Does that translate as Grandfather of the People?"

"Granfiddich translates as ruler of the goblins," he said in a low growl. "Grandfather means I'm your actual grandfather." He turned on his heel and stomped away.

I glanced at the flower faeries. "Do I need to pay?" The last thing I wanted was to offend anyone else in the Other-Realm. Offending their ruler and my grandfather all in one go was probably enough for one day.

"Negotiate payment with the Granfiddich," giggled the faeries.

Brilliant. I ran after him. The Sparkle Market was back with a vengeance, all bright colours and streaming banners. I could barely keep my eye on the Granfiddich in the crowd. Finally I burst out of the edge of the clump of stalls, coughing on herbal smoke and cinnamon dust. The Granfiddich was waiting for me, sitting on a large rock shaped like a four-leaf clover.

I dropped to my knees. "Granfiddich—grandfather, I'm sorry. I did not mean to say anything out of turn."

"Six months," he grunted.

I frowned. "Sorry?"

"It is fine craftsmanship, the best our people have made in a hundred years."

He was negotiating for the chainmail. "Oh. What does six months mean?"

"Six months here, in the True Realm," he growled, staring at me like he expected me to refuse. "Learning about your past, your heritage. Six months."

"Okay."

He blinked. "You will not haggle?"

"No, six months sounds fair. I want to stay here and learn all those things, grandfather. Any less than six months would be too little."

He nodded, seeming pleased. "Then the gift is yours. Come. Let me show you our world."

Again, I find it difficult to describe. I can only remember fragments—as if thoughts of that place don't belong to the mortal world. The sky was constantly swirling with a hundred different colours, with silver and gold and other metals I'd never seen before or since. Their world went on forever. We broke into fruits that tasted of honey and ice-cold jam. We slept in trees and leaf-green boats. We drank water from grass goblets, then tore them apart and replanted the stalks in the ground. It was like your ultimate health farm, but with fun and fashion parades and three-headed monsters. The land was peaceful, full of music, dance and magic. Magic most of all.

In mortal Mocklore, magic crashes and smashes through the landscape, exploding with abrasive sounds and colours. In the OtherRealm, magic is a pattern, and a vein. You breathe it in and out, you eat it for breakfast, and it consumes you right back.

I spent three days making daisy chains with the flower faeries, a week swimming in the pearl rivers with a gang of macho fish goblins and a fortnight learning elegance, poise and seductive walking skills from Mistress Hazelswitch, an aelf matron who was once concubine to the Faerie Prinse himself. I lost count of the weeks, but it can't have been more than six or seven before I found myself in the cave of the seeing pool. It was the favourite place of the flower faeries. "We love to watch the mortals playing," they giggled. Fair enough. Why not check out how the mortal world was getting along without me? An hour later, I was still gazing fixedly into the seeing pool. How could I tear my eyes away from Luc?

He was a real hero now. Rescuing damsels, slaying the really dangerous monsters, righting wrongs. He was rocking the fairy tale hero aesthetic, but his long curly hair was dyed black instead of tucked under a wig. He had found a sword somewhere and demonstrated a surprising expertise with the blade. I stared in wonder at my boy, my not-quite-brother, my best friend all grown up. "How long have I been gone?"

"Mortal weeks or faerie weeks?" asked Harebell.

I blinked at her. *There's a difference?*

"Of course," laughed Rosehip. "Back when the Faerie Quene ruled, she kept strict control on that sort of thing. She loved to lure mortals here for a day and send them back a hundred years later. The difference isn't so dramatic these days, but the Granfiddich and the other chieftains have been known to play with the hours."

I was stunned. Luc was looking grown up, more than I would have expected after a month or two. How long had I actually been here?

"I hope they don't kill him," said Foxglove. "He's such a nice hero."

I pushed her aside to get the best view of the seeing pool. "Who are going to kill him?" I could see them now, the threat. Goddesses. Three of them. My boy was in big trouble. "Is there sound on this thing?"

"Put your head in the water," suggested Harebell.

I had grown used to trusting these girls. I thrust my head underwater. Voices filled my ears.

"It's a simple choice," said Amorata, sultry brunette goddess of lovelorn lust and unresolved sexual tension.

"Which of us is most beautiful?" asked green-haired, swirling Destiny.

"No harm will come to you," purred the elegant blonde Lady Luck, the most dangerous of the three. "Which is the fairest of us all?"

"Why me?" choked Luc. He was sweating, his Corpse White No. 4 face powder coming off in flakes. "What makes you think I'm qualified?"

"You're a man," shrugged Amorata.

"The most famous and popular hero in the land," said Destiny.

"Choose," snarled Lady Luck. "Give the golden apple to the fairest. One of us. NOW."

Luc held a glowing golden ball. He tossed it back and forth nervously. Faced with an impossible choice, and the almost certain retribution of two goddesses if he chose a third as his favourite, he did the most sensible thing he could possibly have done. He threw the golden apple in a soaring arc in one direction, and ran as hard as he could in the other.

I came gasping out of the water, yanked out by the hair. "You nearly drowned," scolded Harebell.

"You still have to breathe," said Foxglove. "You're half mortal, remember."

"I need to find the Granfiddich," I spluttered. "Now."

"He won't like it," warned Rosehip.

"He doesn't have to like it," I insisted. "He just has to let me *go*."

~

The Granfiddich stood on a cairn of pebbles, his voice grouching down at me. "You pledged six months, Bountiful Julietta Esmereldina Fenetre." I *knew* I shouldn't have told anyone my real name.

"How many mortal months have I been here?" I yelled back. "Six, twelve, twenty? I've served my time and more. You're the one who messed with the time streams, without warning me. I'd happily stay here longer, but not while Mocklore is spinning faster than I am. I have obligations to the mortal world."

"To a man?" he said skeptically.

"To a friend," I shot back.

"Do you promise to return?" asked the Granfiddich.

"Do you promise I won't lose an unreasonable amount of mortal time if I do, grandfather?"

A flicker of a smile crossed his grumpy face. "I make no promises. Do *you* promise to return?" He made a gesture with his gnarled hand and the Sparkle Market appeared around us, warm and inviting. "If you make the promise, you may choose anything you like from the stalls."

I wasn't going to do it. I was going to stand up to him, tell him it was my choice whether I came back or not, and I didn't have to make any stupid promises. But I wasn't ready to burn my bridges with the fair folk yet. Plus I saw something I kind of wanted on a nearby stall. So much for the moral high ground.

"I promise to return."

HOME

I had been gone three years. Three years. Do you have any idea how much can change in three years? Mocklore had certainly changed. For a start, my homeland was ravaged by a massive magical explosion which multiplied the insanity of the Skullcap Mountains and turned a lot of things purple. Plus our hundreds of gods had been decimalised by our mad Emperor, and there were only ten left!

Lia was pregnant.

Ma Fortuna's eldest girl, who had been fourteen and in pigtails when Luc and I left to Seek Our Fortune, had married a Guardsman and got herself knocked up. I stood on the wooden verandah of Ma Fortuna's house, my silver chainmail hidden under a village-appropriate linen dress, and stared at the rounded belly of the girl I had always thought of as my own baby sister. "Gods."

"Bounty!" Lia threw her arms around me, hugging me awkwardly but with genuine affection. "It's been so long. Ma will be delighted to see you. Luco's here, too."

"I thought he might be."

It was worse than I had realised. There were two babies squalling in Ma's kitchen, and an unfamiliar young woman trying to calm them both.

"Bounty." Ma Fortuna emerged from the pantry, immaculate and bustling as ever. She, at least, had not aged a day. She kissed me several times. "You finally came to visit. Meet Diona, Franc's wife."

Franciscus, the brattiest teenage brother of them all, had a wife? Diona smiled shyly at me over the heads of her two enormous babies.

I needed air. "Is Luco around, Ma?"

"Outside with the children," Ma announced, placing a plate of cold chicken sandwiches and chocolate biscuits in my hands and propelling me towards the back door. "Go on with you."

I wasn't prepared to see *more* babies, but as it turned out, the children Ma referred to were her own—baby Alessandro now at least ten years old by my calculations, young Giuno about to descend into adolescence, tomboy Nina on the edge of womanhood and ignoring that fact to the best of her ability. They tore around the orchard like mad things, kicking a football with their big brother. Tia, the middle sister who had to be going on sixteen now, sat to one side and pretended she was too grown up for such games.

I sat next to her and ate a chicken sandwich, watching Luc. He had washed out the black dye for the home visit, scraped his face clean of Corpse White No. 4, left the white ruffled shirt and the black leather trousers elsewhere. Racing around the garden with the kids, dressed in his old scruffy clothes with his light curly hair wild around his face, he looked like my boy again.

"Bounty!" shrieked Nina, the first to notice me. She tore across the grass, throwing herself into my arms.

I hugged her happily. "When did you turn into such a babe?"

She wrinkled her nose. "Don't call me that. Tia's the fashion plate."

"Am not," snapped Tia. "I naturally look this good. It takes no effort whatsoever."

Giuno came forward, all awkward arms and legs, and let me kiss him on the cheek. Alessandro shot me a cheeky smile and squeezed the breath out of me with his hug. "You're my favourite sister," he said solemnly.

"Beast!" shrieked Nina and chased him into the house. The others went howling after them, lured no doubt by the tempting scents coming from Ma's kitchen. Finally, only Luc and I were left.

"So," I said. "You didn't bring the hero home to meet mother?"

"Can you see me walking into Ma's kitchen in leather and face powder?" he said wryly. "They don't need to know about all that. They all think I'm training as a merchant in Zibria."

Yeah, right. Like Ma didn't have a scrapbook somewhere detailing the heroic exploits of Luco the Magnificent? Ma Fortuna's kids always underestimated the way she knew *everything* about them. I suppose it was the only way they could stay sane.

"What's happening with the goddesses?" I asked him.

He ignored me. "Anyway, I'm not the only one who dressed respectably for Ma. I bet you don't wear that frock when you're running around having adventures."

"I'm not dressed that respectably," I snapped at him. "Under this, I'm wearing metal faerie underwear. What about those goddesses, Luc?"

"How did you know about that?" he demanded. "You weren't there."

"I wish I had been," I said, feeling guilty.

He looked furious. "Why? What could you have done? This is *my* mess, Bounty. I'm the one who ran around building up a hero reputation, getting so bloody popular. I made myself too noticeable, that's all. Now I'm paying the price."

"How did you get away from them?" I couldn't help asking.

Luc's face was red now, furious, but not just with me. "I

ran," he said bitterly. "They've turned up every other month since it happened. I know that if I choose one as the fairest, the other two will kill me or curse me or make things ten times worse. I don't know why they always let me run away, but they do—must be in their rules. That damn golden apple turns up everywhere—in my soup, in my bedroll. There's nothing I can do but run away every single time."

"We can figure it out," I said earnestly. "All we need is a plan. I can help."

Luc gave me one of those cold icy looks he had got so good at since leaving home for the first time. "I don't need you to rescue me, Bounty."

I swallowed the instant hurt of his rejection, determined to make my point. "What are you going to do, run away for the rest of your life?"

"I'll think of something," he spat. "When I need your help, I'll ask for it. Until then, keep your nose out of my business." He slammed his way back into the house.

I stayed where I was for a moment, stunned. It was hard to get used to, the idea that Luc and I weren't a team any more, that we couldn't pick up where we left off.

After at least a minute of blinding self-pity, I walked back to the front of the house where I had left my bags. I yanked my respectable dress over my head and tossed it on to the steps to keep it clean. Then, clad only in my midriff-baring faerie chainmail, I swung a muddy hessian sack over my shoulder and went down the hill to visit the pond nymphs.

The pond was the same as ever. Beige, boring, muddy. The few limp lilies that were left entirely failed to perk the place up. There was no sign of my girls. I rummaged in the filthy sack, pulling out some leafy plants. "There I was," I said aloud. "About to make a clean break with the OtherRealm. I was going to leave without promising to come back, without letting them have that piece of me, but I saw these babies on a market stall and I couldn't resist bringing them back to you."

Slowly, I lowered the plants into the murky water of the pond. The first water lily had flowers of a vibrant purple. As soon as it touched the water, the petals exploded in showers of silver glitter, making the pond shimmer and glow. The second lily was pink and yellow candy-striped, heavenly scented with peppermint, straw-berries and cream. The last lily was midnight black with a shimmer of an opal crescent moon in its centre. As I watched, the opal moon swelled into fullness and back again, sliding through its phases in the blink of an eye. I had brought baby seedlings too, a dozen different varieties just waiting to do their stuff. I floated every one of them in the pond.

The nymphs emerged. Maybe it was my imagination, but they didn't look like the fright-wives they had always been. There was a new glow about them, a radiance. They would never be less than terrifying, but the new lilies had sparked some life into them.

Or, perhaps, my definition of beauty had shifted a little.

"Ssssank you," said Globula.

"Presssssy," said another nymph, admiring the new adornments. "Beausssiful," she added, leaning forward to inhale a baby crimson lily.

"Like your boootsss," Globula said shyly.

I grinned, preening in my chainmail lingerie. "Well, I'm glad someone finally noticed my boots." My new outfit went so well with the soft grey leather.

"Ssssat poor hero," she said, laughter bubbling in her watery voice.

I laughed too, remembering the last day I had been here, tricking the wandering hero out of his clothes and horse and troll head... Then I sighed, not feeling cheerful any more.

"Globula, is it true that water nymphs can see the future in their own reflection?"

"Somesssimes," she admitted.

"I'm worried about Luc and these goddesses. If he annoys them too much, they could blast him into infinity with one bat of their eyelashes. He is going to ask me for help eventually, isn't he?"

"Swim firssss," said Globula insistently. "Anssswers afsserwards."

It wasn't a bad offer, and the water lilies had perked up the pond no end. I'd never seen it so sparkling and crystal clear. "Your wish is my command." I pulled off my boots and my faerie chainmail, then plunged into the cool, real water. I missed the OtherRealm already, but I couldn't go back. Not until I got things sorted in my mortal life.

In the mean time, I spent the afternoon swimming with the pond nymphs and trying to forget about my worries. Maybe they would sort themselves out, in time.

Mocklore Survival Guide #7:
Prophecy and Portents

If a pond nymph ever tells you anything about the future, listen. She knows these things. I confidently believed that Luc would give in and ask me for help with his goddess troubles within a week or so, and everything between us would be okay again. Globula told me that I would be waiting far, far longer than that. I told her she was crazy.

Eight years later, I'm still waiting.

<h1 style="text-align:center">QUEEN OF COURTESANS</h1>

Zibria always sounded like my kind of town, even if the streets aren't literally paved with gold anymore. Asses milk, rose petals, sequined frocks and snake-bite suicides…oh, yes. This place had style.

As a half hobgoblin girl with a devotion to chainmail lingerie, I had a feeling I was going to fit right in.

When I finally did get a chance to visit the City of Eternal Wonders, it was festival time. The streets were lined with carousing crowds in weird and wonderful costumes.

I asked a few people what we were celebrating, then tried more seriously to get directions to the building I was looking for, but they all just laughed at me and capered on. After a while I gave up, grabbed a drinking bowl and joined the fun.

I was dancing with a man in a cheetah mask who had gold paint spotted down his arms and belly when a silver mermaid tapped me on the shoulder. "Bounty Fenetre? You were asking about the Courtesan's Academy."

"Word travels fast!" I had to yell so she could hear me.

She motioned me to follow, so I abandoned my dancing partner and bunny-hopped after her. Built over a large hill, the city of Zibria is mostly steps. Luckily for the mermaid, her costume allowed her to unhook the bottom of her tail so she could walk. What amazed me was the exceptional grace with which she moved, despite the constraints of her figure-hugging costume. She glided with an elegance I could never have dreamed of—and for a moment I desperately wanted to know how she did it.

Envy makes me bitchy. "Aren't you a little dry for a mermaid?"

"Aren't you a little tall for a hobgoblin?" she shot back.

I hate that. People expect me to be four foot tall, brown and wrinkly. Just because mortals have drawn us that way for centuries doesn't mean hobgoblins actually look like that. Okay, quite a few hobgoblins look like that, but we happen to come in all shapes and sizes. By all accounts, my father was six foot three and drop-dead handsome, despite the silver eyes and bright green hair.

As for me? Well, you'd hardly know I was half hob if I didn't go around telling everyone. My only legacies from the hobgoblin side of the family are mighty abs, wide eyes, constantly tangled hair and a greenish tinge around my toenails. If it wasn't for my habit of wearing midriff-baring chainmail ensembles, I'd look just like everyone else.

A zillion steps later, the mermaid and I were nearly at the crest of the Zibrian hill. When we paused to catch our breath (this was politeness on her part—she was so poised she probably didn't need to breathe) I asked her what the carnival was in aid of. It was too late in the spring for Bronzfetish or Bridesmorn.

"Our Sultan died five days ago," said the mermaid. "This is his funeral."

Some funeral. I'd seen more depressing circuses. "No one liked him much, then?"

"Local tradition," she explained. "We celebrate his life

through joyous revels, instead of wailing over his death. As soon as the pyre has been lit, everyone in the city dresses up to act out legendary scenes from his life."

I looked down at the streets below. Two centaurs sang a lusty drinking song while setting up a limbo contest for a mob of toga-clad zebras and a cigar-smoking unicorn. "He had an interesting life."

The mermaid shrugged, managing even to make that simple gesture an exercise in extreme elegance. "We take the odd liberty. It wouldn't be much fun if the whole city had to dress up as a middle-aged man who sat on a throne all day and liked his cup of tea every hour on the hour. We only have three teacup costumes in the whole city."

She led me to a building that looked like nothing much in particular—though it would have been grand enough in the old days when every wall in Zibria gleamed with marble, gold or jewelled mosaic. Inside, we followed a grand corridor lit with torches and decorated with grim, matriarchal portraits. If it wasn't for the fact that the old bats in the portraits all wore little but satin scraps and sequins, I might have imagined myself in the wrong place.

"It was good of you to answer our summons so quickly," said the mermaid in measured tones.

"I didn't have anything better to do," I said truthfully. "I wouldn't mind knowing, though, if I was invited at the request of the Courtesan's Academy, or the SPZ? The invitation—" summons, apparently, "—was unclear."

"The Secret Police of Zibria doesn't exist," she chided, her carefully trained voice skills drenching me with her superiority.

"So the rumour that the Courtesan's Academy is a front for the Secret Police…?"

"Is only a rumour."

And I was an Anglorachnid ballet dancer.

-§-§-§-§-§-

The mermaid's name was Demi. I learned this as we walked up and down countless corridors, heading for the inner sanctum of the Senior Mistresses of the Courtesan Academy. We also had time to trade info on hair conditioners, shoe styles, and our favourite costumiers. We were practically best friends by the end of the trek, though she hadn't let anything slip about the SPZ.

Obviously, I was going to have to get her drunk.

First things first. We reached our destination, a mighty and imposing set of golden doors, adorned with fine engravings. I recognised several images from 1012 Zibrian Nights, a famous illuminated scroll which has been banned more times than any other work in the Mocklore Empire. Tiny images of courtesans, djinni, kings and fishermen in various compromising positions (many of them physically impossible in our dimension) were expertly etched into the doors.

"Any advice before I face the dragons?" I asked my new best friend.

"They like an old fashioned touch. Curtseying, bowing, scraping, ma'aming…"

"Oh, they sound *peachy*."

"That's one word for them." Demi knocked on the golden doors. They creaked open a little. "After you."

Next to her calculated perfection, I felt like some random harpy in rusty armour. "Too late to borrow a hair brush, I suppose?"

The golden doors creaked open further, then swung wide. I strode in, expecting some kind of grand hall with polished floorboards or lovely marble tiles that would make a good clip-clop echo under the heels of my long suede boots. That is the sort of thing you expect to find behind huge golden doors.

Instead, I bumped into a large antique sideboard, tripped over a small floral sofa and landed on an ornamental chamber pot with geraniums growing in it. "Crap!"

Demi had the courtesanly grace not to giggle, but I *heard* her suppressing it.

"Not very dainty, is she?" commented a voice out of nowhere, a real grandmother of a voice—and I don't mean that in a nice way. It sounded like the voice of somebody else's grandmother whose best linen tablecloth you have accidentally thrown up on.

Don't ask me where I pulled that simile from, I'm still repressing the memory.

The room was cottage-sized, and packed full of furniture. Somebody else's grandmother furniture. It was a nightmare of floral patterns, lace draperies, and monstrously large cabinets straining under the weight of china dolls and souvenir spoons. There was enough collectible clutter to fill a museum, and none of it was in any logical order. I pulled myself to my feet with the help of a sturdy tea chest giving off a gusty scent of lavender, and a towering bookcase containing only books about cats. I scraped my way around that and almost failed an obstacle course of piano stools, each with hand-stitched embroidery depicting sweet rural scenes. The only sign that this was the inner sanctum of the Courtesan Academy was that the embroidered shepherdesses wore g-string bikinis and fondled their sheep in an intimate manner that I'm sure would be disapproved of by the union.

I had left Demi long behind while making my own ungainly path through the Museum of Old and Dead Furnishings. After staggering through a maze of piano stools, pot pourri and a mountain of crocheted egg-warmers that were, for no obvious reason, teetering on top of a pile of wombat-shaped cookie jars (why would *anyone* need more than one of those?), I rounded another corner and found myself face to face with the Senior Mistresses.

There were three of them, and they were knitting. I don't think that sentence fully conveys the sense of dread and intimidation that I felt in that moment.

The first Senior Mistress was enormous, taking up a whole floral-printed sofa on her own. She was dwarfed beneath a huge red wig and a selection of thick gold jewellery that would have made a Sultan's mouth water. She wore an antique scarlet gown—the kind that scaffolds up the bust, sucks the waist in so hard you want to die, then puffs the lower half into something resembling a piano disguised as a giant pomegranate.

The second Mistress was so thin she was almost translucent, her fingers as scrawny as her knitting needles. She wore a tight, black schoolmarm dress that buttoned right up to the top of her neck, well past her wrists, and several inches past her ankles. If it weren't for the long black wig, black lipstick, black fingernails (extending into long points), slut-high boot heels (it's a style, not a judgement!) and spiky silver jewellery, she might have looked almost respectable.

I mean, not respectable by my foster mother's standards, but that wasn't a fair bar to reach.

Then there was the third Mistress, clad in a sequined brassiere, hot pants and a blonde beehive wig so high that it was in danger of attaching itself to the hanging plant baskets that swung over their heads. She had to be at least eighty years old, and she was evidently the baby of the three.

I curtseyed. With those knitting needles they were better armed than I was, so it wouldn't pay to be impolite. "You called, ladies?"

"What *is* she wearing?" cackled Mistress Blonde.

I clamped my mouth shut so as not to retort 'look who's talking!'

"Shut up, Tiffaine," said Mistress Red. "We've got business to discuss."

"I was only saying…"

"Well, don't." Mistress Red stared me up and down. "Young enough, I suppose," she grunted. "You're a bounty hunter, I hear."

"No, ma'am," I said politely. I'd never said ma'am to anyone in my life, but this seemed like a good time to start. I was out of my depth. There was no one here to flirt with, and that was the only thing I was remotely good at.

She peered disapprovingly at me, through her gold-rimmed monocle. "What did you say?"

"I'm not a bounty hunter, ma'am. People often make that mistake, because of my name. Perfectly understandable."

Mistress Red looked alarmed. She formed a huddle with the other two Senior Mistresses, and they muttered to each other for a while. I stared at the ceiling, pretending that I couldn't hear every word that they were saying.

Demi swayed into my field of vision, posing against the wall to show off her curvaceous, mermaid-costumed body to full effect. I was beginning to feel underdressed.

"So you are not a bounty hunter," said Mistress Red.

"I'm not ruling it out as a potential career, but I haven't been one yet."

"But you *are* a hobgoblin."

"Half," I said uneasily.

They shared glances of mutual scorn so sharp I was glad they weren't pointing them directly at me—chainmail's not great protection against stab wounds. Especially when the chainmail in question only covers a small fraction of your body.

"What," said Mistress Black, enunciating carefully, "do

you know about the Faerie Quene?"

Ah, I was on safer ground here. "Not much."

The scornful glances were directed at Demi now. Her years of courtesan training couldn't stand up to their decades. She writhed and withered under their scorn.

"I mean, not much compared to most fey," I broke in hastily. "I probably know more than your average mortal. What did you want to know?"

"We want to know how to destroy her," said Mistress Red.

My mouth opened and closed a few times. There was so much wrong with that sentence I didn't know where to start. "Wha-at?"

"This one's loyalties are obviously to the fey bitch," said Mistress Blonde. "Let's kill her."

"Shut up, Tiffaine," said Mistress Red. "Why are you surprised, Bounty?"

"Well," I said, coughing a little on a dry throat. "For a start, she's powerful. The strongest and mightiest of the fey folk are all terrified of her. No mortal would have half a chance of doing her damage."

"You said for a start," Mistress Black said, tilting her head in curiosity. "What else?"

"She's also *gone*. She was trapped in another dimension behind the Icewall more than twenty years ago, and it's not due to reopen for at least another thirty. She's cut off from the OtherRealm and the mortal realm—no threat to anyone. The only way to assassinate her, even if you could, would be to free her first, which is not the world's best idea, not to mention being impossible. Or you could wait thirty years, in which case the urgency of your summons seems...unwarranted."

"Obviously you are lying," said Mistress Red. She sighed. "You disappoint us, Demitasse. We asked you to find us someone of fey blood who would not have any loyalties to the Faerie Quene."

Demi looked crushed, and scared. I couldn't help wondering what kind of punishment she was in for.

"She's not lying," broke in Mistress Black.

Demi looked hopeful.

"It was our understanding," Mistress Red addressed to me, "That the Faerie Quene prefers the mortal world to believe that she is gone, but in truth she remains in the OtherRealm as she always has, stretching out her poisonous talons to toy with mortals from a distance."

"That's not true," I said firmly. At last, something I knew something about. "The OtherRealm is suffering from a major leadership crisis. With the Faerie Quene gone, all the fey races have descended into something like tribal warfare. From what I've heard, she was never the most subtle of rulers, and she'd have no reason to hide from her own people."

Somewhere in mid-babble it occurred to me that this was privileged information that I only knew because my grandfather was stuck in the middle of it, and I probably shouldn't be spreading it to all and sundry, but hey. Since when have I been able to keep my mouth shut?

"Still not lying," said Mistress Black, her voice slow and surprised.

"Our Valeria knows things about body language that would make a contortionist sweat," said Mistress Red grudgingly. "If she says you speak the truth, we must believe you." She glanced at the others. "If we are dealing with an imposter rather than the true Faerie Quene, this changes everything."

"It changes nothing," said Mistress Black. Hard not to peg her as the brains of this operation. "Whomever this imposter is, she is powerful and dangerous. The only thing that has changed is that our enemy has no name."

I opened my mouth to ask for an explanation, but thought better of it. My eyes are bigger than my stomach when it comes to dangerous missions. They look so tempting and exciting on the outside, and yet I always emerge from them with bruises, broken limbs and/or major psychological damage. I would be so impressed with myself if I could get out of this room without volunteering.

The Senior Mistresses were scary. I really didn't want to meet anyone who could scare them.

They talked to each other now, ignoring me.

"She will be an ideal member of the team," said Mistress Red.

"By her own admission she knows nothing of any use," said Mistress Blonde.

"Someone with experience of the fey may still be of value," argued Mistress Black.

"Hobgoblins are notoriously unreliable!"

"So are humans, Tiffaine, that's hardly persuasive."

How nice. Now they were arguing as to whether or not I was going to volunteer. Apparently, I didn't get a vote.

Somewhere beyond the tea cosies and elephantine sideboards, doors slammed open and closed. We heard the muffled sounds of someone striding confidently into the room, tripping over a small floral sofa and crashing into a series of ornamental chamberpots. Damn!" said a male voice.

The whole thing made me feel quite nostalgic for ten minutes ago.

Our intruder's noisy antics at least put an end to the squabbling of the Senior Mistresses. They sat up with straight backs and arched eyebrows, pure courtesanity dripping from their elaborately costumed bodies. I took the opportunity to sidle away from centre stage, folding myself behind a display of crocheted undergarments.

Various shufflings, trippings and swearings later, our man

emerged from the chintz and mahogany maze to stand before the three Senior Mistresses. He was in disguise. Don't ask me how I know that, but he wore gold and white festival clothes with frivolous beading and ribbons at the neck and sleeves, and they were obviously not the kind of clothes he naturally chose to wear.

That, and the black dye he had used on his hair was that awful stuff that takes months to wash out properly, and looks like you have dipped your head in a bucket of tar.

"How interesting," said Mistress Red, her tone so scathing that even I felt bruised. "To what do we owe this honour, Sir Silversword?"

He looked annoyed. "The disguise isn't working, then."

"Hardly, my dear."

"If you want to travel the country covertly," broke in Demi, "perhaps you should try to be less of a romantic figure. Half our first year students have pin-ups of you on their walls."

He didn't even glance in her direction. His attention was firmly fixed on the terrible three. "Fine, you know who I am. You know, then, whom I represent."

"Naturally," said Mistress Black, with a predator's smile. "How may we contribute towards the greater glory of the Empire, Sir Silversword?

I was missing something, as I didn't have the faintest idea who this bloke was, but I was impressed. He was being blasted by higher courtesan skills from all sides, and didn't even flinch.

"Let's not waste time," he said. "The Emperor wants you know that he knows about the Sultan."

Innocence radiated from the Senior Mistresses, so bright that I had to resist the urge to shade my eyes. "The Sultan?" said Mistress Blonde in a baby doll voice.

"The one you had assassinated five days ago," Silversword

said in a dry voice. "I'm sure you remember." He surveyed the three of them with such withering scorn that I couldn't help wondering if he had courtesan training himself. "You're trying to break the tithe." It wasn't a question.

"Tithe?" asked Mistress Red. I swear, she batted her eyelashes.

"The tithe, Mistress Malisand. The tithe that Zibria has been obliged to pay to the Faerie Quene since she came to your aid during the 57 Years War. It was fruit and flowers at first, but around the time that the Faerie Quene was rumoured to have been imprisoned in an alternate dimension, the tithe became more demanding. Human sacrifice. A group of seven youths and maidens to be sent into the OtherRealm every seven years, into the waiting arms of the Faerie Quene. Is any of this sounding familiar?"

All three Senior Mistresses batted their eyelashes simultaneously. I winced at the crack of dried cosmetic paint and synthetic hair.

Silversword continued. There was something deliciously relentless about him. I had already forgiven him for ignoring my presence in the room. "That first year, the Senior Mistresses of the Courtesan Academy advised the Sultan to resist paying the tithe. According to imperial records, Zibria promptly suffered a magical plague, earthquakes and flood. Hundreds were killed. The Sultan was so incensed that he declared that the tithe would be paid by the Academy for perpetuity, and no further attempt would be made to break the tithe during his lifetime. True?"

Again, the crack of colliding eyelashes, batting in perfect unison. I glanced over at Demi, but none of this surprised her.

"Convenient for you," said Silversword. "The Sultan dropping dead exactly five days before the tithe is due to be paid? His son and heir cannot make any official proclamations until seven days after his father's death and you think you can do whatever you want until then." He lowered his voice dangerously. "I know about the assassin, ladies. I know what you hired him to do, and the method he used. I also know that you have contracted him for a further job, along with a hero, a priest and a shoe-mistress."

Crack, went the eyelashes.

For the first time, Silversword looked directly at me, but he let his eyes sweep over me only briefly before he turned his gaze to Demi. "These would be members five and six of your team, I suppose? A talented courtesan, low enough in the ranks to be disposable…" double ouch! "…and a half hobgoblin as your fey expert. I presume she has already informed you that whomever is behind this tithe is not, and never has been the Faerie Quene?"

I opened my mouth to protest that I hadn't volunteered for anything, but why fight the inevitable? I was always going to volunteer. Ill-advised Adventure was practically my middle name.

"Last time the tithe was challenged, Zibria was almost destroyed by this unknown enemy," said Silversword with an air of finality. "Emperor Timregis will not countenance such a risk again. You will *not* attempt to break the tithe."

There was a long pause. "And the Emperor worked this all out himself?" said Mistress Black.

"He is a far more intelligent ruler than most people give him credit for," said Silversword without hesitation.

"He is a fool and a lunatic, with no interests beyond which shade of purple satin he shall commission for his next wardrobe," said Mistress Red. "He has never shown any interest in the welfare of Zibria."

"You are the imperial champion, man," Mistress Blonde broke in. Oh, so that's who he was. Explained a lot, really. "How can you and your precious Emperor countenance such blatant otherworldly tyranny? Would you make a stand if *fourteen* youths were demanded every even years? Fifty? A hundred? Would you draw the line if it was your city's young people who were at risk, or is it only our students that are disposable?"

"If you resist and fail, you doom your whole city, perhaps the entire Empire," Silversword said between gritted teeth.

"Well, then," said Mistress Blonde, her eyelashes working into overdrive. "You had better join our team so as to make sure that they do not fail."

There was a flat silence in the centre of the room, as Sir Silversword realised the nature of the trap he had walked into.

I leaned forward and tapped him helpfully on the shoulder. "Don't look now, mate, but I think you just volunteered."

~

Even then, I could have gotten out of it. I could have held up my track record as a ditzy bint who wanders into dangerous situations and somehow manages to make them so much worse. I could have emphasised my frivolous nature, my short attention span, my inability to follow simple instructions.

When it comes down to it, I could have said no. I could have shrugged my shoulders, waltzed right out of the Courtesan's Academy and devoted the rest of the day to something worthwhile, like a massage and pedicure.

But I didn't. Not for any heroic reasons, or because I felt an obligation on behalf of all fey folk. To be honest, if you asked me to isolate the specific moment when I decided I was going on this stupid little mission, I'd have to say that it was about three seconds after I realised that the yummy Sir Silversword was coming along for the ride.

Sad, but true.

~

So there were seven of us standing on the city canal bank at midnight, waiting for the otherworldly vessel that would whisk us away to our doom. We were the strangest bunch of sacrificial victims you ever did see. To keep up the deception that we were students from the Courtesan Academy we wore their official uniforms—gymslips, fishnet stockings and pigtails for the girls, open-necked shirts and short breeches for the boys—all in leather and silky, slippery satin.

Chas, the assassin, was doing this for the money. What other motive would an assassin have?

"Surely there are easier ways to make a living out of killing?" I said skeptically when I heard his reason for joining the mission.

He flashed a gorgeous smile at me. "If I cared about easy, I wouldn't be an assassin."

Fair point. Chas was just about the cutest cold-blooded killer I'd ever met in my life. If I hadn't already been half-smitten by the fascinating Sir Silversword, I would have been flirting my bits off.

"This is Eliander," Chas added, introducing me to a sandy-haired and freckle-faced hero. I could tell he was a hero, because he had entirely missed the point of our disguise. His satin and leather courtesan uniform was mix-and-matched with the traditional Zibrian costume of the hero profession—a lion skin, sandals and a stout club. He had a slightly less traditional sword strapped to his back as well, in case of emergencies. He looked about as dangerous as a chicken sandwich.

"My brother was taken in the last tithe," Eliander said

before I could ask, and I caught a vengeful gleam in his boyish face.

"What about you, Bounty?" asked Chas.

I preened and took my time about answering, well aware that Silversword was nearby and listening. "I want to be a courtesan when I grow up."

I saw Demi's mouth twitch. If she wasn't so well trained, I'm certain she would have burst out laughing at that point.

"Really?" said Chas. He was puzzled, like that didn't fit in with the image he had constructed of me. This was someone who prided himself on reading people.

"Not entirely," I confessed. "I *really* want to join the Secret Police of Zibria, and I heard they have a courtesan-only policy. Not that the SPZ exists, of course," I added for Demi's sake. "Anyway, some training in poise and charm couldn't hurt. I have a few rough edges to rub off." I waited for someone to valiantly disagree that I needed such training.

"I would have thought your kind had little need for the mortal arts of false blandishment," broke in a bitter voice. "Can you not use your evil goblin magics to manipulate honest men?"

This had to be the priest of Raglah, patron god of Zibria. It must be hard dedicating yourself to religion when the only god you had left to worship was a womanising reprobate of a deity who never turned up to ceremonies on time. The priest was a grim drip of a man, uncomfortable in the silly leather and satin uniform we all wore. He had strung various godly sigils around his neck, and glared at us all as if it was our fault the cosmos hated him.

"You'd be surprised how many evil magics I don't have," I assured him.

The priest spat in my direction, and turned his back.

"Don't mind Fredo," Chas said cheerfully. "I think he only

joined the team in the hope of wiping every fey creature off the face of the earth."

How reassuring.

"Can't blame him, really," muttered Eliander.

Chas elbowed him and looked meaningfully at me, the half-hobgoblin *completely selfless volunteer*.

"No offence," the freckle-faced hero added hastily.

None taken, I'm sure.

Demi had de-mermaided herself for the occasion, golden in the lamplight as she waited, poised and calm, to be taken hostage with the rest of us. Her hair, cosmetics and manicure were all perfect. Her uniform was professionally tailored so as to highlight her body's every contour.

I had a desperate urge to rumple her hair, or possibly throw a pie in her face.

The third woman in this merry band was Georginne. She was small and meek-looking, with a soft whisper of a voice and a heart-shaped face. She was the only one who came with luggage: a carpet bag full of shoe-making tools and a giant sack stuffed with footwear. Dancing slippers for the most part, though I spotted a boot or two when I had a peek inside earlier. Silversword had called her a shoe-mistress. Apart from cobblers, I didn't have the faintest idea what he meant.

Still, you have to respect a woman who comes on a perilous adventure bringing every shoe she owns.

Just as we were starting to think our evil unknown enemy had forgotten us, a black gondola swished out of the shadows and drew alongside us in the shallow canal waters. Mistress Red, who had come to wave us off along with the other Senior Mistresses, gave a self-important and utterly false speech about the honour of sacrificing ourselves in the name of the tithe. I'm surprised she didn't wink loudly at us after every other line. (Just kidding really, darlings, don't forget the seek, locate and vanquish plan we discussed earlier!)

There was no one but the seven of us on the gondola as we clambered aboard, unless there were invisible gondoliers steering the thing. Now *that* was a creepy thought. As soon as we were settled, the gondola shoved itself off and swished back the way it had come.

"Unnatural," sneered Fredo the priest.

I could have argued that magic was the most natural force of all, but I didn't. Even I know how to keep my mouth shut sometimes.

"What can we expect?" Demi asked me as soon as we were all settled on the cushioned benches in the boat.

I blinked at her. "I know I'm here as the resident fey expert, but I've never volunteered as a human sacrifice before. I haven't the faintest idea what's coming next."

The gondola sped up. We swooshed through the water, faster than was strictly safe. Even at midnight, there should be cargo boats and transporters on the canals. Crashing into a merchant or two would put a swift end to our little adventure.

But of course, we were no longer anywhere near the Zibrian canal network. Spindly vines and trees loomed at the water's edge as we swept past, and they did not look like they belonged to the world we knew.

The stars were gone. I swear, they had been there a minute ago.

"This isn't the OtherRealm," I said aloud. "That's not where we're going." I could contribute that much, at least.

Silversword moved towards me so fast I felt dizzy. "What do you know, Bounty?" Somehow, though he was the last of us to join the team, he assumed he was in charge and we were letting him assume it.

It was cold. There was frost on the overhanging branches

that whipped past our speedy gondola. I hate being cold. I was almost grateful for the protection of the leather gymslip, compared to my usual chainmail ensemble. "It's not the OtherRealm," I repeated. "We're going in the wrong direction, but that doesn't make sense because the OtherRealm isn't in any particular direction, it's just Other. This is Other too, but not in the same way."

His grey eyes were locked on mine, as if he found me fascinating. I found it hard to breathe. "Is that all you can tell us?"

"It's more than anyone else can tell you," I said irritably. I couldn't stop shivering. "How are we going to fight this?"

Alarmed, he put his finger to his mouth, glancing around —for what? The invisible gondoliers?

Demi's cool courtesan exterior was visibly cracking. "If it's the Faerie Quene…"

"It isn't," I said firmly. "The Faerie Quene didn't fake being banished. She's not within sniffing distance of the mortal realm or the OtherRealm."

"But you already said we're not heading for the Other-Realm," said Silversword. "How do you know we're not going to wherever she was banished to? It might be her after all."

I stared at him. There was frost on his eyelashes.

The other side of the Icewall? By gondola? "No," I whispered. "Not that."

My whole body heaved suddenly, and it was only when I crashed back against the little wooden seat that I realised I wasn't the only one. The whole gondola had been shaken by something.

Silversword looked shaken. "What was that?"

The other three boys drew their weapons and looked around like they expected us to be attacked. I couldn't blame them. *I* expected us to be attacked. I couldn't see how Eliander's club, Chas's long knives and Fredo's sacrificial truncheon with extra gutting blade were going to be of any use, as we didn't have an enemy we could see.

Georginne the shoe-mistress busily sewed silk ribbons on to a pale pink dancing slipper. She didn't seem to feel that anything was wrong. I wanted to live in her world.

The gondola slowed, though we were still moving forward. Water swished along our sides. I can usually see pretty well in the dark, but right now I saw nothing beyond our circle of lantern light. "Kill the light," I told Silversword. "I need to see what's out there."

He hesitated, but did what I said. "I hope you know what you're doing."

Me too, honey bunch.

Silversword quenched the lantern, and everything went black for a moment.

Now I could see the trees outlined along the bank of the canal. There was no moonlight, no stars, so how could I see them? They glowed faintly silver and gold in the darkness, and from the hushed exhalations from my fellow sacrifices, I wasn't the only one seeing them.

"This is new," I said.

"What does that mean?" asked Silversword.

"It means don't trust your weapons, don't trust your eyes and ears, don't trust each other, and sure as hell don't trust anyone or anything that you meet here."

Chas swore softly.

"You said it," I agreed. What else could I say? Humans didn't have any place in the worlds outside our own. I only survived my occasional visits to the OtherRealm because I was acknowledged as half fey. This strange land wouldn't extend the same favour to me.

"How did the Senior Mistresses think we'd have a chance?" Demi asked in a whisper.

"Maybe they didn't," I said. "Maybe they thought we'd

provide a more entertaining tithe this time around." I suck at morale-boosting platitudes.

The gondola bucked, so violently that we actually left the water and smacked back down. The current dragged us urgently along, speeding up again towards our destination.

"You," a vicious voice snarled at me in the near-darkness. Fredo the priest of sunshine and happiness. "You are of the same kind as this evil queen of the fey. You have betrayed us to her!" His truncheon whistled past my face. I grabbed his wrist and disarmed him swiftly, throwing the damn thing overboard. Someone grabbed him and pulled him back before he could retaliate. "Get your hands off me, wench!" he snarled.

My rescuer was Demi, chic and dignified as she gripped the struggling priest. "Do shut up," she said in her usual silken tones. "We're in the Faerie Quene's boat, and we came here of our own accord. No one had to betray anyone."

"Only it's not the Faerie Quene," said Silversword thoughtfully. "So who is it?"

I had been wondering that myself. Why would anyone pretend to be the Faerie Quene? Okay, that was obvious. She was the most powerful fey figure anyone had ever heard of. If you convinced people you were the Faerie Quene, you could scare anyone into doing anything. Even sacrificing seven people every seven years.

But why a sacrifice? That was the part that didn't make any sense. Gods are the only ones who have a taste for sacrifices, but they aren't into pseudonyms. They like atrocities to be committed in their name, or not at all.

Maybe we weren't supposed to be killed. That was a comforting thought, most unlike me. But what were they going to do with us?

The canal widened. We couldn't see the tree-lined banks

anymore. We went into a slow spin, the gondola turning with the force of the water.

If a sacrifice is made in an empty river, does it make a noise? I thought giddily.

Something hit us from beneath, thrusting us up into the air. I heard something cracking and saw something black as it slammed into my field of vision, and then I didn't have a field of vision anymore.

Everything was gone.

~

I woke up feeling like seven different kinds of idiot. What had I been thinking? It would be a lovely adventure, we'd stroll into an otherworldly dimension, slay the wicked old witch and be home in time for cream buns and ginger beer?

Dream on, Bounty.

As the resident fey expert of this team, I should have advised everyone to stay home and forget about it instead of jumping in boots first. The fey are not to be messed with.

Had I really gone along with this because of Silversword's intriguing grey eyes? Fourteen different kinds of idiot. I didn't deserve to live.

I was so cold that I hurt from skin to spine. I was lying on something even colder. *Get up,* I told myself. Naturally, my body didn't listen to me. I've always been the rebellious type. *Get up, stupid cow, or you'll die,* I tried, but the only response was that my eyes flickered slowly and opened.

I lay on my back, staring up at silver trees. They were genuine silver, glossy and firm. Jewels twinkled down at me from the branches. Pretty.

There was a deep pain somewhere inside me. Probably my kidneys shutting down. I was lying on snow.

Get up, stupid cow, or you'll die wearing a fake leather gymslip and pigtails. That was enough to kick my limbs into gear. I shoved myself painfully upwards. The fishnet stockings were soaked through, and I was so cold that I wasn't even shivering anymore. Bad, bad sign.

I got to my feet, glad that I wasn't wearing my favourite boots. They would have been ruined. Instead, I had ruined an ordinary pair of buckled schoolgirl shoes. They sagged on my feet, pathetic little swollen articles. I put one in front of the other, and started walking.

There was no sign of the canal, or the gondola. No sign of my six fellow sacrificial victims. It wasn't dark anymore, but that didn't help. All I could see was snow, more snow and a forest of silver and gold trees, their glittering branches dripping with precious jewels.

My feet had stopped hurting. Another bad sign.

Someone was humming. I followed the sound, struggling to make my limbs work. Finally, as I staggered up a slight rise of a snowdrift and looked over the other side, I saw another living soul.

She was wrapped in thick furs, and sat near a crackling fire. Mm. My favourite kind of hallucination. As I got closer, I saw that the fire was burning without any obvious signs of fuel except for a small black object. As I got even closer, I saw that the object was a shoe.

"Georginne?" It took me a few moments to remember her name, but when she turned her head I saw that it was, indeed, the little shoe-mistress.

"Hello," she said calmly, her hands working on a new dancing slipper, this one pale green with a pattern of jewels on it. I wondered if she had harvested them from the trees. "Where did you get those clothes?" I asked.

Georginne reached into the large sack beside her and pulled out a pair of slippers. They were flimsy with pompoms of fur on the front, and break-your-neck high heels.

"Wasn't exactly what I had in mind," I said sourly.

"Try them."

Anything was better than the soggy school shoes currently freezing to the flesh of my feet. I pulled the flimsy pompom shoes on over my own, thinking they wouldn't fit, but they did.

When I straightened up, I was warm and dry, clad in a fur cape and hood, long fur and leather trews, and boots so thick and fluffy that it felt like I had a grizzly bear on each foot. "Wow," I said, feeling at a loss for anything more. "You're good."

"I do shoes," she said, with a small shrug, concentrating on her work. "There's a pair for every occasion."

"Do you know where the others are?"

"She took them," said Georginne.

I wanted to ask who 'she' was, but wasn't sure I would like the answer. "She didn't take you?"

Georginne held up her hand, curled around something I couldn't see. "Invisible slippers. She missed me."

I was starting to get some idea of what a shoe-mistress was capable of. Maybe the Senior Mistresses actually knew what they were doing when they assembled this team. I wondered what hidden talents the others had to offer. "Which direction did they go in? And do you have another pair of those invisible slippers?"

Georginne smiled.

～

We walked for ages, invisible. There were no footprints in the snow, which was another clue that we were in a land with entirely different rules to the mortal realm.

I didn't ask how Georginne knew we were heading in the

right direction. I could only assume that she had a shoe-compass of some kind. In any case, we kept walking until I heard the music.

I'm not the kind of girl who spends a lot of time in bars making goo-goo eyes at the minstrels—well, unless they're extremely cute. Music has never interested me; I hear nothing but a bunch of notes put together in silly patterns. I always thought it was a fey thing, until I met a bunch of genuine fey folk and found out that they like a good old singalong as much as the next creature. Being tone disinterested is just a Bounty thing.

When I heard the first strains of that music though, there in the snowfields of gods-knew-where, I took it all back. This music was the most amazing substance I had ever taken in through my ears. It was like chocolate and melted marshmallows and good sex and the top ten happiest moments of your life, all rolled into one glorious combination of sounds.

It made me want to dance.

I hurried forward, and Georginne moved with me. We could see each other while we were both invisible, don't ask me how or why. Her little brown eyes glowed with something fierce and beautiful and I didn't doubt that my eyes were the same. I didn't care.

We burst out of the silver and gold trees, finally, and saw where the music was coming from. A huge glass pavilion, beautiful and improbable, sat upon the snow. It was draped with silk ribbons and winter-blooming red roses, and it was so beautiful that for a moment I just had to stand and stare.

Dancers moved across the pavilion floor in elegant patterns, with swirling fabrics and glittering shoes. I wanted to be one of them.

Georginne went first. She was such a meek little thing that part of me had thought that she, of all of us, was the least likely to be corrupted. But her carpet bag fell from one hand,

and her shoe sack fell from the other. A few slippers spilled out into the snow. She ran forward, pulling off her invisibility slippers as she ran, then her fur-making shoes, until she was on the glass steps of the dancing pavilion in her original student courtesan outfit, pigtails askew. She kicked off her schoolgirl shoes, and her fishnet stockings, and stepped barefoot up on to the glass.

I saw what had lured her in. A line of dancing shoes stood waiting at the very edge of the dance floor. Georginne hesitated for one long moment, but only to choose which slippers she most wanted to slide on to her feet. One pair of shimmering silver shoes later, she was on the floor, clad in a silver gown that matched her shoes. A partner had been waiting for her, a dark man in a silver, princely costume, whose face I could not see no matter which way he turned. Georginne was lost in the swirling pattern of the dance.

Part of me knew this was bad and wrong and stupid. Even as the music bubbled up inside me, I knew that I was being tempted, and that if I followed Georginne on to the dance floor, I would be lost too.

I went anyway. Hey, there was a free frock on offer.

On my way to the glass pavilion, I tripped over one of Georginne's spilled shoes. I shouldn't have; it was nowhere near me. Perhaps it reached out and grabbed my foot? Stupid. Anyway, I landed awkwardly in the snow and for one shocked and insensibly frosty moment, the spell was broken. The shoe was a small leather thing, slightly lopsided and too small for a human foot. It looked like something my grandfather would wear. A hobgoblin shoe. In that stunned moment of freedom, I scooped up the shoe and stuffed it inside my gymslip, managing to lodge it in my breast-band.

Then the music had me again, and I didn't care. I tore up those glass steps, yanking off my other shoes and flinging them all over the place in my haste. At the edge of the pavilion, the dancing slippers were waiting for me. I picked red ones, ruby red. Don't ask me why. I never wear red, it's totally not my colour. When your hair is mousy and your eyes are muddy green, bright scarlet doesn't just wash you out, it throws you out with the wash water.

Nevertheless, I chose ruby slippers, and before I had moved three steps on that dance floor, I was clad in a whispering, swishing ballgown in that same vivid blood-jewel colour, and a dark prince swept me into the dance. His suit was ruby red too, and he wore rubies in his earlobes and at the curve of his throat.

He was beautiful, and he was mine. I gazed into his eyes. He gazed back into mine. Even in that moment, I couldn't see his face.

We danced, and it would break your heart to see how well we did it. I'd never managed such effortless grace before, not while negotiating dance steps and music and someone else's arms and feet. I usually mess up at least one of the three.

We were dancing like we were born to it, like we were the dance champions of the world, like it was easy. I felt like a goddess—hell, I felt like a courtesan. I loved the dance and I loved him and I loved the music. Happy, happy, happy.

Until I saw *him*, and suddenly my dance partner seemed a little bit less perfect.

Sir Silversword, champion of the Mocklore Empire, danced with a faceless dark princess every bit as glamorous and effortless as my own faceless dark prince. She wore green, from her silk gown to her emerald slippers, and something inside me went a little bit green when I saw her. In a brief, intense moment, I wanted him more than I wanted my dark prince.

Ungrateful, or what?

For a moment, I felt something sharp and leathery inside my bodice, like a body twinge. It was enough to make me change my steps, push the dance in a different direction. My prince followed obediently. What a man!

As we swirled and glided past Silversword and his green lady, I reached out a fraction—just an itty bit—and touched his hand, where it rested on her shoulder.

His hand shuddered for a moment, and then caught hold of mine. The manoeuvre was done expertly, before I could even say 'may I cut in?'

Dancing was made for the swapping of partners. My dark prince in his ruby suit and the dark princess in green moved into each other's arms, and I was in Silversword's, without much effort at all.

It was a good place to be. Nice to be looking into the eyes of someone with a face. It occurred to me that if he was *Sir* Silversword, he had been knighted. I'd never danced with a knight before. Ma Fortuna would be so proud.

Silversword looked better in a formal suit than he had in his trashy festival clothes, or the courtesan boy outfit. The black dye had vanished from his hair, leaving it a nice dark blond. His eyes were grey. Emerald green was so not his colour, but he still looked pretty spiffy. My green knight.

We danced, and that was all that mattered.

But we had spoiled the perfectly arranged pattern of colours, and it wasn't long before we came to the attention of the artistic mind behind this little display. I'd like to say that I had done it deliberately, to goad the queen bee out of her hive, but I hadn't really considered any consequences other than being held in the arms of the most interesting man in this whole winter wonderland.

Call it a happy accident.

The music stopped. To be strictly accurate, the music stopped only for me. I stood still, and Silversword politely stood still too, but his head and fingers still moved to the rhythm of the music that I could no longer hear. Around me, the couples continued to step and whirl each other around in formal patterns. Eliander the freckle-faced hero swung past in a bright sapphire suit with a sapphire girl in his arms. A few moments later, Chas the assassin glided past, his girl shimmering in midnight silk and jet beading to match his dramatically black outfit. Even grim, hostile little Fredo the priest was dancing with a strangely neutral expression on his face. He didn't suit the purple he was drenched in, but the faceless woman in his arms shone with amethysts.

All three of the boys—all four if I had bothered to look at Silversword's feet—wore dancing shoes, equivalents of the ones on my own feet, on Demi's and Georginne's. I couldn't help wondering where the mistress of this place had her shoes made—did she have a shoe-mistress of her own, churning out magic slippers by the bucket load?

I would be able to ask her for myself, soon enough. Silversword and I stayed still, though he still held me loosely in his arms as if we were dancing.

Not only the music had stopped for me. I could no longer hear the sound of dancing slippers ringing against that shiny glass floor. I heard nothing but a single set of stiletto heels, clicking menacingly towards me.

Oh, help. Was it too late to pretend I was another dancing sheep? Part of me longed to hear that music again and drown myself in it. The hobgoblin shoe poked itself forcefully into my left breast, reminding me who I was and why I was here.

Because I was fourteen different kinds of idiot.

The dance changed. They were still swirling and parading and quick-quick-slowing and the rest, but instead of dancing in a series of circles, they fell back to form two distinct avenues.

As the last couple—Demi in a rose-quartz dress and her matching pink prince—drew back, I finally saw what all the fuss was about. The Faerie Quene flowed across the floor of the glass pavilion, a floating mass of amber jewels and golden silk. I couldn't tell where the threatening clip-clop of heels was coming from, because her feet did not move. She moved like she was liquid, like elegance made into a wine and spilled slowly across the glass floor.

The Faerie Quene had been banished in the same year I was born, so I had never seen her in the flesh. Every portrait or statue of her portrayed a different woman, as if the artists had seen her face, body and style in entirely contrasting ways.

Nevertheless, the first thing I was sure of as this creature's grace and beauty smacked me between the eyes was that this was not the Faerie Quene. There was no hint of fey about her, no scent of grass or moonlight. There was no breath of magic in her presence, for all that she was moving like a goddess with a diploma from the Courtesan Academy.

And just like that, I knew what she was.

I had no allies, no one to help me save the day; certainly no one to ride to my rescue. As the mistress of the glass pavilion poured towards me, I curled my fingernails hard into the back of Silversword's hand.

The moment of pain brought him briefly awake. His grey eyes came alive again with that sharp intelligence. How had I even thought I was dancing with Silversword? This was the real thing. "Bounty, what's happening?" he asked urgently.

She was coming, it was too late, she was already here. I drew my nails away and his face returned to that awful neutrality.

Amber and gold filled my field of vision. An exquisite hand uncurled from the mass of warm silk, reaching not for me but for my dance partner. "May I cut in?" she requested in a glorious voice, so very polite.

I let go, and she took him. I sank to my knees on the glass, the ruby dress spilling like a bloodstain around me. I wanted nothing more but to hear her voice, to worship this woman, to dance to her music for all eternity. The twisted piece of leather in my breast-band dug more firmly than ever into my soft flesh, but I could barely even feel it.

The music flooded back, and I almost wept at how relieved I was to hear it again, at how good it was in my ears. A hand reached down to me, and it was an amber and gold consort, as bland and faceless as the other dark princes. His lady danced with my green knight, so he was free to give me a whirl around the dance floor.

I let him draw me to my feet, and we danced, red and gold. Silversword was gone, dancing in the arms of our enemy, and I didn't care. I just wanted an excuse to keep listening to the music.

Don't ask me how long we danced. It could have been days.

Now that our queen had graced us with her presence—and there was no doubting that she was a queen, for all that she wasn't the one we'd been told she was—there was a new purpose to the dance. We weren't spinning and twirling for our own sakes. She danced with my green knight—her green knight—in the centre of the stage and we whirled around her in formation, paying court to them both.

She poured herself over him, not only the gold and amber silk of her gown and the pale ivory of her hands, but her whole body. Her mouth found his eyes and throat, and she melted into him so stylishly that we applauded her.

Maybe in that moment I didn't see anything wrong with the way she was blatantly molesting him in front of us all, but the shoe in my breast-band thought otherwise. It rolled around down there like a mad thing, desperately trying to get my attention.

I lost track of the music for a split second, just long

enough to see the face of my dark dancing partner in amber and gold.

He had freckles.

It shouldn't have meant anything to me, but in those three seconds before the brief image was wiped from my head, Eliander the hero waltzed past with his sapphire princess, and I twigged.

His brother had been paid in an earlier tithe, and if the man in my arms was not his brother, I would eat the little misshapen leather shoe currently trying to punch its way through my ribcage.

I might eat it anyway. It might shut the little bugger up.

Reaching out blindly to the nearest dark prince, I allowed the dance to swap him for my own. This one wore a shining pink suit, and rose-quartz Demi slipped easily in the arms of the golden boy. It was a start.

I grabbed for another dancing partner, and ended up with the jet-suited Chas in my arms. Excellent. Assassins were supposed to have strong willpower, weren't they? I dug my fingernails into his hands and neck until I drew blood, but he didn't flinch, let alone wake up from the dancing reverie as Silversword had.

I would have to look elsewhere for a partner in crime, and unfortunately Silversword was the only one completely out of my grasp. His dance with the Queen of the glass pavilion had developed into something even more sensual, her gold and amber-clad limbs like a spider wrapping its victim.

The switching of partners had now been incorporated into the dance pattern, and I barely had to nudge the blank-faced Chas into handing me on to Georginne's silver prince. Three faceless princes later, I was dancing with Eliander.

My nails had no effect on him, and nor did my whispered suspicions about his freckled brother being alive and faceless in a golden suit. I considered biting him on the neck, but the dance changed and I was already being exchanged for Fredo's faceless princess.

Great. Even if I did wake this little zealot from his stupor, he would be just as likely to blame me and my hobgoblin blood for this whole mess, then try to shove a stake through my heart.

Before I had a chance to try the fingernail thing on him, I realised that he was already reacting to me. His hands quivered where they touched mine, and there was something in his eyes—distaste? Hey, anything was better than that blank expression.

It occurred to me that no matter how unnatural this whole set up was, I was the thing most likely to disturb him. After all, I was the only fey for miles around. I leaned in and kissed his froggy little mouth, putting plenty of oomph into it. That did the trick.

He pushed me off him, sputtering. "Get away, unclean harlot!"

I kept hold of his wrists even as he shoved at me. I managed to drag him out of the dance and to the very edge of the glass pavilion. As he struggled more violently to detach himself from the evil hobgoblin wench, we slid beautifully off the edge and fell in a tangled, thumping heap on the snow below.

I took the opportunity to kick off my ruby slippers. The ballgown vanished, leaving me in my gymslip and pigtails. I lunged for Fredo's feet, but he was too fast for me.

"What are you doing, witch?"

"Saving your life! Look around! I'm not the enemy here."

He looked up at the pavilion, and I saw the exact moment when the music recaptured him. He ran for the glass stairs. I tried a tackle, but I couldn't do much but lunge at his knees and let myself be dragged back up to the place I'd been working so damn hard to escape from. At least I was close to his shoes. Before he set foot on the pavilion, I had pulled one of his dancing slippers off and hurled it into the snow. He turned on me, furious, and I went for the other shoe.

With a snap, he was back in his mock-courtesan outfit, leather breeches and silk shirt, holy symbols rattling at his throat. He growled at me, and ran after his shoes.

I ran faster, toward Georginne's fallen shoe sack, and started throwing the contents at him. There was a shoe for every occasion in that damned sack. I just had to find the one that would fix him.

When the first stiletto hit him between the eyes, Fredo roared and lunged at me, the thought of killing me obviously more tempting than anything the music had to offer. I kept pelting him with shoes. One of them exploded into talcum powder when it hit him, and another covered him in strawberry jam. One unfolded into a pirate's cutlass before I even had it out of the sack, but I tossed it aside. No point in asking for trouble. Fredo trod on one of the many shoes that now littered the snow around him, and was suddenly costumed as the rear end of a pantomime horse.

As he grabbed for my throat, I pushed a fuzzy slipper at him and it unfolded into a giant feather bed that burst, sending feathers everywhere. The next shoe turned into a huge, burning candle. I blew it out and hit Fredo over the head with it.

He went down, dazed.

In about two moments, the music would get hold of him again. It wouldn't be long before it got me too. Already I was feeling the pull of the ruby slippers. But I'd had a brainwave, and none too soon.

There was enough soft wax in the top of the candle to make two sets of ear-stoppers. Once mine were secure, I shoved the second pair in Fredo's ears. He glared at me, but I put a finger to my lips and pointed to the glass pavilion in the hope he would remember where the real threat lay.

Silversword was no longer visible. Only his emerald-slippered feet stuck out from the elegant, writhing mass of gold and amber silks of the mistress of the glass pavilion. We didn't have time to waste.

Fredo's eyes widened at the scene, and he promptly dropped to his knees in prayer to his god, the mighty Raglah the Golden.

I rolled my eyes. Somehow I didn't think that a god who spent most of his time chatting up maidens while pretending to be a giant swan was going to be much help here. I brandished the sack of shoes, and pointed at the glass pavilion.

Fredo stared suspiciously at me, but our duel had at least shown him the versatility of this sack of random weapons. Grudgingly, he nodded. We were allies, for now.

As we reached the top step of the glass pavilion, I saw Silversword's emerald slippers disappearing under the gold and amber silks of the mistress of the glass pavilion.

"War!" I shrieked, and started throwing shoes on to the dance floor. Fredo followed suit, grabbing three or four at a time. Before the mistress had even figured out she was under attack, we had created complete chaos.

Boom!

There were shoes everywhere. The dancers stumbled on to them, and into them. The rose quartz prince stepped in a stray boot and suddenly found himself wearing a full suit of armour. Demi stumbled on a sandal and ended up flat on her back in a large pile of custard.

Fredo and I kept throwing. We weren't even halfway

down the sack. I was beginning to suspect that it was bottomless.

Some of the shoes were musical, rattling out cheery little tunes that disrupted the siren song of the dancing music. Those dancers who tried to battle on regardless soon found themselves stepping out of time, slipping on custard, and generally having a bad time of it.

Chas was the first to free himself, snapped out of his reverie by an exploding glitter bomb of an evening pump with attitude. His assassin's skills returned with a vengeance, and he slithered so fast off that glass pavilion I barely even saw him move. Demi too, once she was free of the custard, thumped her current dancing partner in the snoot and leaped down into the snow, heading for the silver trees.

Fredo was indiscriminate with his shoe hurling. I had a specific target in mind. Every shoe I threw was aimed straight at the bitch queen who was still wrapped around Silversword. My aim sucked, so very few of them had hit her, but you can't blame a girl for trying. Finally a pink lady's dress-boot cracked the queen across the top of her head, spilling chilled champagne in such abundant froth that her silks were soaked into a dripping mess.

I'd hit her where it hurt, right in the wardrobe.

She came up off him with a raging howl that resounded deep inside the glass pavilion. "Who are you to challenge me?"

Her voice was still poised and perfect, even in the depths of rage. I fought the urge to throw myself on her mercy and beg to be forgiven.

Silversword rose up behind her with a pair of ceremonial Zibrian dancing clogs, one in each hand. They were a miracle of modern engineering, pointed metal and jagged edges. He shoved one in under her ribs and used the other to slice her throat open. Her blood bounced against the cold glass of the

pavilion floor as she fell, and she even did that with calculated beauty and grace.

We ran. What else could we do? I tried counting to make
sure all our people were safe, but it was hard to be certain in
the chaos. Silversword rolled free of the glass pavilion, grabbing Georginne as he went. I heard her trying to convince
him that they should stay to pick up all her shoes, but he just
grunted and pulled her away.

The faceless dancers remained on the pavilion, still trying
to dance to the music that even they could no longer hear. I
made a try for Eliander's brother, catching his arm. "You
could come with us. All of you. You could come home..."

His eyes glowed red, and he snarled at me with teeth that
were no longer human. So that was why she'd gone to so
much trouble to hide their faces. I tried to pull free, but he
flashed those fangs of his and came in for my throat. His
gold-suited body jerked twice, then fell back, sliding from
the sword that Eliander had been carrying on his back this
whole time. I stared for a moment at the grim, freckle-faced
hero, wondering if he knew he had just killed his brother.

He knew. He also knew that I knew that he knew. And so
on, and so forth, but there wasn't time for all that. Time
to run.

We raced through the snow. Silversword and Georginne
were ahead of us, Fredo and Demi ahead of them. Chas was
already over the first rise, where the silver trees were thicker.
Behind me, I heard the sound of sharp stiletto shoes ringing
on glass, and I ran even harder.

Bounty Fenetre, World Track Champion of the Cosmos.
Who'd have thought it?

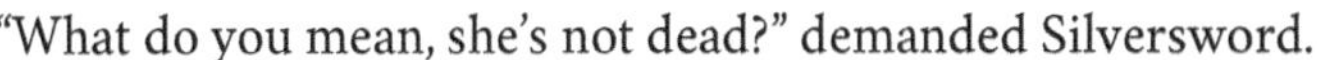

"What do you mean, she's not dead?" demanded Silversword.

The seven of us were sheltering in the silver and gold forest, around one of Georginne's shoe fires. Eliander scrubbed at his sword, all traces of boyishness now eradicated from his freckled face. Fredo sat huddled on a rock, glaring at all of us, but especially at me. I might have saved his life, but he still hated my entrails.

Silversword was outraged by my certainty that the Bitch Queen was still coming after us. "No fey creature walks away from two fatal wounds from cold iron."

Good to know someone still read the old ballads. "She's not fey," I told him. "Not even a little bit."

"Two fatal wounds from cold iron wouldn't do a human much good either," said Chas in a professional tone of voice. He was doing a weapons check, systematically sliding every blade out of concealment on his body, then snapping it back into place. I'd stopped counting after thirty.

"She's not human, either," I sighed. "Not anymore. She's running on pure energy. Liquid elegance." I looked hard at Demi, waiting for her to contribute. "You know what she is. You probably know who, as well. Don't tell me she isn't one of those portraits on the Academy wall."

Demi looked miserable. She barely lifted one graceful shoulder in response.

"She's a courtesan?" said Silversword in disbelief.

"More courtesan than I've ever seen all at once," I said grimly. "I can't think that she's anything else."

"She doesn't have to actually be a courtesan," said Chas brightly. "Maybe she's just eaten so many over the years that we can't tell the difference."

I was still looking at Demi. "Who were the Senior Mistresses before our current lot? This has Academy Retirement Plan written all over it."

"Mistress, not Mistresses," she said quietly. "There was

only ever one Senior Mistress at a time, and the position was won by duelling."

"How do courtesans duel?" Silversword asked with a frown.

"Sequins and hairpins at twenty paces?" suggested Chas, not entirely joking.

"Anastazia was a Senior Mistress who was so powerful that no one could beat her," Demi went on, staring at her feet. Georginne had outfitted us all with furry winter-clothes boots, though she disapproved of how many of her precious shoes I had already wasted. "The more ambitious ladies of the Academy resigned themselves to waiting until she died of old age before they could have a chance at the top spot, but two generations passed and they realised that she wasn't getting any older."

"Magic," grunted a disgusted Fredo.

"Anything but," said Demi. "Anastazia had access to the deepest secrets of the courtesans. It's a different kind of power to magic—order rather than chaos, a form of elegant energy. They discovered that she had been feeding from the younger students. Drinking their life force, their poise and beauty and youth. At least one student every year since she came to power had just—disappeared."

"Seven every seven years, to be exact," said Eliander in a harsh voice. They were the first words he had spoken since killing his brother.

"How did they get rid of her?" Silversword asked.

"No single courtesan could duel her and win," said Demi. "Three of the most powerful and ambitious members of the Academy—Malisand, Valmont and Tiffaine, combined their powers and took her down together in the duel to end all duels. It was the worst kind of cheating, but no one said a word against it. Anastazia was banished from Zibria, and had her courtesan's license revoked. Now we have three Senior

Mistresses, and they have vowed that there will always be three. If one gets too powerful, the other two can intercede. It's too dangerous any other way. Her portrait isn't on the Academy walls any more, Bounty. She represents our greatest shame."

"Did the Senior Mistresses know this was who we were facing?" I asked.

Demi looked startled "I don't think so. They would have come themselves—they've beaten her once. What chance did we have?"

"Assassins have lousy luck against courtesans," muttered Chas. "Somehow they always talk us out of killing them."

Eliander regarded his own weapons, the sword and the club, with some disgust. "If slitting her throat had no effect, I don't suppose hitting her over the head would help."

"If she is not of the fey, my god has given me nothing with which to fight her," said Fredo, sounding genuinely distraught. I made a note to myself to keep clear of the holy symbols he *was* wearing, if they were designed to combat the fey.

Georginne was rummaging through her shoe sack, but with an air of despondency.

"I killed her once and it barely slowed her down," Silver-sword said bitterly.

I interrupted. "Stop feeling sorry for yourselves. We know what she is now, and that means we *do* know how to vanquish her. We need a courtesan to beat her in a duel." There was only one courtesan among us, and we all looked at her.

Demi crumpled. There was little left of the immaculate professional she had been when we set out—the snow and dancing and blood and fear had knocked her calculated training out of her. She shook like a leaf. "I can't. Bounty, I just can't! I'm not strong enough. I'm not good enough! I can't even stand up to Mistress Tiffaine without breaking out in spots. What makes you think I can beat a courtesan who needed all three Senior Mistresses to knock her down?"

"You're a courtesan," I said firmly. "It's what we need right now."

"I'm not courtesan enough!" she wailed, and it was true.

Silversword looked to Georginne a second before I did. "What do you have?"

The little shoe-mistress emerged from her sack with a pair of shabby looking high heels. "These amplify the skills of the wearer," she said.

"Excellent," I breathed. "Any way to make them more specific to courtesans?"

Georginne reached for her carpet back. "I have some beads that belonged to Queen Clio of Zibria."

Demi's smile was heartbreaking, but hopeful. "*Really* Queen Clio?"

"Of course," said Georginne, already threading a needle. The beads were perfect little pearls, almost as white as the snow around us.

A howl reverberated through the woods, the howl of a courtesan on the warpath. "Better hurry," said Eliander, drawing his sword again.

Silversword was frowning. "What has Queen Clio to do with courtesans?"

"She founded our profession," said Demi, almost babbling with enthusiasm. "She declared that there should be a more independent order of concubines, who could not be owned or controlled by others. She even trained as a courtesan herself, saying that the skills would make her a better queen."

Silversword pulled a knife from somewhere and sliced his palm in a rapid movement, holding his own blood out to Georginne as she worked. "You'd better use this, then. Queen Clio of Zibria was my great-grandmother."

Everyone was full of surprises today.

Georginne accepted the palm full of blood without flinching, and drew the blood into the shoe she was stitching. "Demi's, too," she said after a moment, and Silversword passed his knife to Demi so she could also put her blood into the shoes.

We all shivered as a breeze passed over us. It worried me. There had been no wind here the whole time—it was too natural somehow, like stars. It didn't fit with this artificial little place. "She's coming for us," I said.

Demi took the completed shoes from Georginne with trembling hands. They were lopsided little things, all blood and pearls and faded silk, but they were strangely beautiful. Slowly, Demi reached down to slide them on to her feet. She hesitated. "They don't fit."

"Don't be an idiot," I said impatiently. "Just put them on."

"I can't!"

"Take your other shoes off first," I snapped.

"It won't make any difference," Georginne said in that placid, calm voice that I was really beginning to hate. "I didn't make them for her, Bounty."

Everyone looked at me. I had a horrible sinking feeling in my gut. "Oh, no, no, no! I'm not even the beginning of a courtesan!"

"You are now," said Demi, sounding so relieved that I wanted to bite her.

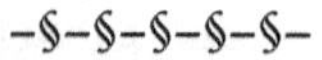

The shoes fit perfectly. In retrospect, I should have been more worried about that, but I was too busy being worried about the overwhelming power that they bled into my body.

Stand up straight was their first command, and I wasn't sure if the words were in my mind or in the shoes themselves.

You are glamour, the shoes told me. *You are queen of the world. You are Courtesan.*

Hear me roar, I thought back at them. They didn't laugh. Shoes have no sense of humour.

Walk as courtesan, they thought back at me. *You are elegance. You are arrogance. You are beauty.*

In that instant I was all of those things and more. I walked across the snow as the haughtiest glamourpuss that ever lived. I breathed poise in and elegance out. My limbs were soft, liquid silk and my spine was so straight and proud it was practically screaming in pain.

I am Courtesan. Hear me purr.

Demi was in my head, that perfect silver mermaid she had been when she first greeted me at the Academy, before she collapsed into self-doubt. Silversword was there, the cool exterior that had protected him from the power of the Senior Mistresses. Georginne was there in every stitch, but I wasn't sure what qualities she was adding to the mix apart from the vital knowledge of how to walk in exceptionally high heels, and I was already pretty good at that.

Behind all of them was another voice, a queenly presence that hovered in the pearls of my shoes. I didn't know much about Queen Clio of Zibria except that she had been the second most beautiful woman of her era, and that she was so glamorous it made everybody's teeth hurt.

Except, apparently, Silversword's great-grandfather.

Was it Queen Clio's imperious voice telling me to face my enemy as one woman to another, to begin the duel by arching my eyebrow and end it by crushing the bitch's face into the ground? I don't know, but the voice was starting to get on my nerves.

I glowed with glamour. My enemy glowed even more

brightly. She emerged through the silver and gold trees, slowly enough for me to see that she had changed her costume. She was as white as the snow, gleaming so brightly that it hurt to look at her. She was the Queen of Courtesans, and what the hell was I?

I was Bounty Fenetre, a half-hobgoblin ragamuffin in a borrowed pair of shoes, a battered leather gymslip, torn fishnet tights and tangled hair that just wasn't willing to stay in pigtails any longer. How could I face the Queen of Courtesans on equal terms when she was dressed so much better than I was?

On the other hand, I was wearing a truly kick-ass pair of shoes.

She stepped closer, and I saw her cheekbones sneering at me. Her mouth was so perfect that you'd think it belonged to the Goddess of Pretty Pink Mouths. Her eyes were wide and deep, a colour so original that they belonged in a museum.

And, oh crap, her eyebrows were starting to arch. I had no chance.

The shoes had other ideas. They walked me towards her, so stylishly that my feet almost dissolved with their own smugness. The spirit of Queen Clio filled my skin, and damn it all if I didn't arch my eyebrow first.

"You cannot defeat me," slinked Anastazia, Courtesan of Courtesans.

I almost opened my mouth to agree with her, until the shoes reminded me that by breaking our mutually haughty silence, she had conceded a point to me. I said nothing, following up my first victory with a pout to end all pouts, and a head tilt so subtle that my chin almost fainted with pride.

Her nose lifted in chilly challenge.

I breathed, conveying my own self-importance in the soft cloud of air that enveloped my face.

She lifted her lashes, as if to ask how I dared meet her on anything like equal terms.

I let a soft, graceful sneer envelop my face so slowly that she might almost think herself to have imagined it.

She radiated exquisite indignation without moving a muscle, and her power was so fierce in its subtlety that I wavered on the verge of collapsing, declaring my submission, craving her pardon.

The shoes would not let me submit. Silversword's pride mixed with that of his ancestress, and they both held me upright, unflinching. Demi entered the picture with a brief hint of a move that could win me this game before I gave away that I had never done this before.

As the afterglow of Anastazia's indignation burned around me, I swivelled my shoes in an agonisingly sophisticated manner, and turned my back on her.

It wasn't subtle, but boy did it make her furious. She moved frighteningly fast, and was there in front of me by the time I had completed my turn. With outrage burning in her uniquely-coloured irises, she slapped me hard across the face.

If I had fallen, she would have won. It was a bold move. But the shoes caught me, and Queen Clio's spirit bled from her pearls into my flesh, and she gave me the confidence to do what needed to be done.

I did nothing. I did not even flick an eyelash. I ignored the slap with such pure, poisonous abandon that it was as if she had never touched me. It was, in fact, as if she did not exist.

She sneered at me from on high, but it was too late. The moment had passed. She was not perfect anymore, she was not unbeatable. With haughty, casual disinterest radiating from every pore of my skin, I glanced away from her, as if something slightly more interesting had caught my eye.

Power poured from her, the terrible energy of a courtesan

scorned, and I was all but flattened by the pressure. I fell to the snow, crushed by the beauty and grace and perfection that she had cultivated for so many decades. She was strong enough to annihilate me, and we both knew it.

Nevertheless, I had won. It was a strange thought. Stranger still was the way that I was able to move so gently, sliding my hand down the neckline and pulling the little, twisted hobgoblin shoe from my breast-band. It came free easily. I pulled it out and extended my arm as if I had all the time in the world, plunging it quite casually into the flesh of the Queen of Courtesans.

The shoe slid into her body like a sharp knife, exactly where her heart would be if it still beat like a mortal's. She shattered, her skin as brittle as ice, and her poise bled on to the snow. When she fell, it was a graceful movement, but somewhat less than exquisite.

The Queen is dead, long live the Queen... I rose to my feet with slow, liquid motion. I was Courtesan, the Highest Courtesan in the world. Grace, elegance and exquisite beauty ran in my veins, and my whole body throbbed with how perfect I was.

I took one flawless step, then another. My power filled me from edge to edge, and I gloried in it. There was another courtesan here, crouching in the snow. She would be easy pickings, an after dinner mint following the magnificent spectacle of the main course.

Demi saw me coming for her, and cringed. I could obliterate her with one bat of my eyelashes. I poured towards her, glowing with the marvellous precision of my own movements.

Silversword stepped between us, standing up to me. The man was like a bucket of ice water, his whole body language screaming that my radiant lusciousness left him unmoved. "It doesn't impress me, Bounty," he said in a voice so cool that it pulled me apart.

I hesitated for just a moment, and my power wavered. The new Queen of Courtesans had been vanquished in a new and interesting way. In the moment that I hesitated, four people lunged for my feet. Chas and Eliander worked together to separate me from my left blood-and-pearl slipper, while Georginne and Demi practically took their teeth to my right foot. When they had finished, I stood barefoot in the snow, and the chill was enough to bring me back to reality.

"Oh, bloody, bloody hell!"

Silversword looked meaningfully at Georginne, who grudgingly produced a new pair of shoes for me to wear. "Don't throw these at anyone."

I was so cold I was willing to promise anything. "Yes, yes! Hand them over."

Only when my feet were all snuggly and dry did I think of looking at the fallen body of my vanquished Queen of Courtesans. She wasn't that anymore, of course; the loss of her power had rendered her Anastazia again. She was an ordinary corpse of an average-shaped woman lying there in the snow.

"We should cut her head off, to be sure," said Fredo.

"Her limbs as well," said Eliander. "We could bury them in separate places."

"Good plan," said Chas, producing a truly wicked set of chopping knives from gods-knew-where.

"Leave the shoe in her heart," said Georginne, in a small voice. "You don't want it to start beating again."

My, they were a bloodthirsty little mob.

"No one's cutting anything off!" I said loudly. "She's a conquered, dead old lady. Leave her be."

"We'll take her back with us," said Demi in a clear voice. "We burn our dead in Zibria."

There was a long pause.

"Works for me," said Silversword.

"I suppose we could scatter the ashes in different places," said Eliander.

"I could do a cleansing ritual to prevent her from reconstituting herself," suggested Fredo.

Chas weighed his chopping knives wistfully. "Are you sure I can't just cut her head off?"

And then what? We went home. Seemed like the thing to do. We went back to the glass pavilion first to see if Anastazia's death had released the remaining dark princes and princesses from their demonic bondage. In a way I suppose it had, because we found nothing but little heaps of dancing slippers, and tatters of the costumes they had worn.

Georginne collected up those shoes along with her own, and her sack was seriously bulging by the time we left.

It wasn't that easy, of course, to leave the snowy realm of the Queen of Courtesans. We had to find the gondola—and also, the river—and the only way to do that was to search the whole damn silver and gold forest until we found where it had been stashed.

Then there was the problem of how to get the gondola to move upriver given that her Majesty's invisible gondoliers had retired, or faded from existence, or whatever. We managed eventually, poling our way against the current with branches hacked from the silver and gold trees.

It was a long and laborious journey home, and for a while there we all thought there would be no escape, but finally we emerged into the Zibrian canals of the mortal world, and our quest was at an end.

We drifted up the canals so slowly that the Senior Mistresses were informed of our return in plenty of time to be standing on the bank in true stately manner to welcome us home.

There were streamers. Even talk of a parade. Hard to enjoy it, when our only trophy (apart from the silver and gold branches) was an old woman's body on a makeshift bier.

"You said you weren't a bounty hunter," said Mistress Red to me when she saw the corpse of Anastazia.

I almost stuck my tongue out at her, but the vestiges of courtesanry that still lingered in my blood transformed it into a withering stare. Damn it, that was a bad sign.

Back in the Courtesan Academy I was ushered into a dressing room to find my real clothes waiting for me. It was such a relief to scramble into my chainmail lingerie and big grey suede boots—to feel like Bounty again. Was it my imagination, though, or was I throwing on my clothes a little more carefully and gracefully than I used to? There was a quiet knock on the door, and Silversword stepped inside. For the first time, I saw him dressed as himself, rather than in some costume or disguise. Clothes do make the man—or, at least, they tell you an awful lot about him. He was all in grey, with his Emperor's livery on his arms and chest. Sombre, dignified and business-like.

His boots were grey leather, but not as cute as mine. Thank goodness. A girl has to have some pride.

We looked at each other for a moment, the serious imperial champion and the flighty hobgoblin adventuress.

Another knock, and Demi poked her head in. "There you two are! The Mistresses want to see you."

"They do?" Hard to get excited about that.

"To present your rewards, of course. Especially you,

Bounty. They were very excited when they heard about you channelling Queen Clio to conquer Anastazia. I think they want to offer you a place here, in the Academy."

Interesting. "I'll be along in a minute."

"Don't be long!" She withdrew.

I looked at Silversword again. Was it my imagination, or had the distance tripled between us since Demi's announcement? "Come on. You can help me find a window to climb out of."

He lifted his eyebrow a little. "I would have thought joining the Courtesan Academy was just your sort of thing. Power, glamour, the chance to find out if there really is a Secret Police of Zibria..."

I would have thought exactly the same thing not so long ago. "And end up like Anastazia, all frocks and glitter and desperately trying to out-glamour everyone for eternity? No thanks."

He was gazing intently at me. "What?" I said defensively.

"People don't impress me very often, I was appreciating the moment."

"Moments are one thing," I said firmly. "Windows are another. Let's get out of here."

One window later, we were on our way out of Zibria. Together. I found myself wanting to take my time. "So, I impressed you, huh?"

"A little."

"Impressed enough to walk a girl home?"

Was that a smile I saw on his face? A flicker, anyway. A very promising flicker. "I think I can manage that. Where's home for you?"

"I don't currently have one." There's a flaw in every plan.

"Ah. Well, I have to get back to Dreadnought eventually."

"Sounds like as good a place as any." Mm. Dreadnought was right at the other end of Mocklore. It would be a good long journey, with plenty of opportunity for all kinds of interesting developments along the way.

"Excellent," said Silversword, and he sounded like he meant it.

I had a thought. "I didn't stop you picking up *your* reward from the Senior Mistresses, did I?"

"I didn't do this for a reward," he said pointedly.

"Well, now you've impressed me."

"Stab me, my life is complete."

We continued on our merry way, bantering a little and flirting a lot. So he was impressed with me turning down a potentially lucrative and glamorous career as a courtesan, was he? I'd better not tell him that I had souvenired the pearl-and-blood slippers. They were currently stashed in my travel pack between my pillow and my wash bag. I might not want to be a courtesan now, but that doesn't mean I won't change my mind. I'm not sure if I've mentioned it before, but I'm a very fickle person.

After all, they are very cute shoes.

II

DELTA VOID IS NOT A MERCENARY

DELTA VOID AND THE UNICORN SOUP

In Skullcap, a little seaport on the edge of nowhere, there's a street where only the beautiful people go. Not a formal rule, but one of life's natural laws: dragons are flameproof, emperors are crazy and you need a beauty licence to get into the Beautiful Street. Even the most beautiful people don't venture along that particular stretch of cobbled asphalt unless they are looking their tip-top best—wearing their prettiest tunics and their sleekest boots, faces prinked and painted with various colourful metallic compounds. And that's just the men.

The irony is that it isn't a particularly attractive street. Oh, it's clean enough, so the beautiful people won't get their beautiful shoes dusty, but there are nicer streets to be seen in Skullcap—or anywhere else, for that matter.

Still, a custom is a custom, so when I was summoned to one of the most exclusive hotels in the Beautiful Street, I decided to wear Benedetta for the occasion. Of all my jumbled personae, Benedetta is the most attractive. She exudes a certain warmth, an indefinable air of quality. I do have more beautiful personae to call upon, but they're either totally psychopathic or just plain brain dead, set aside in my Absolute Emergency (don't ever go there) category.

So it was Benedetta in her red and white polka-dotted frock with built-in bodice straps who breezed into the bar of the hotel, and slid into a marble-tiled booth.

It was several minutes before the Chef came over, and I was already furnished with a high glass of bubbles and ice cream that a passing waiter had spontaneously given me, no charge. I love being Benedetta.

"Are you ze agent from Claddius?" the Chef growled in an accent I couldn't place at all. The Beautiful Street probably demands its food service professionals display fake accents so that the clientele can feel superior.

I batted my eyes at him (well, Benedetta did) and toyed with my straw. "Who would you like me to be?" That's the main drawback with being Benedetta. She flirts like it's her job.

The performance had little effect on the Chef. "What eez your name?"

"Benedetta," I said coyly. Damn, but the novelty soon wears off with this one. I hate being coy.

He dropped his accent like a hot mouthful of stew. Ha, I knew it. "Your real name, doll. Think I don't know a Switcher when I see one?"

Doll? I looked around to make sure no one would notice the sudden appearance of my less than perfect nose in the midst of the Beautiful Street glamour. Then I switched to my original form, with less sex appeal but more brains and a better sense of humour.

The Chef nodded, his theory had been confirmed. "Name?"

"Delta Void," I told him in my most business-like voice, squirming in Benedetta's little polka-dotted dress. Those bodice straps fit her a lot better than they fit me. "DV for short. Claddius said you had an assignment."

I'm an odd job agent (not a mercenary, they're illegal you know) and Claddius handles the business side of it. He gets me the weirdest gigs, especially when he muddles me up with his other main client—Barko the circus act.

"I need a unicorn," the Chef hissed at me. "Soon as possible, yesterday at the latest."

I would have laughed out loud, but I didn't want to draw attention towards my less than perfect nose. "Are you serious?"

Nervous, he retreated to his obscure accent. "Ze gossip minstrels 'ave announced ze latest diet fad to ze Street, and a unicorn eez ze main ingredient. I must 'ave eet."

"Of course it's a good diet food," I snapped back. "Extinct animals mean zero calories. Can't you just slaughter something and say it's unicorn?"

He gasped, wounded to the quick. "Weez ze discerning palates in zis street? I zeenk not!"

I tried to spell it out for him "There aren't any unicorns left, except in—" The bastard was grinning. "Oh, no. I'm not going there!"

"Where ze bluegums grow," said the Chef.

"There are no more bluegums," I told him desperately. "The last plantations were wiped out by the Glimmer—they were all turned into clockwork typewriters or something. Purple clockwork typewriters."

"Zey are plentiful in zee Outback," the Chef told me smarmily.

"And that's where I'll find you a unicorn, I suppose," I sighed. "Do you know what that place is like?" It was worth a shudder, so I shuddered.

"Obviously you do. You 'ave been zere before, yes?"

"I had the personae to cope with it in those days," I growled at him. "My collection is more depleted now."

He named a figure. A big one.

I drew my eyebrows together and named an even more exorbitant figure, hopefully one that would make his legs fall off in shock, so he would forget the whole idea.

He added the two numbers together, scribbling the result on a scrap of parchment, and handed it to me.

I'm a sucker, I know I'm a sucker. But 212 is my lucky number, and a girl can't resist an offer like that, not when her boot soles are worn as thin as mine are.

You did realise that we were talking about free meals, didn't you? 212 meals in the Beautiful Street is 212 damn fine meals, even if I had to dress up as Benedetta every time to claim one. And maybe I could trade some of them for a new pair of boot soles.

~

That's how I ended up wandering through the multi-coloured peaks of the devastatingly weird Skullcap Mountains, looking for a gateway into the most bloody horrible alternate dimension ever devised. And that is how I met Lance.

I was wearing Herna the Huntress at the time and she spotted him a mile off, marching along in his brown leathers and dull grey furs—he stood out like a beacon among the bright, acrylic leaves and tangles of this part of the Skullcaps, which is mostly fuschia and fluorescent green.

Since Herna was dominant I couldn't prevent her from throwing a spear at him, though at least I deflected her aim so it only struck him in the leg. I switched to DV and hurried over to see how he was. I can be caring! Well, actually I'm not that good at caring, so I switched over to Bettany the seamstress (I haven't had any healers in me since the Year of the Superflood).

Still, Bettany did the trick, stitched him up and kept him happily drugged on lionsbane (don't ask me how she knows what these herbs do, she has a weird background) until he was fixed. By this time it was almost sunset and I was willing to do almost anything to avoid going into the Outback, so I let Bettany set up camp and cook a nice stew, then I switched over to DV in order to eat it. I'm no fool.

Lance was still groggy, but I managed to get his name out of him and some soup into him before he lapsed either into sleep or a coma.

Sleeping on the ground isn't all it's cracked up to be. They never mention that in epic poetry, do they? "And the hero was extra bad-tempered because he had a crick in his neck and dust in his shoes from a night with a dead log as his only pillow, so he slew them all, including the damsel in distress…" Now there's a bedtime story with some realism.

Morning came, and my newfound knight in grubby leathers awoke. As the smell of sizzling bacon overpowered the annoying smell of nearby bluegum, he told me what he was doing in these parts.

I stared at him, gobsmacked. "You're a what?"

"A dragon hunter," he replied, smacking his own lips around a piece of bacon.

I laughed at him. "You're kidding! You hunt dragons? What, were the sheep a bit much for you? Got bored of stalking kittens with long spears?"

He was disgruntled, as if I had mortally offended him, which I probably had. DV may be my natural form (well, as natural as forms get for a Switcher like me) but she doesn't have much tact.

Anyway, this Lance person swelled up his chest. "Dragons

are a ferocious and deadly beast, milady. Only the bravest and the noblest of heart can slay a dragon."

I gave him a slow and steady look. "You're not from around here, are you?" The only dragons I know are farmed for their scales, docile as bunny rabbits.

He ignored that, biting savagely into his bacon. "What are *you* hunting, pray? When not spearing strange knights in the leg, that is."

"I'm hunting a unicorn," I said glumly. "Fool's errand, but a job's a job."

He smiled beatifically. "Ah, the chaste young maiden seeking to capture a unicorn to be her love slave."

"I beg your pardon?" I grabbed my own piece of bacon and blew hard on it to cool it to eating temperature. "Not a maiden, thank you very much, not particularly chaste, and I don't need a love slave. What book of epic poetry did you pull that one out of, mate? I'm snaring a unicorn for the cooking pot."

He stared at me in horror. "You mean—to eat?"

"Gods know why. It'll taste terrible, tough as old boots." I stuffed the rest of the bacon in my mouth and wiped my hands on my trews. "Now if you'll excuse me, I've got a terrifying alternate dimension to ransack. Have a nice day."

He grabbed my arm, almost apoplectic with shock. "B-B-but unicorns are beautiful magical, aethereal creatures. Precious to the gods, symbols of purity!"

I gave him a long, hard stare. "You're really not from around here."

The long and the short of it is that the well-meaning clot decided to come along with me, in search of his big ferocious dragons (I don't know who spun him that tall tale) and in the hope that he could convince me to give up this idea of catching a unicorn for the dinner table. And miss out on all those free meals? Not likely. Besides, I knew something he didn't about unicorns.

Once the fire was doused and the scent of bacon washed away, the bluegums were easy to smell. The Skullcap Mountains are a weird place—so many magical explosions and mystical convergences have happened here that mysterious portals are stacked three-deep, tucked between the cracks in reality.

I have a good nose for these things. Well, Sadonna does. She's my most mystical persona, a willowy creature with long hair and trailing jewellery. She can get high on one incense stick, and does so too frequently for my liking, but she's good at sniffing out doorways to other universes, which was just what I needed.

No one really knows what the Outback is. It's a broad land with desert up to your neck and sky down to your ankles. A land where the bits and pieces of reality go when they're no longer needed. I went there, once upon a time, for some stupid reason or another, and at least six of my personae got themselves killed. I wasn't looking forward to this trip. But the bacon had been the last of my supplies, and I didn't plan to go hungry this winter, so…

Sadonna moved forward, trailing wisps of sea-green lace and sniffing healthily.

Lance followed, his eyes squarely on her prominent cleavage, which was boosted by various arcane means. I've never understood the whole underwire thing, myself. "How do you change like that?" he asked eagerly. "Your whole body, features, personality. How do you do it?"

Sadonna gave him a much more tolerant smile than I ever would have. "It's ma-agic," she said dreamily, and stepped forward. Into the Outback.

I switched back to DV and took a deep breath to clear my head from Sadonna's vague personality. "Well, here we are." I swung my rucksack back over my shoulder. The smell of bluegum was intoxicating, only slightly toxic. "Seen any dragons yet?"

"Nay," said Lance, in his know-it-all voice that told me a lecture was on the way (I knew him so well already). "The beasts only nest in the mountain tops and the deep caves, they would never be seen out in the open like this, and at night."

It was night here, did I mention that? The moon was succulently full and everything seemed blue, even the gritty ground. There was a glow of something like fire in the distance. I shaded my eyes, trying to make it out. A moment later, I realised what it was.

Even before Lance could tell me 'I told you so' about dragons being large and ferocious, it was already on top of us. Don't ask me where it came from—maybe it was a left-over from the old days, when knights were bold and stupid. Maybe there were other doors that led from the Outback—doors to distant lands, where dragons were too bloody big for their own good. Then again, maybe the daft berk had conjured it up out of his over-active imagination. I wouldn't put it past him. Trust me, the claws and teeth were real.

Lance threw himself forward with a crow of triumph, sword in hand. He was going to get himself killed. I sifted my mind for a persona who could cope with this situation, but most of them lay cowering in the back of my subconscious. Only one came to mind, and it was a full moon too, damn it, damn it. I could feel her rising to the occasion, swelling up in my over-crowded psyche.

"Excuse me," I called out apologetically to my travelling companion, and switched.

Into Miss Lunatic.

The moon filled me up with light and I tore forward, clawing, shrieking, ten foot tall. I ate into the dragon, bit his flank and felt the blood drip down my body—Miss Lunatic always leaves me with excessive dry-cleaning bills.

The distraction allowed Lance to fit together his namesake, a long pointy pole that I presumed he was planning to stick into the dragon at some point. I was thwacked from behind by a tail (or a wing) and went flying, my werewolf senses momentarily dazed.

Lance charged the dragon full on, but the canny beast simultaneously sidestepped and sideswiped him. As he fell, Lance yelled my name or something very like it, but it was too late for me.

Miss Lunatic gets easily distracted, and while Lance was fighting for his life with the overgrown lizard, Miss Lunatic was off with the faeries, dancing the werewolf dance across the desert floor of the Outback, baying to the moon. More trouble than she's worth, that one.

～

Sunrise came to the Outback, and I woke up (DV again, and none too soon) with a fit of coughing, spitting up hairballs and feeling like death warmed up. I crawled back to the mouth of the overgrown desert dimension, half-expecting to find several little wet pieces of Lance that would need burying.

He was still alive, though he had an oozing claw wound in his side. The dragon was dead.

Feeling seedy, I nudged the beast with my toe. "Need help harvesting?"

Lance stared up at me, looking worse than I did. "Harvest?" he croaked.

I picked a handful of bluegum leaves and passed them to him to staunch the wound. 101 uses, you know. "Sure. The meat and the scales—though gods know what use the scales will be, they don't seem to hang together nicely like normal-sized dragon scales do."

Just as well, really, or you'd get the burly drakherd sons up here, trying to catch a beast to mate with their Flossies and Shirlies, and I know for a fact that they shear the dragons every year by whirling them around their heads and frightening the scales off them—having crossbred their little Flossie with Draco here, the drakherd boys would break their backs come harvest season, though I doubt if even that would stop them.

"What a horrible idea," Lance said distastefully. "There will be no desecration of this body."

I stared at him. "Why did you kill it if you weren't going to harvest the meat and scales? You could have run away. Why provoke it?"

He shifted slightly, to give me a better view of his belt. And the notches on it.

I was too horrified to speak, too horrified even to think, and I probably would have hit him in his pretty-boy face if the unicorn hadn't chosen that moment to come out of the bushes.

From a distance, unicorns look aethereal and lovely. Close up, they look more like me after a hard night's were-wolf rave. This fellow was greyish rather than pure white and he had a straggly little beard that trickled down to his knobbly knees. His nasty yellow eyes were bleary. His horn was at a disreputable angle. Still, he was definitely unicorn shaped.

Lance's face was beatific, and he reached longingly out to the creature. "Oh, beauteous one. Cleanse me, heal me. Let me share your magnificence."

The unicorn stepped towards him and I readied myself, because there's one thing I know about unicorns that Lance, being from well out of town, doesn't. The thing about unicorns is, they're evil bastards.

Perhaps Lance realised from the horrible glint in its eye, because he flung himself aside at the last minute and the horn caught him smack in the left shoulder instead of through his heart. I suppose that was a good thing. As he screamed with pain and the horn was temporarily occupied, I switched to Herna the Huntress and wielded my trusty machete, chopping the horn off at the stem.

The other thing about unicorns is that once you remove their horn, they're totally lamblike. Old Goat-Features didn't even mind carrying a wounded knight on his way to the soup pot (we dropped the blighter off near the Skullcap docks to catch a boat back to wherever he came from).

So the Beautiful Street ate soup, and the unicorn's horn was a trophy displayed to prove that the unicorn soup was the real thing (although I know for a fact that the Chef thickens his stock with farmed dragon meat, to make it go further) and everyone was happy until the new fad came along.

As for me, I ate well that winter and I had new boot soles too, the kind which go click-clack on the cobbles, because I'd finally figured out a use for over-sized dragon scales.

Hey, I call it a happy ending.

DELTA VOID'S DAY OFF

It was the middle of the afternoon when I stepped on to the docks, surveying the city of Skullcap. I'd been away long enough that even the usual dockside scents of salt, grease and *fish fish fish* were welcome to me.

I walked with purpose towards the Business District (which, thanks to the small size of our city, is also the Theatre District, the Restaurant District, the Palace District and the Strangely Fashionable Little Antique Shop District).

My manager Claddius has an office on the ground floor of a skinny brick building in Chartreuse Street, which just goes to show that he's wealthier than he claims to be. Ground floor rents are sky-high around here because the tightly packed buildings, narrow streets and houses built out of oil-soaked driftwood make the city a major fire risk. Ground floor tenants are the ones most likely to survive when Skullcap inevitably goes up like a bonfire on heat.

My routine goes something like this—I stroll into the office and harass Claddius's secretary to pay me for the last job I completed. She in turn smiles sweetly and pretends not to have the faintest idea who I am. We exchange insults, threats and blows. About the time that I'm on my knees, trying to scratch her eyes out while avoiding her talon-like fingernails, Claddius will pop his head in from his back office, express surprise at seeing me and then express even further surprise that I think he owes me money. He offers me barter goods such as eggs, dried fish and live goats, reminding me that Mocklore is mostly a cash-free society. We exchange insults, threats, blows…and I eventually get paid, because he fights like a limp kitten.

The secretary was noticeably absent today, probably off getting her fingernails waxed or her armpits decorated with glue-on sequins. I knocked on the door of Claddius's inner sanctum and strolled right in.

"DV," he said in a friendly voice that made me instantly suspicious. "Nice to see you, my dear. Good trip?"

"You mean your feathered spies haven't already notified you how many times I was seasick on the way home, and how many sea monsters attacked the ship between Northport and Skullcap? You must be losing your touch."

He's a fine figure of a man, my agent—assuming you like your men soft around the middle and fraying at the edges. He wears a toga like they didn't go out of fashion two hundred years ago, and some moronic female must once have told him that he looks good in profile, because he constantly tilts his head back and forth when he talks to you, as if inviting you to comment on the aristocratic length of his nose.

Oh, yes, and he has a voice like cream. The kind the cat got.

"Problems, DV? You sound moody. Over-emotional, I expect, home sweet home and all that. I know just what will take your mind off it…"

"Four jobs in a row not enough for you, Claddius? I didn't even get to stay for the Middens wedding, after all that work

I did finding the bride, then you sent me a homing pigeon about the Dreadnought silk theft before I'd even finished the Zibrian murder mystery. I'm home now and I deserve a damn good holiday!"

Claddius did his best not to go pink at the mention of the dread word, 'holiday'. He tried to look understanding—at least, I think that's what he was trying to do. Either that, or he was suppressing a hiccup. "DV. Honey. Sweetpea. I know you've been rushed off your feet, but it's a madhouse around here. Fenella quit to get married, Guido got headhunted by the Rat Runners, and no one's even heard from Vander since he went up against that two-headed goblin colony on the East Coast. There just aren't as many reliable mercenaries around as there used to be."

I stood up quickly. "Okay, that's enough. I can cope with being hassled to do more work and I can cope with being spied on by freaky talking birds, but now you're mentioning the m-word, you know, the illegal one? That worries me, Claddius, it really worries me."

Mercenaries have been illegal since Emperor Timregis figured out they were the reason that the Fifty-Seven Years War lasted so long. There hasn't been a war in Mocklore since he made the decree, generally regarded as the only sensible decision he has made in his fifty-four year reign. I am *not* a mercenary. I do random jobs for pay. It's totally different.

Claddius put his hands up defensively. "Honeycake. Relax, please. Slip of the tongue, nothing more. There just aren't so many odd job agents available right now, and you're the best. I can't trust anyone else with my sensitive cases."

I smiled one of my nastier smiles. "Sounds like I have something to bargain with."

His shoulders sagged a little. "What's it going to take?"

I was enjoying my brief illusion of power. "I want full

payment for the last four jobs—in actual money, not hair-dressing coupons or baby rabbits. I owe my landlady some serious rent. I also want a substantial bonus for accepting new jobs while still in the field."

Claddius opened his mouth as if to argue, then shut it. "Anything else?"

"Yep. I want a day off."

I was expecting him to go green, but he took it quite well. "Just the one?" Damn. I should have tried to squeeze a week out of him. "So you'll be in bright and early tomorrow for your next assignment?"

Ooh, nice try. "Uh-uh. Today is travelling time. Tomorrow is my day off. I'll be in bright and early the day *after* for my next assignment."

Claddius sighed. "Fine. See you then."

I waited. He raised his eyebrows, tilting that damned profile at me again. "Something else, DV?

"My *money*, Claddius."

I emerged from his office with a spring in my step and a rattling purse. Squeezing actual coinage out of Claddius was an achievement in itself, but I'd also scored a whole day off of my very own. I'd forgotten what it was like to have time to myself.

Next, I went to visit my dealer. Gallicon hangs out in the Docks District (also the Market District, Pawn Shop District and Seedy Bar You Wouldn't Take Your Grand-mother To District). He owns a bar the size of a broom closet, with a shiny marble counter opening on to the street. There's never any produce in sight, only Gallicon's elbows propped on the clean counter as he watches the world go by.

"DV," he croaked in a gravelly voice as I approached. "What's your pleasure?"

"The good stuff, of course. What's special today?"

He grinned at me with his disturbing mouth. Every second tooth was missing. "I wouldn't trust just anyone with this, DV, but you're a good girl. I think I can let you loose on it." He vanished behind his bar. I heard a few gloppy noises. Gallicon emerged in a rush, hauling something large, white and flabby on to the pristine marble counter. It flopped winsomely on the hard surface, tentacles splayed.

"Squid!" Gallicon yelled proudly, as if identifying the gender of a firstborn baby.

"I can see that." I leaned forward and sniffed. "Is it going to taste like it smells?"

Gallicon tapped his nose knowingly. "Maybe if you cook it hard and fast, kiddo. But if you work it slowly, the flavours will be beyond all previous experience." He kissed his fingers extravagantly.

"If it's so good, why aren't you busy stewing it up for your wife and sixteen children?"

"I got another twelve just like it out the back," he confessed.

I tossed him a heavy coin. "Wrap it. Throw in two dozen oysters." I paused. "The oysters *are* good today, aren't they?" I had been craving oysters since Dreadnought.

Gallicon kissed his fingers again. "Fat as pigs and fresh as newborn little daisies."

"Make it three dozen."

Ten minutes later and I was home, opening up the windows of my cozy attic room and letting the chopped squid simmer in spices on the top of my stove. Most people in upper floor apartments aren't allowed any kind of cooking apparatus because of the whole setting-the-city-ablaze possibility, but my stove involves no naked flames. My mad Uncle

Imago built it entirely out of clockwork. At least, I think it's made of clockwork. I definitely hear whirring when I start it up.

I rinsed and swallowed several oysters before getting to work on the sauce. I had bought a bag full of Chiantrian fruits from a market stall on my way home and now busied myself pulping oranges, pale reds and yellowish greens before hacking my way into a coconut and draining the milk into a bowl. Whipped together with a slug of lionade (a sweet white liquor brewed in the back streets of Zibria), it made a satisfying sizzle when I poured it into the squid pot. The most amazing smell filled my attic, wafting out the open windows on the cool spring breeze.

A moment or two later, someone wafted in through my windows, a bottle of wine tucked under each arm. He somersaulted neatly and placed the bottles with reverent care on my sideboard. "Hello, ducks. Long time, no fish."

Stamp lives on the floor below me, and is usually the first to smell dinner happening. Windows are his favoured method of transport since a) he's a cat burglar and b) he and his roommate Chas (who has an equally dodgy profession) boarded up the doors of their apartment long ago so you can't tell it's there unless you count the windows from the outside.

Stamp has a theory that if you don't look like a cat burglar, people don't think you are one even if you climb in their bedroom window and pinch all their valuables. I'm pretty sure that's also the reason that he cultivates an accent that's far too posh to be real. Today he was wearing a striped silk suit, a bright green cravat, and an actual goddamned boater hat. "It's terrible," he complained. "You've been gone for the entire scallop season. I expected at least one decent curry out of you this year." I tossed him an oyster in a half shell and he slurped at it with relish. "Fine, I forgive you. What smells good?"

"Squid. What are we drinking tonight?"

"No idea, pet, but the bottles were heavily guarded when I stole them from Lord Rynehart's cellar, so they must be good." He peered at the dusty bottles. "Could be Gazpartan red."

"Fancy. Set the table?"

While Stamp located my tablecloth collection and complained about the moth-holes, I turned the heat down and covered the squid, letting it bubble away satisfactorily.

Kaitlin arrived next, through the conventional door with a giant bowl balanced in her arms. "Hi Delta! Heard you on the stairs, so I chucked a salad together. Hope I made enough."

"Because we could never have enough lettuce," sighed Stamp. His tone changed instantly when he spied the pristine tablecloth folded over Kait's shoulder. "Civilisation, at last! DV, you and your threadbare rag collection are an embarrassment to us all." He shook the cloth over my squeaky but serviceable dining table.

"You're rather precious for someone who has no idea of the price of milk," I complained.

Kait put her salad on the counter and came to give me a hug. "I hope that old bastard paid you what you're worth. Three and a half months away!"

"Never fear," I grinned at her. "I talked him into giving me actual money." I nodded towards the large leather pouch near the door.

"Really, truly? No dairy cows or counterfeit diamonds or baby rabbits?" My housemates have never let me forget the baby rabbits. "Astounding. Shall I take it with me when I go?"

"You'd better, or I'll end up spending it on fripperies like vegetables." Kait is our landlady and my banker, which is a surprisingly sensible arrangement as long as you trust both your landlady and your banker.

Stamp fussed with the cutlery. "I'm going to steal you some better forks," he said sternly. Another minute and he would be whinging that I didn't own linen napkins. (I did, but I kept them in my first aid kit when travelling, so useful for mopping up blood and gore!)

A screech came from the door as Aimee made her entrance. She dumped a plate of cakes in the middle of the table and bounded towards me, sweeping me up in an enthusiastic hug. She smelled of strawberry perfume. "DV, it's been ages! Where have you been?"

"Everywhere," I said, laughing at her exuberance. "Mostly the Middens, not my favourite place to spend winter."

"Umm," she said, inhaling deeply. "Squid? I could smell it from all the way downstairs. Luckily the goddess has received lots of dessert-style offerings lately."

Aimee is a priestess of Mocklore's one remaining lust-goddess, Amorata. She had the bedroom of her first-floor apartment consecrated as a temple a few years ago.

"Are we allowed to eat cakes that were offered to the goddess?" Kait asked. "Won't Amorata complain?"

Aimee shrugged. "As long as I save her anything with macadamia nuts in it, no problem. She's sick of cream cake and rose jelly; there's been a glut lately. She prefers buttered toast and a pickled onion whenever I summon her."

"DV, you glorious peasant," yelled Stamp from the table. "When are you going to put all of us out of our misery and invest in some double damask table napkins?"

Seriously, double damask napkins, so absorbent for minor flesh wounds.

We were sitting down to eat when a long loaf of bread sailed through one of the open windows, followed by a gorgeous young man with soulful blue eyes and a killer smile. Only Stamp moved fast enough to catch the bread. He's lived with Chas a long time.

"Chuck it on the table," I said.

"Straight on the tablecloth?" said Stamp.

Chas shook his head disapprovingly at me. "DV, that's cruel. How many tablecloths do you have to kill right in front of him before you learn the error of your ways."

Diplomacy and sarcasm are such similar skills, I'm never sure which one he's using at any given time.

Stamp glared at me until I fetched a basket for the bread. Chas joined us at the table and we relaxed into the last and best bit of my coming home routine, chatting aimlessly while stuffing ourselves with seafood and drinking our way through Stamp' mystery wine collection.

"So," said Kait as we made coffee to go with Amorata's cream cakes. "What's next for Delta Void?"

"More work. I'm irreplaceable, according to Claddius."

"There are worse things to be," said Chas. "I wouldn't mind being irreplaceable. In my industry, there's always cute young things coming up behind you with a knife to stick in your back."

"You should try DV's job," Aimee said slyly. "It's a little more respectable than yours."

"My job isn't illegal, last I looked," he shot at her.

"It's not illegal to be an odd-job agent either," I said quickly.

Chas smirked at me in a way that would have been unforgiveable if he wasn't so damn cute. "That's what you're calling it these days? Here was I thinking your job title began with M?"

"Don't start that again," complained Stamp. "Semantics gives me a headache. We don't care what DV does for a living. We'd still like her if she was an evil overlord, or a lawyer..."

"Or an assassin," said Aimee.

"Fair enough," Chas laughed. "Go wash up, Stamp. You know the rules. If you insult Delta's crockery, you have to clean it."

"Worth it!"

While Stamp stacked plates, I moved with some satisfaction to the couch. It was nice to sit on furniture that wasn't nailed to a pirate ship. Cushions were a great invention.

"You look done in," said Aimee, leaning over the arm of the couch and rubbing my shoulders sympathetically. "When do you go back to work, tomorrow?"

"I bargained myself a day off. Not sure what to do with it, but I hope it will involve me, my bed and very little else."

"You can't spend your one day off in bed," said Aimee, working into my shoulders more emphatically. "It's the Big Market Day tomorrow. Come shopping with me. Kait, do her feet."

"I wouldn't do this for just anybody," teased Kait, pulling off my boots.

I sighed. With this kind of treatment I might agree to anything, even shopping with Aimee. "Have I mentioned how much I love you people?"

"Even me?" called Stamp from the kitchen counter.

"You're doing my washing up, what do you think?" I called to him.

Chas settled into the armchair opposite me. "I'm too full to do anything but gaze adoringly at you."

I closed my eyes. "I'll settle for that."

Aimee rapped me sharply on the shoulder blade. "Stop changing the subject. Shopping."

"Shopping for what?" I protested. "I don't need anything."

Chas made a valiant attempt to save me. "If you're short of something to do tomorrow, you could come along with me. I've got tickets to a matinee at the Gilded Showpony."

I looked at him in alarm. "The theatre? I don't have the kind of clothes you wear to the theatre."

"Hence the shopping!" Aimee squealed in triumph.

~

There was no getting out of it. I rolled out of bed the next morning to find Aimee in my kitchen, fixing us an energy-filled breakfast. "We need to plan our morning," she said.

Still in my pyjamas, I yawned at her. "Didn't we already plan it?"

"Of course not. You need a proper schedule if you have less than four hours to shop for something specific."

"That's okay," I said. "I figured I'd just wear Oleandra, she's dressy enough for a matinee."

Aimee looked at me in horror. "You can't wear Oleandra."

"Vampyra, then. All that black velvet, she'll be fine as long as I make sure she's fed before the show."

"DV, this is crazy. Chas asked *you* to the theatre, not one of your fake personalities!"

"They're not fake," I said. "They're as real as I am."

"That's not the point. What's so wrong about dressing up?"

"DV doesn't suit dress up clothes," I said plaintively.

She leaned over and smacked with in the head.

"Ow!"

"That's for talking about yourself in the third person. Don't let it happen again. You have to watch yourself, DV. You rely on your other selves way too much and it wouldn't hurt to remind yourself of what it's like to be a real person. A real person, I might add, who has been invited to the theatre by a cute boy and is going to frock up for the occasion if it *kills* her."

"It's just Chas," I grumbled.

She eyed me severely. "Are you trying to tell me that Chas is not a cute boy?"

She had me there. Truth is, we were all half-in love with Chas. It was probably the beautiful smile that did it, plus the bright blue eyes, plus the fact that he's brooding, mysterious, and an utter sweetheart.

Romance, of course, is out of the question because a) relationships with people you share a house with are always a bad idea and b) Chas is an assassin. One of the best hired killers in his field. It sounds glamorous and dangerous if you don't think about it too much, but there's no getting away from it. Chas is cute, but he kills people for a living.

❧

I thought about what Aimee had said as we elbowed our way through the market stalls. There are markets aplenty in Skullcap any day of the week, but Big Market Day—the first day after full moon—is when the streets fill with so many trestle tables and fried-fish vendors that no one is safe. We had to shove an entire second-hand spice stall out of the way before we could even get out of our front door.

Was I using my personae too often? It was hard to tell, since the only people who share my power to switch bodies at will belong to my own family, and they're all too weird to act as role models. I used my gift more responsibly that the rest of them—my twin sister was legendary for her abuse of it, once spending a whole year as Agatha the elephant-rider, only to discover when she finally reverted to Theta Void that I was four inches taller than her, and a year ahead at school. She's never quite forgiven me.

Maybe I should lay off the switching for a while. It was my day off.

The next two hours passed in a blur of spangly fabric and

plunging necklines. Aimee conspired with various beautifully groomed frock merchants to criticise my posture, the length of my legs (both too long and too short, apparently), the width of my waist, the angle of my hips, the shape of my shoulders (don't ask me what shape shoulders are supposed to be) and my inability to wear pink.

I was half-out of a cranberry crinoline and half-into a primrose petticoat when a tall, distinguished silver-haired gentleman in a long grey robe and matching top hat wandered into the changing-tent.

I knew who he was. He'd been on a few Wanted posters in his time, and a few Commended by the Imperial Crown posters too. A whole generation of adolescent girls (the generation before mine, thankfully) swooned over miniature replicas of his image, which they concealed lovingly under their pillows. I would have recognised him without all that, since my childhood home was dwarfed by a massive oil portrait depicting my parents with silly grins on their faces, one arm each slung around the shoulder of the Silver Warlock.

"Delta Void?" he said politely. "I have an offer of employment for you."

I froze. "Um, it's my day off. Have a word with my manager, Claddius in Chartreuse Street?"

"Of course," said the most renowned magic-wielder in the history of Mocklore. "My apologies for disturbing you." He tipped his hat to me, and vanished. Not vanished into the milling crowd vanished, but poof! Vanished in a shower of sparkling silver lights.

"Right," I said to myself. A horrible thought struck me, and I stared down to check that all relevant bits of my body were covered up, whether by cranberry crinoline, primrose petticoat or boysenberry bodice.

Aimee rounded the corner with another outrageously frou-frou garment.

"No feathers!" I yelled.

~

When I met Chas outside the Gilded Showpony, I was suitably sleek and fashionable, my wrong-shaped shoulders concealed by the flattering cut of a green satin gown with a wide enough skirt to disguise my peculiarly long/short legs. Under the relentless influence of Aimee, I had acquired new shoes, a tiny handbag and antique pearl ear bobs. My hair was pinned up, and my scruffy nails had beautiful fake ones glued over the top of them. Transforming yourself the way ordinary people do is a lot of work.

"Nice," was what Chas said when he saw of me. He was wearing one of his usual all-black suits, with slightly fancier buttons than usual.

"You'd better come up with something better than that when Aimee asks," I warned him. "She put in a lot of effort to squeeze an insincere comment out of you."

He took my arm. "Stupendous?"

"Keep working on it, she'll expect at least three adjectives."

"Bedazzling."

"It had better be a bloody good play," I muttered.

It was. The local Wagstaffians were putting on *Orthandro*, the story of a cross-dressing monk who has an affair with his alternate personality and strangles himself in a fit of jealousy. It was a classic production with full period costume and all the original song-and-dance numbers.

Chas had a private box, which meant we could look straight into the other box across the theatre. It contained several members of minor royalty (I counted at least four tiaras), their hanger-on friends and a bunch of uncomfortable-looking bodyguards. Watching them bicker and flirt was almost as much fun as the first act, so I switched my attention regularly between the two.

During the interval, I sipped champagne and watched the people in the twelve-copper seats file out to queue for their chocolate bits and cups of flat beer. When I glanced over at Chas, I noticed him fitting several small pieces of ivory tubing together.

It was a blowpipe. "What are you doing?"

"It's your day off, Delta, not mine." Chas pulled a tiny dart out of his pocket, handling it carefully.

I felt cold all over. I'd never seen him working and didn't want to start now. "You can't do this *here*."

"It won't take a minute."

"That's hardly the point!"

He held the blowpipe steadily in his lap, the dart already nestled inside. "I thought you'd be okay with it."

"How can you possibly have thought I would be okay with this?"

There was a scream from the royal box. A gentleman in a puffed red velvet hat slumped over the gilded railings at the side. Before anyone could grab him, he slid horribly over the edge. The crowd below lunged out of the way, and he hit the ground with a thump.

I shot an accusing look at Chas. He rolled his eyes and indicated the blowpipe, which still lay in his lap. "I'm good, but not that good. That was someone else."

"Was that your target?"

He made the blowpipe disappear into his sleeve. "Act natural. Scream a bit and look shocked."

"But—"

"We've done nothing wrong, Delta," he said urgently. "Act like it."

"Assassin!" screeched a voice from the royal box. "Assassin!" A plump red-haired girl in a tiara (who shared my inability to wear pink but seemed blithely unaware of that fact) bounced up and down, screaming and pointing straight across the theatre at Chas. "Assss-assss-innnn!"

"Are you wearing a badge?" I demanded. "Why can't you wear colours like a normal person?"

"Don't panic," said Chas.

"You have a murder weapon in your sleeve!"

"I didn't kill anyone with it!"

"*Today!*"

"DV, calm down. Take a deep breath."

"Then what?"

"Then we run away. Very fast."

You'd think it would be simple enough to leave the box and hide ourselves among the panicking crowd. Not a chance. For a start, the crowd didn't panic. The theatrical patrons of Skullcap have strong stomachs and nerves of steel. They sat in their seats, politely waiting for someone to clear away the dead body so they could get on with watching the second act.

A corpse was a corpse, but Wagstaff was Wagstaff.

Chas and I felt extremely visible as we tore out of our box and squeezed past many rows of people in the balcony seats. It didn't help that redhead was still shrieking "Assassin!" and constantly stabbing her finger in our direction.

Would you believe, there was actually a whole troop of uniformed constabulary in the back row? They regarded us with some interest, but the redhead's accusation had worked in our favour—assassination is not a crime in Mocklore, so the constables had no reason to pursue us.

Not so the half-dozen armed bodyguards whose job it was to protect the royal family of Skullcap. Letting one of their charges die was a bit of an embarrassment, so they had swords at the ready as they pursued us. Luckily, their attempt to clamber over a row of elderly women in wombat-fur stoles slowed them down when the old dames started whacking them with their programmes and telling them what rude boys they were.

Chas and I made it out into the foyer. "Hide somewhere and switch," he ordered me as we flew down the staircase.

"What about you?"

He shot an icy look over his shoulder.

"I'll get out of your way, shall I?" As we reached the ground floor, I hurled myself into the privacy of the Ladies Room and took several long, slow breaths before switching into Benedetta, my pert flirt in a polka-dot dress.

Everything was instantly better. Benedetta has a rose-tinted brain. Everything is fluffy and adorable in her world. I peeked out of the Ladies Room to see Chas (armed with a sword I was pretty sure he hadn't brought in with him) fighting for his life against the royal bodyguards. He got to the front doors and away, the bodyguards hot on his heels.

I straightened my polka-dot dress and stepped out into the foyer, prepared to pass myself off as a stray audience member. Benedetta was a foot shorter than DV, with shinier hair and bouncier cleavage. There was no way anyone would recognise me. I still felt like I had 'Assassin's Accomplice' engraved on my forehead.

The bodyguards returned grumpily through the front doors. "Can't believe he gave us the slip," complained one. "Bloody assassins."

"Gave him something to think about," drawled another, and they all laughed and patted him on the back as he brandished his sword, which was wet with blood.

It was all too much for Benedetta, who squeaked and fainted.

~

I regained consciousness in the ticket office, hemmed in by all six bodyguards, three concerned male ushers and several constables, all of whom were arguing over who would bring me tea and biscuits, and who would walk me home to make sure I was all right. Being Benedetta, I couldn't help fluttering my eyelashes at each of them, giggling at everything they said and dutifully writing their names and contact details down in my glittery heart-shaped address book (each persona comes with her own props). I only escaped when one of them suggested they wrap me up warm to prevent me suffering shock or coming down with a cold. They all raced off to fetch blankets.

It's embarrassing, being this adorable. I'm glad I hardly ever have to resort to it. I trip-trapped out of the theatre as fast as my strappy stiletto sandals would carry me, and switched as soon as I was a block away. I didn't feel like taking the risk of appearing as myself, so I settled on Flavia, a brisk school teacher who was a dab hand at knitting and crossword puzzles. At least she wore sensible low-heeled shoes and didn't faint at the sight of blood.

Even with calm Flavia at the helm, I was so steamed up I couldn't think straight. I could not believe Chas had done that to me on the one day I had counted on not having to deal with dead bodies, run away from things and switch personalities. He had invited me along to divert suspicion, I suppose—a young man booking a whole theatre box without a female companion might have looked suspicious. Bloody men.

I could have gone back to the house and waited for him to limp home and apologise, but I wasn't in the mood. Let Aimee and Kait bandage him up and kiss him better. They'd do a better job of it.

Flavia's feet automatically turned towards Chartreuse Street. That wasn't a bad idea. My day off was officially a disaster. I couldn't go home without running into Chas, which left me with one option to redeem the afternoon —work.

Claddius's secretary was absent from her desk again. Too much to hope he had fired her? I switched back to DV and strolled through to the back office. "Hey, Claddius, it's your lucky day!"

It really wasn't.

Claddius was dead. I've never seen anyone deader. Several spiky weapons protruded from his limp, toga-clad body. Blood stained his clothes, the floor, the papers on his desk and all four of the walls.

This wasn't just murder. Someone had enjoyed killing him.

I backed out of the room, slamming the door on the horrible sight. I stared at the polished panels of the door, muttering under my breath. "You are not Benedetta, you do *not* faint at the sight of blood, you are not Benedetta—"

"Delta Void?"

I screamed and spun around to face my attacker. It was the Silver Warlock. He wore the same elegant attire as before, including the grey top hat that he tipped politely in my direction.

"Isn't it your day off?"

"He's dead!" I squawked. It was horrible to see someone whom I argued with on a regular basis, reduced to an empty-eyed lump of meat in a toga.

The Silver Warlock calmly opened the office door and then closed it again. "Indeed he is. Shall I call a constable?"

"Yes please," I said, then had a sudden attack of paranoia. I couldn't afford to be identified as one of Claddius's employees—everyone knew he ran mercenaries. "Hang on a minute." I switched to Flavia. Respectable client enquiring about the private investigation service Claddius used as a front for his real business dealings. Much better. "Okay, now fetch a constable."

The Silver Warlock grinned boyishly at me, letting the dignified facade slip for a moment. "I never did get used to your father doing that. Wait here." He vanished in another shower of sparkly lights, these ones green.

I sat on the secretary's desk and calmed myself by allowing Flavia's personality to swamp my own. She had never had direct dealings with Claddius, so she was able to view his gruesome death with a dispassionate attitude I desperately needed.

She also fancied the Silver Warlock, which I found highly disturbing. He had to be getting on for sixty (*although he doesn't look it*, Flavia insisted, *more like a young forty, one of the benefits of being a powerful warlock, I suppose, and what's wrong with older men, anyway?*) and I drew the line at fancying men who were friends with my Dad.

Flavia was obviously deranged, so I switched instead to Kally, a gum-chewing chick with a rebellious attitude and several piercings in uncomfortable places.

The Silver Warlock reappeared in a shower of purple sparks, accompanied by a senior constable (higher in rank than a junior, ordinary or medium constable, lower than a super, extra, chief or major chief constable) who looked queasy at the method of travelling. "Bloody hell," he groaned, grabbing a desk for support. "You didn't have to do that, mate. Our precinct is only three doors down."

"You know this office, then," said the Silver Warlock.

"Yeah, this is Claddius's joint. We've been trying to nab him for years. Slippery little bastard makes a fortune hiring out mercenaries. Never been able to prove it, though, he's canny with his job descriptions." He looked hard at me. "Work for him, do you?"

"Messenger," snapped Kally, bristling at his tone. Not the best choice for dealing with authority figures, but at least she didn't look like a mercenary. "It's my first day at work, right, and the boss is all blood and guts all over the floor. Don't reckon I'll get paid now."

"I'll need your name and address," said the senior constable.

"I will vouch for the young lady," said the Silver Warlock, passing over a business card that glowed faintly.

"Right you are, sir." The senior constable opened the door into the back office, shuddered slightly and closed it again. "You two had better get out of here. I'll need to get a team in. I'll call on you if we need your statements."

The Silver Warlock extended a hand to Kally, but I sidestepped it neatly and headed for the door. "None of that sparkly stuff, grand-dad. I like to walk with my own two feet."

"Don't blame you, miss," grunted the senior constable.

Outside the office, the Silver Warlock and I walked for a few blocks in silence. "Could I speak to Delta for a while?" he asked finally. "I'd like to buy her a cup of coffee."

"I know a place we can go." I'd had enough of the respectable half of Skullcap for one day.

～

In a seedy coffee house near the docks, I switched from Kally to DV with some relief. I now had to deal with the stress of finding Claddius dead, but at least I didn't have a safety pin in my eyebrow.

"What will you do now?" asked the Silver Warlock. "Sign on with another manager?"

"There aren't that many around," I admitted. "They don't advertise. I suppose I'll go freelance and hope to be head-hunted again." Yikes. My pre-Claddius years had been difficult, roaming from job to job with long, impoverished months in between. Okay, my post-Claddius years hadn't been much better, but at least someone else had handled the paperwork.

"I have a proposition for you," said the Silver Warlock. "I would like you to work for me."

"Full time?" I said in surprise. "I tend to prefer a… varied work environment."

"I had something flexible in mind," he assured me. "Odd jobs, unusual errands, the same sort of work Claddius set up for you. I'd have you on retainer, available whenever I request your services. You'd be free the rest of the time to handle any work you arrange for yourself."

It didn't sound like a bad idea. A retainer could ease the burden of being freelance. "What kind of fee are we talking about?"

"Your rent paid all year around, plus a small bonus for each job you actually do. I'd only need you half a dozen times a year at the most."

Hmm. It could be a really good idea or the worst decision of my life. Hard to tell. "Contract?"

"For ten years."

Ouch. That could get nasty. "There are some things I won't do," I warned. "Killing people, for a start."

"Of course not. If I ever ask you to perform anything that is beyond your capacity, or which you find morally insupportable, our contract will be terminated." He handed me several pages of parchment. "Look this over and let me know what you think." He vanished, not in a shower of sparkles this time, but in a cloud of fuzzy blue bubbles.

I read the contract carefully. He had given me something

to think about. But if he was so keen for me to work for him, he had a good motive for putting Claddius out of the way.

Nasty suspicious mind I have, don't I?

I headed home. It looked like the rest of my day would have to be devoted to finding out who killed Claddius, so I could be certain my potential new boss was not responsible. First things first. I needed a change of clothes and a bath.

～

The trouble with sharing a house with lovable housemates who look after my attic room when I'm away is that they get into the habit of using my attic as a general living room. All four of them were in residence when I got home.

Kait and Aimee were fussing over Chas, who had made it back despite a gashed leg. Stamp was brewing tea. They all looked nervous as I walked in. So much for my bath.

"Are you still pissed off?" Chas asked, wincing as Kait yanked hard on his bandages to tighten them.

"Yep." I kicked off my shoes and opened one of my cabin trunks, pulling out some nice sensible DV clothes: trews and a linen shirt. I'd leave the heels and satin to Benedetta and the others. "I have more to worry about than missing the second act of *Orthandro*, though. Claddius went and got himself murdered."

"That's horrible," exclaimed Aimee.

"Bad day for mysterious deaths." I pulled on my trews under the green satin dress and then pulled the silly garment over my head, tossing it in a far corner of the room before I shrugged into the shirt. Aimee automatically went to the corner, picked up the dress and smoothed it out before folding it over the back of a chair. Cruelty to clothes is never tolerated in her presence. I looked at Chas. He seemed edgy. So did Kait, which was odd. "What's up with you?"

"The man who died in the theatre today," said Chas. "He was my target."

"I figured that. Someone must have really wanted him dead to send *two* assassins after him. Who was he?"

"Arch-duke Harry, Lord Rynehart's cousin. It's not just that." Chas looked like he had swallowed a live newt, all wriggly and uncomfortable. "Claddius was on my list too," he blurted out.

"*What?*"

"I had until the end of the week, so I was putting it off, kind of hoping you'd be out of town before... well, before I did it."

The others moved slowly and casually, positioning themselves between us in case I tried to strangle him. "Why are you telling me this?" I said wildly. "Why do you think I want to know?"

"I need your help, Delta. Someone's killing my targets before I get to them. I have to find out who it is."

"What am I supposed to do when I find this other assassin? Shake him by the hand and thank him for killing my boss before my friend had to do it?"

"You're good at finding stuff out, DV," Chas said earnestly. "Someone knows way too much about me, and is stealing my kills. I want to hire you to find out who it is."

Aimee and Stamp both shook their head warningly at him, but too late.

"Suddenly everyone wants to employ Delta Void!" I yelled. "Who said I was for sale, you cold-blooded *killer*?"

Stamp reached me first, shaking me firmly by the shoulders. "Deev, calm down. You're being a bitch, which is definitely not your colour." He pushed me into the couch, which had no immediate effect except that my feet stopped hurting. Strangely, it helped.

"I've had a really bad day," I mumbled at no one in particular.

"I know," said Stamp. "I'll bring you a cup of tea and we can all figure out who is stalking Chas, okay?"

It sounded reasonable. "Lots of sugar," I told him.

Chas sat in the armchair opposite. He looked guilty and nervous at the same time, like an eight-year-old boy who is painfully aware that his big sister will crucify him when she finds out he has shredded her favourite party dress.

I sighed. "You're only talking about two victims, right? It could be coincidence. I'm sure Claddius had more than one person who wanted him dead. Maybe the Arch-duke did too."

"Two in one day could be coincidence," Chas agreed, but he didn't sound convinced.

"Okay, we'll assume foul play." It suddenly occurred to me that there was a bright side in all this. If someone was killing Chas's victims before he got to them, then the Silver Warlock was less of a suspect. He had no motive to hassle Chas, or to kill Arch-duke Harry. Maybe I could sign that contract with a clear conscience after all. It then occurred to me that I wasn't a very nice person for thinking such a thing. Claddius was dead and I was hoping that the murderer would turn out to be the least inconvenient option for me?

Maybe it was time to stop giving Chas a hard time. "So who knows about your targets ahead of time? Do you have a booking manager?"

Kait coughed and put up her hand. "That would be me. Sorry."

Stamp was prepared for this. He closed my hand around a cup of hot, sweet peppermint tea. The aroma was wonderful.

I took a few deep breaths. "I thought you were a banker. You have my life savings!"

Kait looked a bit embarrassed. "It's not a real bank, that's my cover. I keep your life savings in a box under my bed. There's not much after I take the rent out every month."

I wondered why I wasn't screaming at her. "This is very good tea, Stamp."

"Hand-dried by very calm monks," he grinned.

"Assassination isn't illegal," I said to Kait. "Why the big secret?"

"People don't like it to be known that they are hiring assassins. They're always worried that their third cousin's great-aunt will spot them going in. My business tripled the week after I took down the Assassins for Hire sign."

"How nice for you."

"I didn't mean to lie to you, Delta. I just never tell people when I first meet them. By the time we were friends it seemed too late."

I glared at Stamp. "You knew, obviously. Do you work for her, too?"

"I'm an independent cat burglar, thank you very much," he said haughtily. "Mind you, she's a wicked fence."

"No one ever told *me* any of this," said Aimee huffily.

At least I wasn't the only one. I took a deep swallow of the tea. It really was very good. "Okay, let's work through this. Could anyone have found out who Chas was due to kill this week?"

"Our office was broken into last week," Kait admitted. "It happens all the time. Paid-up members of the Profit-hood know it's not a real bank, but there's always some amateur who thinks they can pull off a smash and grab. They usually give up and go home when they see that the vault is empty."

Chas glared at Kait. "So anyone could have read my file?"

"Why would they want to?" Kait shot back. "There is no earthly reason why someone would figure out who an assassin was due to kill and get in first. Why bother?"

"I have a better question," I said firmly. "Who's your next victim?"

Chas and Kait glanced at one another. "Prince Rorey," said Chas.

"Big week for you," I noted.

Stamp clapped his hands in delight. "Royalty! Bags I come."

~

We forced Chas to stay at home, since his wounded leg would slow us down. Stamp and I headed for Lord Rynehart's palace, which (due to the space restrictions in Skullcap) is a semi-detached house in Lordling Street.

I wore Helene, a slinky almond-eyed burglar in a black jumpsuit. She was Stamp's favourite, but I didn't let them play together often. Stamp wore a fur-lined cape and a pearl-encrusted doublet over white hose and cavalier boots, an outfit that had taken him forty minutes to assemble. If Prince Rorey was already dead, it was his fault.

We crawled across a succession of roof gardens, finally arriving at the one that had to belong to the palace—little golden crowns had been stamped on everything from the water features to the potted shrubs.

I switched back to DV as soon as I no longer needed Helene for the roof-climbing. She's athletic, but only speaks in a language no one has ever heard of, which makes communication difficult.

"I didn't think we had any princes left in Skullcap," I hissed to Stamp as we concealed ourselves behind an orange tree carved into the shape of two swans mating. "Didn't Lord Rynehart's children all die in freak accidents?"

"The legitimate ones had the freak accidents," Stamp whispered back. "Rynehart had to resort to illegitimate offspring after that. Prince Rorey and Princess Ranessa were officially inducted into the First Family of Skullcap last year."

"How do you always know this stuff?"

"I'm a cat burglar, ducks. We're *all* into royal gossip and tea. That's how we find out where the best diamonds hang out. Ooh, speaking of royal gossip…"

I peered over the top of the orange tree. A pale, flabby young man lay in a deckchair, snoring. It could only be Prince Rorey. He wore an over-sized coronet, multi-coloured boxer shorts, and a gormless expression.

"Should we warn him?" Stamp whispered.

"Warn him about what? That our friend Chas is going to kill him sometime this week if a mysterious stranger doesn't get in first?"

"Good point. Why are we here, then?"

"You want this day to start making sense *now*? So far I've been mauled by shop assistants, chased out of a theatre for being in league with an assassin who didn't kill anyone, and…" I broke off, thinking furiously.

"What's up?"

"How did she know he was an assassin?"

"Who, pet?"

"*Her.*"

The redheaded girl who had screamed and pointed at us in the theatre was here, on the rooftop. She stepped out from behind a fake waterfall, wearing a black leather dress that looked like a handbag with armholes. She wore a tiara, and held a nasty-looking length of razor wire in her gloved hands.

"That's Princess Ranessa," whispered Stamp. "Maybe she's pruning roses."

"Or not," I said as the princess reached Prince Rorey's deckchair. "Get her!"

Stamp was faster than me, and reached her before she

looped the wire fully around the prince's neck. A moment later I crashed into both Stamp and the princess, my momentum knocking all three of us into a miniature ornamental lake.

Prince Rorey woke up with a jolt. "I say, what's going on?"

"Your sister tried to kill you," announced Stamp.

While he pinned the struggling princess to the ground, I extracted the razor wire and handed it to Prince Rorey.

"Oh, that," said Rorey. "She's always trying to kill me. Not very good at it, are you, lovey?" He chuckled. "I even heard she hired an assassin to bump me off, can you imagine?"

I leaned over and secured Princess Ranessa into a firm headlock. "Did you kill Arch-duke Harry and my manager Claddius?" I demanded.

"Of course," she grunted, still struggling.

"Why would you kill Cousin Harry, old girl?" asked Rorey in astonishment.

"Practice," snarled the princess. "I knew Daddy would never let me inherit Skullcap as long as he had a male heir, so I moved into a different profession. After the Assassins turned down my application, I hired an accredited assassin to kill you, then broke into the office and found out who else he was due to kill this week. Beating him to his victims should be impressive enough to make the Board of Assassins reconsider my application."

"Assassins have a Board?" said Stamp in surprise. "Why don't cat burglars have a Board? All we have is a book club."

"So no one hired you," I said, staring at the princess. "No one paid you to kill those men."

"So what?" said Ranessa. "I'm not doing it for the money. I have pots of money. It's all about *professional pride*." She looked pleased with herself.

"You're not a professional," I said. "If no one hired you to do it, you're an amateur. What you did was not assassination. It was murder."

This was an important legal distinction. Unlike assassination, murder is a crime in Mocklore. Princess Ranessa stared blankly at me.

The expression on Prince Rorey's face was beatific. "My dear fellow," he said to Stamp. "You wouldn't mind dashing off and fetching a high-ranking constable, would you? I'll have a chat to Daddy. I rather think he'll be interested in what my darling little sister has confessed to."

~

It took hours to sort everything out. I sent Stamp home, since he was likely to be recognised around the Palace thanks to his many wine-pilfering expeditions. I stayed to explain everything to his Lordship as well as to various constables, and finally to the major chief constable himself. Princess Ranessa's daddy was quite happy to put his troublesome daughter in the hands of the judicial system, and he made a point of mentioning she would have to pay for the lawyers herself.

I had to agree to appear in court as both Delta Void and Kally Pierced-Eyebrow, but I got off pretty lightly since none of the constables could prove I had ever worked for Claddius. Lord Rynehart even hinted that he might hire me next time he had a situation that required discretion.

It was late when I got home. From outside I could see lights flickering in my attic room, which suggested a welcome committee lying in wait. I was fine with that as long as they didn't expect me to cook.

Orange sparkly lights twinkled beside me and the Silver Warlock appeared. "Have you thought about my offer?" he asked.

Flavia was right. He was a bit of a looker, for an old guy. I decided not to think about that. "Everyone wants to hire Delta Void," I said aloud.

~

When I finally made it to the attic, Aimee was putting the finishing touches on a fearsome chocolate cake, Kait was ladling pasta into bowls, Stamp was fussing over table arrangements and Chas was opening yet another bottle of Lord Rynehart's finest.

"Did Princess Ranessa pay in full for the assassination of her brother?" I asked Kait.

"That's confidential," she said primly. "And no, just a deposit."

I helped her carry the dishes to the table. "You'll have to write that one off. Her daddy reduced her pocket money for being a horrid little psychopath, and she has to sell all her tiaras to raise her own legal fees." I handed Kait a medium-sized pouch that had a promising clink to it. "His Lordship would like the matter of Prince Rorey's impending assassination to go away."

"Fair enough," said Kait, taking the money. "We can always be bought off, can't we, Chas?"

"Trademark of the profession," he agreed.

We sat down to dinner, eating mostly in silence. Aimee broke first. "Are you going to forgive Chas or not?"

I looked to my left. Chas was looking anxious. I leaned over and kissed him on the forehead. "We're fine," I told him.

"Really?" He didn't sound convinced.

"As long as you refrain from killing people I know, we're fine."

"I can't guarantee that, Delta."

"I know. Let's deal with that when we come to it."

He flashed that gorgeous smile of his at me. I threw a piece of bread at him. Everyone relaxed.

"I was thinking," said Kait. "Are you going freelance now Claddius is gone? I could always add you to my books. I've had quite a few requests for m– for odd-job agents."

I grinned at her. "Thanks, but no need. I've signed a ten year contract."

"One job?" said Aimee in alarm. "Only one job for the next ten years? Delta, are you crazy?"

"It's random work," I reassured her. "For the same person, that's all. A maximum of six missions a year, and my rent is paid all year round."

"Score," said Kait the landlady.

"So who's the new employer?" asked Stamp. "Is he cute?"

"Pass," I said hastily.

"Must be cute," giggled Aimee.

"Spill it, pet," said Stamp. "Who has the wit and brain to shackle himself Delta Void on a permanent basis, and is he hiring cat burglars?"

"Can you trust him?" Chas added.

"You know me. I don't trust anyone. I even half-suspected him of murdering Claddius just to get me to work for him. Is that a suspicious mind at work or what?"

"Who, who, who?" demanded Stamp.

I gave in. "The Silver Warlock."

Aimee squealed loudly. "I've seen his portrait, he's a fox!"

"He's practically royalty," said Stamp excitedly. "Does he have a wine cellar?"

During the hubbub, Kait and Chas exchanged a look that only I saw.

～

Some time later, while Aimee served up the cake and Stamp

squabbled with Kait about whether her new cake forks were made from real silver, I collared Chas. "What do you know about my employer?"

"You don't want to know, and I can't tell you."

"What if I demand it as the favour you owe me for inviting me to the theatre and making us leave before the big duet between Orthandro and his split personality?"

"Delta, I *can't* tell you," he said pointedly. "Assassins are honour-bound not to reveal the names of their clients."

Everything went grey. I fell back against the arm of the couch. "The Silver Warlock hired you to kill Claddius?"

"I didn't say that, DV. You didn't hear it from me."

My mouth opened and closed a few times. I'd spent the whole day freaking out about being friends with a killer. Now, as of half an hour ago, I was employed by one. For ten years.

"Aimee," I called faintly from the couch. "Can I have a really big piece of that chocolate cake?"

"With whipped cream," Chas advised.

Tomorrow. I'd think about it tomorrow. In the mean time, there was cake.

DELTA VOID AND THE CLOCKWORK MAN

No one has the right to be that good looking. I mean, seriously. We're talking long, golden limbs, a good strong chin, sky-blue eyes and a stomach you could do press-ups on. I circled him slowly, looking for flaws and not finding any, impressed as all hell. "Are you sure he's made of clockwork?"

Rynehart, Lordling of Skullcap, looked as pleased as if he had built the thing himself. "That's right. Amazing, isn't it?"

I peered into the unmoving blue eyes of the clockwork man. "Can it talk?"

The eyelids lowered and rose again in a single slow-motion blink. "Three languages," said the clockwork man in a deep, reproachful voice.

I tilted my head to look at the Lordling. "Wow."

"He can walk, talk and protect you from harm," said Lord Rynehart, clapping his hands merrily.

"So what's the job?"

"The old Jarl of Axgaard was a great friend of mine," said Rynehart, assuming as many clients do that I was actually interested in his motives. "We both had bad luck with heirs, unfortunately."

Bad luck? Lord Rynehart had made the crucial error of marrying a woman famously known as the Accident-Prone Wench of the Languid Isles. Her tendency towards accidental self-destruction was passed on to her three children, who were all killed in freak accidents: one was squished by a spontaneously-appearing city, one was trampled in a stampede of frightened hedgehogs and one accidentally fell down six flights of poisoned stairs.

Jarl Erik's children had met more violent fates, but that was due to the fact that parents in Axgaard provide their children with edged weapons before potty-training them. No wonder Jarl Erik, who had sired children on an entire harem of women, only had one son left to inherit his city. "I may not approve of Erik's heir," Lord Rynehart continued, his voice droning on. "But I must provide a suitable gift. All you have to do is present it to the new Jarl at the coronation ceremony."

Hmm. That meant a trek across dangerous mountains and treacherously boring swampland to reach the most violently crazy city that this little Empire has to offer, accompanied by a devastatingly gorgeous man built entirely out of metal. "I'm in," I said aloud. "But there's one thing you have to do before we set off."

"What's that?" asked the Lordling eagerly.

I ran my eyes up the length of the tall, handsome metal man. As far as I could see, everything was in perfect proportion. "He needs pants."

~

As I escorted the clockwork man (now fully clothed) out of the city, it occurred to me that he didn't have a name. "Can I give you one?" I asked. "Or is that up to your new master?"

"There are no specific traditions," Mr Clockwork said politely. "If my new master wishes a different name for me than the one you choose, I will not mind."

"I should call you Touchstone," I laughed. "You know, from the ballad? Hero of the world and saviour of women everywhere."

He didn't get the joke. There are some things even living clockwork can't replicate. We headed in silence towards the big pointy mountains.

My name is Delta Void, DV for short, and I do stuff for a living. You know, stuff. People need a job done, I do it. It works for me because I'm not suited to just one career path, I'm suited to about a hundred and thirty. I have a highly original physiology (shared only by my nearest and most dearly loathed relatives) that allows me to switch personae at will. I can be a fierce warrior one minute and a highly skilled witch the next.

Well, I lost the highly skilled witch a few years ago, but I still have a permanently vague witch who looks cute in velvet. Sometimes I'm a huntress, sometimes I'm a seamstress. I was an elephant trainer once, but that's another story.

Escorting a metal man to a party should have been child's play.

Mountains bore me, which is a problem because I live in Skullcap, a tiny seaport city surrounded by huge, dangerous mountains on all sides that aren't ocean. The only way to get to the rest of Mocklore from Skullcap is by climbing up rocks at steep angles using ropes and pointy implements— that's when I get bored. I have easier routes for getting through the mountains, but I'm not allowed to use them in mixed company, so Mr Clockwork and I were going the long way.

I had switched to Herna the Huntress, my meanest and toughest persona. She eats rocks for breakfast, which is why I never let her eat breakfast. She grunted and girl-powered her way up the mountain no problem, and Mr Clockwork matched her pace well. I was quite enjoying being Herna, right up to the point when she put her hand on a stinging nettle, screamed, and fell three feet.

For some reason, I changed back into DV on the way down, and received the full pain of the fall personally. "Ow, ah! Godsdamnit!" My knee was skinned, but that wasn't the worst of it. I really hate nettle-burns.

Still making pouty pain noises, I looked around. Rock everywhere, above, below and on all sides. No vegetation in sight except that one bloody nettle my girl had put her hand on. Whatever happened to that tidy bit of folklore that says where there's a nettle, a dock leaf grows nearby to soothe the sting? "Oh, yes," I muttered. "Always a freaking dock leaf around when you need one."

Mr Clockwork shimmied down his rope and placed his cold metal palm against mine. "Try this."

The burning pain vanished instantly. I was impressed, even more so when he knelt and did the same to my bleeding knee. "Right, that's it. I'm calling you Doc. Dock leaf, get it?"

He stood up, his gorgeous golden body facing mine, and he stared into my eyes. His eyes were very, very blue. "It is my pleasure to serve," he said in a melty voice.

I backed up, so quickly that I almost went over the cliff. "Are you flirting with me?"

"It is my pleasure to serve," he repeated, sounding a little put out. "I have been trained in all the arts of seduction."

"Yuck!" I didn't have a persona to deal with this. I don't think anyone has ever dealt with a situation like this before. "Why would a Jarl of Axgaard require a flirting robot as a coronation present?"

"I am not only programmed to flirt," said my friend Doc, still sounding peeved.

"Please don't say 'arts of seduction' again."

"I am programmed to fall in love."

"With *who*?"

"That has not been revealed to me."

"When is this miraculous event due to take place?"

Doc considered. "That has also not been revealed to me. It could be any time."

"Right." That made up my mind. "We're taking the shortcut. I'm really not getting paid enough to be romanced by a collection of nuts and bolts. This way."

I led him around the rocks a little way, then stepped off the cliff and stood on what seemed to be empty air. "Come on. This is the path."

Doc was resolute. "I have been programmed with geological information covering the entire Mocklore continent, and there is no path there."

"Yes, there is." I bounced up and down on my bit of empty air, to prove it to him. "See? If there weren't a path, I wouldn't be standing on anything. I would have fallen to my doom two minutes ago."

"I am aware of this," said Doc, sounding agitated. "Please return to the cliff where it is safe."

"Look," I sighed. "This is the Rat Run, a network of secret routes. Only criminals and their favourite family members know about them. Once you know about the paths, you can use them safely. Just because it's not programmed into your bronze-age brain doesn't mean it doesn't exist."

"Please return to the cliff," repeated Doc.

I grabbed his hands. "Close your eyes and obey me. Step forward."

He stepped. For one moment I thought his disbelief would carry us both screaming down the long drop, but his shiny feet stood firm. "Good," I said in relief. "Now another step."

I led him blind until we were in the tunnels. The path was still invisible, but now you could see rock under our feet and that kept Doc happy. "We should be through the tunnel and out on the far side of the Skullcaps within half an hour," I told him.

"This is not correct," Doc said primly. "It must by my calculations take at least a day and a half to cross through the centre of the Skullcap Mountains."

This was going to be a long trip. "Would you stop arguing if I told you the Rat Run is magic?"

"I do not believe in magic," said Doc.

I heroically prevented myself from beating my own brains out on the tunnel wall. "Doc, *you're* made of magic. Clockwork is a magic substance that runs rampant in the wild areas of these very mountains. People trap it, tame it and turn it into amusing objects like fob-watches and argumentative robots. You are entirely made from magic."

I know about these things, since I have an uncle who has been clockwork-crazed all his life.

"I do not believe in magic," Doc repeated.

"Fine," I muttered. "You know, things would be a lot easier if you just said 'Yes, Delta' every time I say something you don't understand."

"Yes, Delta," repeated Doc.

"That's better."

The tunnel opened out into a huge cavern. Moisture dripped from the ceiling, pooling in a silver lake in the centre. I squinted at the two outward tunnels, trying to remember which one we should take. Doc was busy staring at the lake. A glass coffin with a girl inside was floating on the surface. I had been trying to ignore it.

"Is that a princess?" he asked.

"Oh, I doubt it. Mocklore is pretty short on princesses these days. It's probably a damsel in distress. I think it's the left tunnel. Shall we go?"

Doc stood his ground. "Damsels in distress must be rescued," he said stubbornly. "It is a rule. She must be awoken with a kiss."

Resigning myself to more wasted time, I sat down on a handy rock. "Go on, then. If you must."

Doc waded out into the shiny water and grabbed hold of the glass coffin. Moisture from the ceiling dripped on to his golden muscles. Doc opened the lid of the coffin and dumped it in the water, then reached in and kissed the girl.

From where I was standing, it was a hell of a kiss. Her arms came up and around his neck, pulling him in for the full workout. She was wore a white lacy dress, which is standard when rescued from glass coffins. As they came up for air, which was very gallant of Doc since he didn't need any, I noticed that the damsel's hair was what epic poets call 'raven black'.

Doc lifted her effortlessly out of the coffin and started carrying her across the water. When she saw me, the silly bint started screaming. "You! You locked me in the coffin! Aaaahhh!" Luckily for my eardrums, she then fainted. Gracefully, of course.

"Did you lock her in the glass coffin?" Doc asked, the damsel still all swoony in his arms.

"Of course not," I said defensively. He gave me a funny look, like he didn't believe me. "I have an evil twin sister who looks a lot like me, she probably did it." And who could blame her?

"Yes, Delta," said Doc. I think he was being sarcastic.

"Fine, don't believe me." I stood up, brushing cave-crud

from my backside. "Let's go. And don't think I'm helping you carry that cute little armful."

"I need no assistance," said Doc, holding his damsel protectively. Anyone would think he was worried I might do her harm. Well, if she started screaming again, I just might.

~

By the time the cute armful deigned to reopen her pretty lavender eyes (tinted glass, I bet you) we were well and truly outside. It was a nice sunny afternoon. The first thing she saw was me. "Oh," she said, wrinkling her nose. "I thought I saw the horrible witch who locked me in that coffin. But you're not like her at all."

"That's all right, love," I said soothingly. "Just a nasty nightmare."

I had figured it would be prudent to switch personae so my ordinary face didn't set the damsel screaming again. My first impulse was to choose Sadonna, my vague and dreamy witch who looks good in velvet and sniffs out magic like a hog hunts truffles, but I wanted my mind clear for the journey so I selected Mandra instead, a simple soul who cares genuinely about the wellbeing of others. I don't usually wear her, because creepy!

I don't remember much of the rest of that day. Mandra was being so sweet and helpful it made me sick, so I pretty much tuned out. When I woke up the next morning, back in DV's body and my own sarcastic self, I was horrified to discover that we (i.e. Mandra and Doc) had volunteered to go half a day's travel out of our way to return the damsel to her true love.

The damsel's name was Lirabel. She was so busy going on and on about the virtues about her darling Tybalt, from whom she had been separated by a nasty witch, that she seemed to have forgotten I had the same facial features as that 'witch'. Nothing like a short attention span to simplify life.

I tried to talk Doc into abandoning her in a handy bit of swamp, but he refused. I couldn't argue, since my short cut had saved us so much time. Plus returning Lirabel to darling Tybalt would get rid of her, so I went along with their plan.

Darling Tybalt lived in a hut in a thick foresty part of the Midden Plains (yes, I know plains don't usually have forests, but trust me when I tell you that Mocklore isn't like most places). He was chopping wood when we arrived, his back to the path so he couldn't see us coming. I had expected some young fop, especially since Lirabel had told me in great detail how he was practically a prince, fourth in line for the Zibrian throne because his grandfather had been cousin to the current Sultan's grandmother—anyway, I was expecting a sort of male equivalent to Lirabel, a pouty youth in satin shirts who wrote bad poetry.

He wasn't like that at all. He was whistling as he chopped the wood, a merry-looking blond bloke in his mid-thirties. An ordinary, likeable sort with some seriously firm muscle in the upper-arm department.

"Tybalt!" screeched Lirabel, running towards him.

He turned, dropped the axe and looked horrified. I couldn't blame him, really. Lirabel threw herself into his arms, kissing him wildly. Over her grasping arms, his eyes met mine and he mouthed 'help!'

I mouthed, 'What?'

'Get her off me,' he mouthed, with some desperate hand signals as Lirabel moved in for the kill.

I took pity on him. "Lirabel, don't you want to say goodbye to Doc? He did save your life…"

Lirabel broke off from darling Tybalt and spun around to lavish her attentions on the Knight in Shining Clockwork. "Oh, of course, darling Docky." She kissed him on both cheeks, then on the metal mouth. "My hero, so brave and courageous, saving my life and reuniting me with my betrothed. I'll miss you terribly!"

Darling Tybalt looked sick. "What the hell did you bring her here for?" he demanded in a hushed whisper.

"I don't recall being given much of a choice. Don't fancy her, then?"

"That's not even funny," he growled. "You know I've been trying to get rid of her. The wench doesn't listen. You said you were going to talk to her."

This was intriguing. He seemed to know me. Either I was suffering from major amnesia (which does happen from time to time) or the evil twin sister had struck again. I decided to go along with it until I figured out which it was. "Talking to that girl is a losing battle," I said casually.

Darling Tybalt gave me a look that could kill. "I have to be at Axgaard in time for the coronation, and I do not have time to drag Miss Whiny along in my wake!"

"But that's where we're going."

Lirabel, breaking away from her clockwork hero at last, overheard that last bit. "Tybalt, sweetie, are you going to Axgaard too?" Doc must have told her about our destination, the fool.

"Well, *I* have an invitation," Tybalt said darkly.

"But that's just marvellous!" she exclaimed. "I don't have to say goodbye to dear old Docky and Mandra after all. We can go together!"

As she enfolded Docky in another hug, I glared at Tybalt. He glared back. "This is your fault!" we both hissed in unison.

~

We reached the far end of the Middens by nightfall, but it was too late to get to Axgaard unless we wanted to arrive at the castle well after midnight. Doc, Tybalt and I set up camp while Lirabel talked at us. You wouldn't believe how much that girl could talk. Every time an empty little thought entered that empty little brain of hers, she felt the need to share it with the rest of us—at length—in her piping little voice. I was ready to throttle her with my rucksack. Judging by Tybalt's white knuckles, he felt the same.

Later, as we munched roast something-or-other around the fire, Doc made a suggestion. "I believe it is customary to tell stories around a campfire. Do you have a story, Delta?"

"I thought her name was Mandra?" said Lirabel in a loud whisper. "Or is that when she's wearing the nice-person face?"

I let that go. "I'm not much of a storyteller, Doc. I always get the punch-line wrong. Why don't you ask our new friend?" I looked at Tybalt.

He scowled. "I don't tell stories."

"Oh, you do!" exclaimed Lirabel, taking over the conversation yet again. "Of course you do, you told me that wonderful one about the Ballad of Touchstone, the hero who saved all those girls from that nasty old god!" Without waiting for him to chime in, she started relaying the famous story. Badly. Really, really badly.

"It was back when we all still had lots of horrid gods running around, before the Emperor decimalised them, and there was this really mean god called, um…"

"Panthas the Heartless," Tybalt muttered, looking embarrassed.

"He kidnapped five women and put them all on this huge

big rock, and lots of heroes got killed trying to rescue them because Panthy always saw them coming, being a god!" Lirabel said in a big rush.

I rolled my eyes. How she could butcher a story that any six-year-old knew off by heart was beyond me. "Why did they do that, Lirabel?"

"I can't remember," she said, biting her lip. "Oh, yes. They were famous women—the daughter of the Sultan of Zibria, the last Sultan, not the new Sultan, your cousin, isn't he sweetie?" She simpered at Tybalt, who put his head in his hands. "Anyway, her and one of the Jarl of Axgaard's wives and her little girl."

"Jarls don't have wives," I corrected. "They have an official harem of wenches."

"Whatever," said Lirabel. "There was the Chief Profit-scoundrel who was a woman then—that's odd—and some pirate's wife."

"Black Nell," Tybalt interrupted darkly. "Wife of Bigbeard Daggersharp." The most famous pirate couple in the cosmos, so no surprise Lirabel hadn't heard of them. "The point of the story is that they were all women who were important, so everyone tried to rescue them. Profit-scoundrels, pirates, princes—dozens of them tried and failed."

"But then this young pirate called Touchstone had a magic rock that killed the god and it was a happy ending!" Lirabel said excitedly.

Tybalt looked outraged. He stood up suddenly and tossed some moss on the fire, damping it down. "We should get some sleep."

"He was only called Touchstone after the god was defeated," I told Lirabel. "Because his 'magic rock' was a touchstone. It made him invisible to gods, it didn't kill anyone."

"Whatever," Lirabel said dismissively. "It was like a hundred years ago."

I looked at her in amazement. "It was *fifteen* years ago! In living memory of everyone here except Mr Recently-Constructed-Out-Of-Bronze."

"Whatever," Lirabel sighed. "I'm sleepy."

Doc slept that night, or at least pretended to. I suppose it would be disquieting if he sat there with his eyes open all night. Lirabel slept too, after the obligatory half hour of describing her lovely soft feather bed at home, and how horrible it was to sleep on the ground. I lay awake for ages, trying to remember exactly how that Touchstone story went anyway. Just as I thought I had figured it out, darling Tybalt climbed on to my bedroll and stuck his tongue in my mouth.

What with all the adventures and travels, it had been a while since I had been properly kissed, so I went along with it for a moment. His mouth was hot and heavy, and he seemed to know what to do with it. "What are you playing at, Theta?" he whispered. "Or is it Mandra, or Delta this week."

Too late, I remembered that he thought he knew me. I strategically removed his hands from various curvy bits of my body and stuck out my hand for him to shake. It bounced off his firm chest. "Mostly I go by the name Delta. I think you're mistaking me for my evil twin sister?"

He stared at me in horror and then threw himself back, putting some much needed personal space between us. "You're Dee."

"DV, short for Delta Void." I hate being called Dee.

"What happened to Theta?"

I took a deep breath. "She seems to have spent some quality time with you, and then to have lured our friend Lirabel into a glass coffin in an underground cave, which would count as a great service to humankind if my pal Doc hadn't rescued the dear child. Other than that, she could be anywhere doing anything. But nothing good."

"Up to some scheme again," he muttered. "I thought she'd changed."

I laughed at him. "You thought the love of a good man would turn Theta Void into a productive member of society? That's unreasonably optimistic. Now, I have some sleep to catch up on. So, good night."

He crawled back to his own bedroll, grumbling to himself.

I lay back down and stared up at the murky night sky. It really was too bad my sister had got to him first. He was a hell of a kisser.

~

We travelled on in the morning, on track to arrive at lunchtime, which is the best time to arrive anywhere. Tybalt was sulking, occasionally shooting a grumpy look in my direction.

Doc was back to his old tricks, flirting happily away. Luckily, it wasn't with me. Lirabel was the lucky girl in question. She flirted right back in a loud, obvious kind of way, but the effect was spoiled every time she looked around to see how jealous Tybalt was. (He wasn't.)

Since Tybalt was the only sensible person in the group, I decided it was time to make friends. I sidled up to him. "Can you think of a good reason why Lord Rynehart would send a flirting robot to the new Jarl? Doc says he's programmed to fall in love, and I can't see what use that's going to be to Prince Thorfried."

"Svenhilda," Tybalt said shortly, not looking at me.

"Sorry?"

"Princess Svenhilda is going to be the new Jarl, not Thorfried."

"Since *when?*"

"Since Thorfried died of alcohol poisoning during a celebratory beer-drinking competition two weeks ago. He's the last of Jarl Erik's sons, which leaves his sister Svenhilda. The next Jarl of Axgaard is going to be a girl."

So Lord Rynehart had sent a walking, flirting clockwork man to a female Jarl. Nope, still didn't make sense. "Svenhilda. Where have I heard that name before?"

"I know!" exclaimed Lirabel, proving she wasn't entirely self-absorbed. "Svenhilda was the little girl in the story."

"The Touchstone ballad," I agreed, snapping my fingers.

"She's all grown up now," scowled Tybalt, moving away from me.

"Hang on," I said, grabbing his sleeve. "One more question before you go back to honing your sulking skills. Do you expect my sister to be at the coronation?"

"I don't know what to expect from your sister," Tybalt said. He started walking more quickly, putting distance between us.

Now I was worried. Not because my mission didn't make sense—they rarely do. I was starting to get one of those feelings of dread that I always get when my sister is involved in something dodgy, which she almost always is.

～

The first thing you see of Axgaard is a big wooden wall. Usually you hear the city before you see it, what with the shouting and the screaming and the clashing of swords. Not today, though. Today, all we could hear was music.

"That doesn't sound like Axgaard music," I said. "Axgaard music is all thumps and crashes and ballads about glorious battle. Songs you can sing along to with a lot of beer inside you. This is—dancing music."

"Oh, goody," said Lirabel. "I hoped there would be dancing!"

Tybalt was smiling, for the first time since I first ran into him. "Good old Svenny. I thought she'd give it a try."

"What are you talking about?" I asked him.

"Svenhilda's a modern girl. Spent a lot of time outside the wooden walls. She told me once that if she was in charge, she would turn Axgaard into a proper centre of civilisation."

I blinked. "Civilisation? You mean, not setting fire to people who know about table manners?"

"That sort of thing. I never thought she'd go through with it. Mind you, I never thought she'd be Jarl. No one did. Even when she started running out of brothers." He shook his head. "Old Jarl Erik would be turning in his grave if he knew he was being succeeded by a girl."

"Lord Rynehart didn't seem too happy either," I said, remembering the Lordling's comment about how he didn't approve of the new Jarl. That made sense if he knew she was a girl. Rynehart was like Erik, a bloke of the old school. Female Lordlings in Mocklore were rare enough without conspiracies keeping daughter out of the succession!

I was feeling vaguely empowered by this whole thing.

Tybalt led the way through the Town Square, which was usually full of bearded warriors competing to see who could drink the most beer and throw the greatest number of axes at live targets. The children would be doing much the same but with smaller axes. The only decoration you would expect to see at a special event would be severed heads on spikes, with a bit of gore dripping down for colour.

Today, the rough, tough Axgaard populace prepared for a different kind of party. Grim warriors hung yellow streamers from the rooftops, and others nailed flower arrangements to anything that moved. Women with long braids manoeuvred a huge, sizzling roast beast from the spit and hacked it into small, dainty pieces that they threaded on cocktail sticks along with pineapple chunks. A group of small, bearded children went through the motions of a Maypole dance, weaving ribbons in and out as they skipped through the jolly little steps and whistled the jolly little tune. Only two of them got knifed in the process.

"Whose nightmare is this?" I muttered.

"Theirs," said Tybalt. "Look at the expressions on their faces! If she keeps on with this, she'll have a revolt on her hands."

"I'm revolted already. Where is this princess of yours?"

Tybalt surveyed the square, and pointed.

A group of ladies (not a term usually applied to Axgaard women, believe you me) sat on a dais, threading flowers into each other's braids. A pretty, pastoral scene. Sure, they were also braiding in thistles, nettles and the occasional root vegetable, but they were new at the whole 'lady-in-waiting' gig. Svenhilda, next Jarl of Axgaard, sat on a velvet stool in their midst.

She was a large, buxom lass with solid curves in all directions. Her braids were a bright flaxen blonde, woven with roses, ribbons and something from the parsnip family. She wore a crown. It had obviously started out as the traditional Axgaard crown—a small wooden helmet with two enormous horns nailed to it—but having been through the same process as everything else in the square, it was painted gold and glued all over with shiny stones. A third horn, pale pink, had been jammed in the middle of the hat. A long veil of gauze draped prettily from it. Several large rhododendrons, visibly wilting, had been nailed to the crown as had what looked like a dead possum.

When she saw Tybalt, Svenhilda's face broke into the widest grin I have ever seen. She tossed several ladies-in-waiting to one side, bounded powerfully across the dented cobbles and threw her arms around him. "Touchstone!" she declared in a powerful, theatrical voice. "It's good to see you!"

"You too, Svenny," he said cheerfully.

She kissed him in a noisy, lip-smacking manner. "Wait until you see what I've done with the place!"

"I can see it from here!" he said, in a better mood than he had been for our whole journey.

Lirabel, looking put out, came forward to hang possessively to Tybalt's arm. I tugged at his other arm, whispered quickly in his ear. "Touchstone?"

He shot me a grin, peeled himself away from Lirabel and went off with Svenhilda as she pointed out the improvements she had made to the place.

"Well!" exclaimed Lirabel, pouting.

I looked around for Doc, and found him hiding behind a large marble pillar. Don't ask me why a marble pillar was there, since it wasn't holding anything up. "What are you doing?"

"I am a surprise gift. The Jarl must not see me before the coronation ceremony."

"Fine," I sighed. "We've got some time to kill before this evening. Why don't we go find something to eat?"

"I do not eat," Doc reminded me.

"Well, we'll find someone to give you a wax and polish instead." I eyed Lirabel, who was staring after Tybalt and Svenhilda, utterly unable to accept that she had been ditched. "Let's go quickly and quietly shall we?" I suggested to Doc. I didn't want to be around when the damsel started wailing.

The pre-coronation party was surprisingly good. Even the most stoic of the Axgaard warriors had got the hang of swing dancing. I had switched to Laria, a slinky blonde persona who loves to dance, even with scary bearded men. The music had a good beat, the things on sticks were tasty and the drinks were plentiful. Sure, it was mostly beer, but they served it in dainty glasses. The town square was full of merrymakers and not a single axe had been drawn.

The ceremony was due to start in ten minutes and I couldn't find Doc. I climbed some dodgy steps to get a better view of the crowd, but he was nowhere in sight. I switched back to DV and surveyed the scene again. How did one lose track of a shiny man made out of bronze?

Something glinted in a side street and I took off after it, glad to be back in my natural body with its sensible shoes. I stopped in the shadows and listened.

"That's right," said a soft, female voice. "Then you dip me low, still maintaining eye contact, and bring me up slowly. It's very important that when you kiss her, you gaze into her eyes until the very last moment."

"Yes, Theta," said the obedient voice of my friend Doc.

I stepped into the alleyway. "Nice to see you taking such a personal interest in things, Thetes."

Theta Void, my evil twin sister, was still in the 'dip' position of the dance lesson. She stared at me in shock, let go of Doc's arms and promptly landed flat on her back. "Dee!" she said in astonishment.

"Don't act surprised. You must have known I was the one escorting Doc to the ceremony, since the two of you are so close."

"I didn't, actually," she said, standing up with the aid of Doc's gentlemanly arm. She glared at him. "He didn't mention it."

"You did not ask, Theta," Doc replied smoothly.

Theta and I stared at him with what I suspect were identical looks of suspicion. "So what's going on?" I asked my beloved sister. "You provided Doc for Lord Rynehart, didn't you? You got Uncle Imago to build him."

"Maybe," she said defensively. "Lord Rynehart wanted to send the new Jarl a clockwork bodyguard, since she's a weak defenseless girlie, and I knew Uncle Imago had been working on that sort of thing. It all dovetailed nicely."

"And did Lord Rynehart order Doc to be capable of flirting and falling in love?" I still couldn't see where we were going with this, but I pressed on regardless.

"I call him Sebastian," Theta said huffily. "Doc is a silly name. So what if I added a few extra functions? It's not a crime."

"If you did it, it's almost certainly a crime," I shot back. "Why?"

Theta scowled. "To distract that pushy bitch who's going to be Jarl. You should hear her, Touchstone this, Touchstone that, Touchstone rescued me from an evil god fifteen years ago, blah blah blah. That braided heifer is after my boyfriend."

I laughed. I couldn't help it. "You went to all this trouble to keep Svenhilda away from Tybalt? I suppose that's why you locked Lirabel in the coffin as well, to keep her away from him. What is it with this guy?" You know, apart from his amazing kissing skills. "Never mind," I said hastily as Theta opened her mouth to start telling me why darling Tybalt was worth all this trouble. "I don't want to know. It sounds like the ceremony's starting. Once I've presented Doc, my job is over. I can go home and forget any of this ever happened. Okay?"

"Fine with me," Theta snapped. She turned, brushing a little travel dust from Doc and buffing up his lips with her handkerchief. "Go out there and be dazzling, Sebastian."

"Yes, Theta," said Doc obediently.

I grabbed him by the hand and pulled him after me. "Try not to ravish the Jarl until after the ceremony, okay, Doc?"

"Yes, Delta."

"See you, sis," called Theta from behind us.

"Not if I see you first!"

~

As we got back to the square, the music was starting—real Axgaard music, all drums and screeches and thumpy choruses. I suppose Svenhilda wasn't able to throw out all the local traditions in one day. A parade was starting. I found Tybalt somewhere in the middle of the throng, Lirabel securely attached to his arm again. He looked uncomfortable.

"My sister's here," I told him helpfully as Doc and I approached.

Tybalt stared at me. "Really?"

"Back in that side street," I told him, pointing.

He extracted himself from Lirabel and hurried off in that direction. Lirabel pouted. "I didn't know you had a sister," she said huffily.

"Oh, yes. Theta looks just like me—hair a little lighter, that's all."

"Theta," she mused. "That sounds familiar."

"It should do. She's the witch who locked you in the glass coffin, remember?"

"Oh, yes. It's funny, really."

Svenhilda had reached the big galumphing throne, and a long line of Axgaard warriors dedicated their axes and swords to her, laying them in a big pile at her feet.

Lirabel was still talking. "I'm not sure why she went so nasty, we were practically the best of friends at first. She even introduced me to darling Tybalt. He's just as handsome as she described, and fourth in line to the Zibrian throne!"

I stared at her. "Theta introduced you two?"

"Not exactly introduced, but she told me all about him and brought me to the party where I met him. She told me that she thought darling Tybalt was going to be my true love. And she was right! And now it turns out that he's also the hero from that Touchstone story. It's so romantic!"

"When did all this happen?" I interrupted. "When did Theta tell you about Tybalt?"

"Twelve days ago," said Lirabel firmly.

"Are you sure? You could have been asleep in that coffin for any length of time."

"I know I was in the coffin for exactly eight days because I missed morning tea at Matilda's and the fancy-dress picnic, but not the Axgaard coronation and I know it was twelve days ago that Theta took me to that party where I met darling Tybalt because it was just after Bettina's ball, and that was the day after the Spring Festival."

Interesting. The girl's head only gave the impression of being empty because it was packed with a full party calendar.

Theta wasn't trying to push women away from Tybalt, she was throwing them in his path. She had introduced Lirabel to him soon after the death of Prince Thorfried. Why?

A large, bearded warrior stood up and boomed that it was time for ambassadors from the various city-states of Mocklore to greet the new Jarl of Axgaard. Svenhilda nudged him and announced that from now on she would be referred to as 'Baron' rather than 'Jarl,' since it was more modern. Several of the warriors around Svenhilda (mostly the ones with ribbons in their beards) promptly tried to kill her.

Doc leaped into the fray with the casual elegance of a warrior who knows no fear. He slashed, slapped and pushed all the attacking warriors away from Svenhilda. Not one of them got close, although at least twenty tried. It was all very impressive.

When Doc had finished, there was a large pile of groaning warriors at the feet of the new Baron of Axgaard. Doc bowed smoothly, his bronze body gleaming. Everyone who wasn't unconscious burst into applause.

It seemed as good a cue as any. I stepped forward. "On the occasion of the coronation of Svenhilda, fourth Jarl and first Baron of Axgaard, Lord Rynehart of Skullcap presents this mighty clockwork warrior to stand by your side and protect you from all dangers. He speaks three languages," I added. "His name is Doc."

Svenhilda's eyes lit up. She stood, clasping the hands of the highly-polished Doc. "You are welcome to our court, Doc of Skullcap. Come, take your place at the side of my throne. I am greatly pleased by my gift."

Doc gave her one of those smouldering looks he had been practicing on me, Theta and Lirabel. The Baron of Axgaard blushed.

The other ambassadors made their various presentations, but mine was totally the best. Tybalt represented Zibria, giving Svenhilda a gold box full of exquisite jewellery. She gave him a generous smile, but it wasn't quite so dazzling as it had been before Doc came into her life. She kept darting little glances at the clockwork man, as if already smitten.

Tybalt stood beside me as the next stage of the ceremony continued, a long boring bit involving chanting and the promising of pledges.

"Are you interested in Svenhilda?" I asked him in a low voice.

Tybalt looked at me as if I were mad. "What?"

"Like if she asked you to marry her, would you go yippee?"

"She's a child," he said in horror. "Baron or not, she's not even twenty."

"She's older than Lirabel," I said with a smirk.

"I'm not interested in Lirabel either," he muttered.

"You must have been at some stage."

"Okay, yes. I was briefly interested in Lirabel, right up the point where I had a conversation with her. But Svenhilda? I've known her since she was four years old, that's disgusting."

"What about Theta?" I pressed.

He frowned, didn't say anything.

"Tybalt, this is important. Are you interested in Theta?"

"I'm in love with her," he growled. "Are you finished?"

"Does she know?" I persisted. "Does she know she's the only one you're interested in?"

"I've told her enough times. What is all this?"

"Oh, don't mind me. I'm just trying to get a handle on my sister's scary little brain."

The ceremony drew to a close. A few dead animals were tossed around in the name of appeasing the gods and then the dancing started—"modern" dancing with non-Axgaard music. Anyone who complained received a chilling smile from Doc, and decided not to push the point.

Svenhilda took to the dance floor in Doc's arms, dancing cheek to cheek. So he was the perfect gift after all. How had Lord Rynehart known exactly what Svenhilda needed? Why would Lord Rynehart give Svenhilda something great, anyway? He didn't approve of her, I had noticed that vibe even before I knew the new Jarl was a girl. And old Jarl Erik would be spinning in his grave if he knew his daughter had succeeded him…

I tugged at Tybalt's sleeve. He looked at me warily. "You don't want to dance, do you?"

"Pfeh, you wish. You should be up to date with the Who's

Who of Mocklore royal families. Who would be Jarl if Sven-hilda died?"

"She has an elder sister," he said slowly. "But Bjornhilde ran off to join the Sparkling Nuns a few years ago. Then there's their brother, of course."

"There's another brother? I thought she'd run out of brothers. You know, beer poisoning, axe-thowing accidents, fatal tavern-singing incidents."

"There's still Friefried, the eldest. He caused a scandal years ago when he ran off with one of Jarl Erik's wenches. Still, the old Jarl would have forgiven him if he knew he was the only male heir left."

In the middle of the square, Svenhilda's dance with Doc was becoming more romantic. She reeled him in with those powerful upper arms of hers, inviting him to kiss her.

I switched to Sadonna, startling Tybalt. I became a vague and velvet-clad shadow of my former self, but with the handy ability to sniff out magic—and there it was, smeared over darling Doc's mouth. Smeared on by my evil twin sister, I had no doubt, remembering her handiwork with the hand-kerchief. I started running, switching as I did to Herna the Huntress, my tough warrior babe (providing there are no nettles in the vicinity).

Svenhilda and Doc arched towards each other in slow motion, coming in for the long romantic smooch. I reached then a fraction of a second before they made contact, and Herna's meaty fist slammed powerfully into the side of Doc's face. He fell. Several tough Axgaard warriors applauded.

I switched back to DV and dropped to my knees, screaming with pain. "Owwww!"

"What are you doing?" bellowed Svenhilda.

"Get an apothecary," I gasped.

She peered at my battered hand. "It doesn't look that bad."

"For him, you...Jarl. Baron. Whatever." I pointed at Doc,

who was sitting up with a polite and attentive expression on his slightly dented face. Herna packs quite a wallop when she gets up some momentum. "He was about to put a spell on you!"

Svenhilda simpered girlishly. "I think he already has!"

Tybalt came over while we were waiting for someone to bring us an apothecary. "That looks nasty," he said, eyeing my swollen hand.

"Remind me to invest in an axe," I grunted.

The apothecary came, grumbling about being made to work during a public holiday. He did a cursory examination of Doc's lips, and made a few notes. "Fairly basic sleeping spell," he said, cleaning it off with a cotton swab provided by his girl assistant. "The hundred years contract with a four hour delay. The spell would have been irreversible from the moment of the kiss."

"Someone wanted me to sleep for a hundred years?" Svenhilda said in surprise. "Why?"

"Why don't we ask the one responsible?" I suggested, grabbing the apothecary's assistant by the hair (using my unbruised hand, of course) and pushing her down to the cobbles.

She screeched, turning into Theta Void before our eyes. "Ow, Dee!"

"When are you going to learn that I know all your faces? Come on, Thetes. Explain the grand plan to the nice Baron."

Theta scowled. "It was your father," she told Svenhilda.

"Surprising, but not entirely unexpected," I noted. "Go on."

"He and Lord Rynehart made a pact when they realised they were both losing heirs at an alarming rate. They made each other promise to do whatever they could to ensure that a daughter would not succeed either of them. They both had some kind of phobia about women in power."

"Oh well," Svenhilda sighed. "I can't declare war against Uncle Rynehart if he was fulfilling my father's wishes." She stretched. "I'm hungry. Does anyone fancy some things on sticks?" She wandered away, but came back after a moment. "Was Doc in on this?"

"I knew nothing about this attempt to attack your Ladyship," Doc said in an offended voice. "I am programmed to protect, to flirt, to speak three languages and to fall in love. That is all."

"Besides," I added. "He doesn't believe in magic."

"That's all right, then," said Svenhilda, extending a hand to pull Doc to his feet. "Come on, babe. You can hold my plate for me."

"It would be my pleasure," he said politely.

"Looks like you're free to go," I told Theta, giving her hair another good pull before I released her.

She stood up quickly, feeling her scalp. "You're so bloody law-abiding, Dee. I don't know which side of the family you get that from."

Tybalt was staring at Theta, looking hurt. "Am I part of this?" he asked her. "You and me, was that part of your scam?"

Theta shrugged. "Svenhilda was too interested in you, and that was a risk. We needed you out of the picture to give our clockwork boy the best chance of getting that kiss. I thought Lirabel would do the trick, but when that didn't work I put her out of the way and did the job myself."

Tybalt looked disgusted and wounded at the same time. "The job?"

"I was paid," said my darling sister. "That's usually my motive." She slid off through the crowd, her hips swinging, and neither of us did anything to stop her.

Tybalt looked shattered. I knew that expression—I've seen my sister at work before, when she wants someone to fall in love with her. They always end up with that face and I'm left to pick up the pieces.

"I could switch to a more sympathetic persona," I suggested. "I'm sure I've got one somewhere, a nice girl who can be kind and comforting about how you had the bad luck and bad taste to fall for my evil twin sister."

"I wouldn't bother if I were you," said Tybalt.

"No, you're right. Let's find a drink."

DELTA VOID AND THE STRAY GOD

I've mentioned these mountains before. They're pink and yellow, bronze and scarlet, gold and silver, blue and orange, purple-spotted, very rarely green or brown. They are bright with snow, dark with shadows, often cold and deeply threatening. There is so much magic in these mountains, being near them makes your teeth hurt and your hair stand on end.

My name is Delta Void and I hate mountains. More importantly, they hate me.

"Bounty," I said to my companion after we had spent several hours hiking through multi-coloured peaks. "What exactly are we looking for?"

"Something valuable," she assured me brightly.

I grunted, and turned my collar up to keep out the drizzle. It drizzles a lot in the Skullcaps, even in summer. It was summer now, two days before the Solstice. You could tell by the grey clouds, the aforementioned drizzle and the sticky sap oozing from the colourful tree-trunks. In winter, the sap freezes solid. "I can't believe I let you talk me into this."

Bounty Fenetre could talk an army into swapping their bronze swords for ones made out of liquorice. I've known her since we were toddlers, and I have no immunity against her. She's the kind of girl who dresses in chainmail lingerie—no, really—and avoids assassination by widening her eyes and saying, "Who, me?" If she weren't my best friend in the world, I'd have to kill her.

"Sssh!" She grabbed me suddenly, pulling us both into a copse of spiky red bushes. Something purple and slimy hung from the branches—I couldn't tell if it was part of the bushes, or something trying to eat the bushes.

Several heroes walked by us, making loud crunching noises with their boots. I could tell they were heroes because they were all dressed in lion-skins, swinging clubs and chatting about the latest damsels in distress they had rescued (probably from each other).

It seemed to be Open Season in the Skullcaps this week. After the heroes had gone, Bounty pressed a finger to her lips for a second time. Two bounty hunters passed by, only a little quieter than the heroes. They wore chainmail tunics —sensible chainmail, not the midriff-baring concoction that Bounty draped over herself in lieu of clothes. One of the bounty hunters jumped at the sound of a squirrel sneezing.

"Don't be so twitchy," the other one grunted. "Anyone'd think this is the first scalp you ever hunted."

"We've never tried to capture a god before," the first one said nervously.

"The reward's high enough, isn't it? You won't be complaining when the Emperor hands over that gold talent..."

They moved on, out of range. I found my hand reaching out almost automatically for Bounty's throat.

"I meant to explain about the gold," she squealed, jumping back out of range. "Obviously you get half!"

"Not the reward," I growled. "The target. You didn't tell

me we were being stupid enough to try and hunt down a deity. Which one is it?"

"You wouldn't know him."

"There are only ten!" I exploded. "It's not hard to remember all their names."

The mad Emperor currently in charge of the Mocklore Empire had arranged for the gods to be decimalised a few years earlier, reducing our vast pantheon to only ten very over-worked gods.

"It's not one of the legit ones," Bounty said, wiping tangled hair out of her face in order to appear earnest. If she batted her eyelashes, I was going to have to punch her. "The Emperor found out recently that one of the original gods escaped the Decimalisation and has been hiding out in the Skullcaps. They sent out a proclamation two days ago, declaring that whoever captures Aolpho the Apostate and brings him to the palace will be rewarded with a whole gold talent. That's why these amateurs are roaming around the mountains."

"And we're part of the mob," I said flatly.

"But we have inside information," she insisted, sounding pleased with herself. "Plenty of handy details that weren't on the proclamation. I know exactly where he was last sighted, what his strengths and weaknesses are, everything." She waved something that looked suspiciously like a map sketched in lipstick on the back of a table napkin.

"And where are you getting this inside information?"

She had the grace to look embarrassed. "You know how I was telling you about my new boyfriend?

I tried to remember. Bounty's love affairs blend together in my mind, but she had been rabbiting on about this one quite recently. "Intense grey eyes, really good in bed?" Just her type.

'That's the one. He's the Imperial Champion…"

"And talks in his sleep, apparently." I rolled my eyes at her. "I hope you know what you're doing."

"Have faith," she said loftily.

~

A few hours of miserable trudging later, we found a sheltered clearing near a babbling brook and prepared to camp for the night. Sleeping on the ground is something I've learned to cope with, since my travels rarely bring me anywhere close to a handy tavern. My essential props are a waterproof bedroll, a griffin-hair blanket (scratchy as hell, but light and warm at the same time, a rare combination) and a clockwork warming-flask that my uncle invented—a constant supply of hot water is not something to be sniffed at.

Bounty had brought one thing.

"A pillow?" I said in amazement as she squeezed it out of her travel pack and slapped it into shape.

"Of course," said Bounty. "Can't sleep without one."

"What about blankets, spare underwear, food supplies?"

"A pillow takes up a lot of room. I didn't have space for anything else. Didn't you bring food?"

I growled again, sorting through my supplies. "I have oatcakes and hot water."

"Sounds nutritious."

"You can't lie on the bare ground. It'll be damp."

"Then I'll get damp, DV. At least my head will be comfy. How do you cope without a pillow? Don't you wake up all grumpy?"

"People assume it's my personality."

She laughed. "That explains a lot. Now tell me you have chocolate powder in that supply bag of yours."

Well, yeah. What self-respecting woman with an unlimited supply of hot water would travel without chocolate powder? "Don't go all slumber party on me," I warned as I filled my flask from the nearby brook and gave it a shake to start the heating process. "We have a job to do."

Bounty stuck her tongue out at me, and rummaged in her little travel pack. "I lied," she said. "I did bring one thing that isn't a pillow." She pulled out a small paper bag and shook it triumphantly. "Marshmallows!"

You have to admire a girl who goes camping without a change of clothing, but remembers the marshmallows. Everyone should have a Bounty Fenetre in their lives.

~

I woke up grumpy. Well, I would, wouldn't I? I didn't have a fluffy down-filled pillow like Miss Chainmail Knickers. My neck was all cricked out of shape by lying flat on my sensible waterproof bedroll. The ground wasn't damp, incidentally. There hadn't been any drizzle or dew all night, which is unheard of in the Skullcaps. Bounty woke up with her head nestled comfortably on a bone-dry pillow. I woke up grumpy.

It wasn't just my neck. There was the dream, too. I could barely remember it as I awoke to the smell of Bounty doing something horrible to my frying pan, but it had disturbed me all night. I could still hear that trilling giggle, the laugh of a powerful and utterly insane creature with ice-white hair. It chilled me to the bone.

As did what Bounty was doing to my frying pan. She was surrounded by billowing black smoke. I stared at her, then at the messy charcoal that was stuck to the inside of the pan. "That had better not be my bacon!"

Bounty smiled guiltily. "Actually, *that* was your bacon." She pointed to a sad little pile of crispy black lumps near the brook. "You didn't say you had bacon. You said you had oatcakes."

"I didn't want you to wake up first and try to cook." I stretched my neck from side to side in the hope that the numbness would subside. It did, and the soreness set in. "Silly me, I'll trust you in future."

Bounty scraped the new blackened mess from the frying pan on to the grass with the other blackened mess. "This was the oatcakes. I thought it might add some flavour if I fried them."

"Object achieved," I said dryly. "Marshmallows for breakfast, then?"

"I ate the last of them while I was cooking," said Bounty. "I needed the energy. You know, you really are grumpy in the mornings. You should get a pillow."

Along with a new frying pan. I started packing up my gear. "We'd better get moving. Quench the pan in the brook, will you? And dry it on the grass so I can pack it with my other stuff."

"Absolutely," said Bounty. She weighed the frying pan in one hand. "This is very heavy. You carry this with you all the time?"

"I like a hot breakfast." The irony was lost on her. I let it go. No point in instigating a catfight. I tried to bring the conversation back around to the matter of our entirely impossible quest. "Gods tend to be powerful, even unofficial ones. Assuming we can find this Aolpho the Ipostate, how are we going to catch him?"

"Feminine wiles, of course. Gods love that sort of thing. And if it gets messy, well, you do have certain powers of your own, don't you?"

I stared at her. "You had better not be suggesting what I think you're suggesting." The only power I had that could stand up against the might of a deity was something I never wanted to inflict upon the world again. I shivered, remembering the ice-white hair and trilling, insane giggle that my dream had reminded me of. No thank you.

"We can keep her as a last resort," said Bounty.

"Last resort after the universe ends," I snarled. "You know better than that. What else have you planned that doesn't involve your flirtation skills or *my* so-called powers?"

Bounty smiled her sweet smile, the one that comes under the heading of 'feminine wiles'. It did little for me. "I have this." She reached inside the skimpy bodice of her chainmail costume and pulled out a filigree hair net. At least, I thought it was a hair net since it was so fine and light, but it kept coming until it was large enough to cover a person.

I touched it, watching the way that it sparkled in the dim morning light. It smelled faintly of salt. "Is this what I think it is?"

"Property of Oceandra, former goddess of sea-nymphettes. I bought it last year, when the Emperor staged that auction of the abandoned property of the ex-gods. I got it cheap, considering its awesome powers over the mortally challenged. It's strong enough to bind up to twenty deities for a small eternity, according to the auction catalogue."

"Good," I said, releasing the net so she could tuck it back into her bodice. "I'm glad you have that."

"I know," she said, and our eyes met in a brief moment of seriousness.

I knew why Bounty had bought the net long before the bounty was set on Aolpho the Apostate. He wasn't the only god who had evaded the Decimalisation. There was at least one other, and she was the most dangerous creature the Empire had ever seen. Ironically, Bounty was the one taking precautions. It should have been me.

∽

After several more hours of trekking, hiking and clawing our way up one of the Skullcap peaks, we found ourselves up to our ankles in something truly disgusting. "Yuck!" said Bounty, leaning down for a closer inspection. "Are they flowers?"

They did look like flowers, if flowers were strange and gooey and their colours ran into each other. "The Scented Swamp," I said as the smell of rotting roses overwhelmed my poor little nose. "I thought this was on the other side of the Skullcaps."

"Maybe it moved." Bounty sank a few more inches as she tried to step out of the seething, colourful mess.

The muck was up to my knees now, cold and clammy with the occasional soggy lump in it, like week-old porridge. I was close to passing out from the powerful flower fumes. "Are those primroses?"

"Daffodils," gagged Bounty. "And violets, I think. Warped beyond all imagining. How does a smell like this *happen?*"

I tried to ease a leg out of the sucking, scented slime and found myself dragged down to hip-height. "Has anyone ever survived the Scented Swamp?"

"I've never heard any ballads about anyone surviving it. If I survived something like this, I'd write a ballad."

"That's what you said about that plague of mutant hydra-monkeys."

"Have you ever tried to find a rhyme for mutant hydra-monkeys? I agonised over it for weeks. Um, Delta, I'm sort of stuck here." The slime-flowers were up to her waist now. She shuddered as the vibrant muck closed over the lower half of her bare midriff. "Isn't it time you came up with a brilliant plan?"

"I'm not weighed down by a metallic costume. *You* come up with a brilliant plan."

"My plans are always stupid," she said hysterically. "You're the one who's good under pressure!"

My mind was blank, utterly unhelpful. My body was half-immersed in a relentless, multi-coloured swamp that smelled like a thousand funeral bouquets a year after the funeral. What I needed was an alternate brain and body to take over for a while, to give me some breathing space and hopefully spark off some constructive brainstorming.

Luckily, thanks to a rather unique physiognomy, I had an almost unlimited supply of alternate brains and bodies.

Miss Lunatic was no good, ditto for Benedetta. Both were likely to panic and drag us further under the swamp muck. Plus, I'd just had Benedetta's frock steam-cleaned. Herna the Huntress might have the muscle to pull us out of this, but she's a hefty lass and I don't think suddenly weighing twice as much would be a good idea under the circumstances. Sadonna would want to meditate us out of here (not a method I had much faith in). Flavia would waste valuable time telling Bounty how impractical her outfit was. Vampyra would try to *bite* Bounty. Helene would extract herself from the situation neatly then run off and leave Bounty to die. Mandra would attempt to make everyone a nice cup of tea and encourage us to talk about our feelings.

There was one persona who could save us both, no problem. She could do anything, and didn't mind showing off her skills. She edged her way to the front, ready for action, giggling excitedly. For a brief moment, I saw the end of my braid turn ice-white as my most dangerous persona began to take control of my body. I squashed her back as hard as I could, searching for an alternative. *No, not you. Not this time.*

I was thinking it through all wrong, far too distracted by the squelchy feeling under my armpits. I didn't need a single persona to do the entire job of saving us. I needed to pick the one who could come up with the best plan, then switch to the one with the powers to implement the plan.

Chriselda it was.

"Oh, no," Bounty groaned as she saw whom I had become. My body was smaller, skinner, with wiry red hair sticking out in all directions. Gold spectacles perched on my nose, and my teeth too large for my mouth. Bounty slid further into the pungent swamp muck, the pink and purple gunge-petals swallowing up her chainmail-covered breasts. "I *hate* this one."

Chriselda is one of those girls who was born a crone. She is serious, way too smart for her own good and has a tendency to lecture non-intellectuals about how they're wasting their life. She is also good at coming up with plans.

"Okay," said Bounty. "What ingenious plot are you going to devise to drag us out of this mudhole? Impress me."

I looked up, quietly calculating the distance between certain trees. "It's perfectly obvious, Bounty. The fumes from your metallic clothing must have eroded what miniscule intellectual ability you possess if you can't see how we are going to escape this particular predicament."

"How?" Bounty fumed.

I smiled in that annoying way that Chriselda has. "We're going to get rescued by the lady on the rope."

"*What*?" said Bounty, just as an elegant black woman swung out of the trees above us, grabbing Bounty under the arms and pulling her schloop! out of the flowery muck, depositing her on the grass. As Bounty gaped, our saviour kicked off from the grass and swung towards me.

I switched back from Chriselda (with some relief) to DV (my usual self) in time to be rescued with a second schloop!

Bounty and I were both a mess, dripping with the stinky, colourful rotten-flower swamp muck. United, we turned to stare at our rescuer, who didn't have a hair out of place.

And how had she managed that rope swinging trick? Every time I've attempted something like it, I've ended up flat on my face. Where did the rope even come from?"

"Xandra Spydaughter," she said in a business-like voice. "SPZ. Shall we walk? My camp is just ahead." Without waiting for an answer, she strode off through a mass of golden trees. Bounty and I exchanged brief shrugs, then glupped after her.

Xandra Spydaughter wore a far more ridiculous outfit than anything I've ever seen Bounty wear (which is saying a lot!). Not many people can get away with wearing a sarong made of jangling golden coins and knee-high gold stiletto boots without looking like a hooker or a drag queen. This woman looked like a boss.

She had dark brown skin, black hair shaved short across her scalp and a gold (I didn't doubt it was real) torc wrapping her slender neck. She walked across the uneven, lumpy ground in those teetering boots without limping. Or tripping.

"I think I swallowed some of that swamp muck," said Bounty.

"What do you want with us?" I asked Xandra.

"I was thinking of offering you lunch," she said as she strode ahead of us.

That settled it. I didn't care whether she was a criminal, villain or a psychopath. If she was offering lunch, I was listening.

Xandra's camp was as practical as the woman herself. I'm not sure how she managed to get an enormous silk pavilion, a metal barbecue stove and a wide array of cooking gear up the mountain without assistance, but I wasn't complaining. She had a pot of something delicious bubbling on the stove and fresh flatbread warming beside the fire.

"You're not really in the Secret Police of Zibria, are you?"

said Bounty. "I've been trying to join for years, but I could never get anyone to admit they exist—and I've trained as an upper level courtesan in Zibria! I gave up in the end, figured they were mythical after all."

"Only slightly mythical," said Xandra. "Fancy some citrus duck noodle stew?"

Zibrians. They do the best things to food.

~

After Bounty and I had wiped off most of the flowery gunge in a nearby spring and were settled comfortably with large bowls of lunch, Xandra Spydaughter explained who she was, who she worked for, and why she was here.

Why she was here was the most interesting bit, because she was after the same thing that we were—Aolpho the Apostate, stray god at large. At this point, I stopped eating, concerned that if she saw us as rivals she might have spiked the stew with troll sleepy dust, or something even more dangerous. It's hard to spot even the most flavourful poison under the spicy taste of citrus duck. Bounty ate on, unconcerned. Eventually, I did too. Why waste a good meal?

"There's no need to be suspicious," said Xandra airily. "I only want to talk to him. I'm not after the bounty."

I couldn't believe it. "Half the known world is out to capture this god for the bounty, and you want a quick chat?"

"Why rescue us?" asked Bounty with her mouth full. "There are search parties swarming all over these mountains at the moment. You could have allied yourself with any of them." She looked over the rim of the bowl at Xandra. "It is an alliance you want, isn't it? The SPZ aren't known for performing random heroic deeds."

"I chose you because you have Oceandra's net," said Xandra to Bounty. "And I know what you have, too," she added to me. "A god can't be cornered against his will without major powers, and I think you two are the only ones in the Skullcaps likely to have half a chance of neutralising this one. I want to work with you. We capture Aolpho together, and after I find out the information I need, you two can take him to the Emperor and get your bounty."

"What's in it for us?" demanded Bounty. "I have Oceandra's net, and DV has...her particular skills. What do you bring to the party apart from wicked fashion sense?"

Xandra leaned down and slid a gold-hilted knife out of her boot. She placed it in the air in front of her, where it hovered unaided for a moment. Slowly, it began to rotate until the blade was pointing west. "You're not the only one who bought something in the post-Decimalisation auctions. This is the knife of Glorios the Backstabber. It's a god-detector."

~

My clothes still smelt of rotten flower sludge. I tried switching to some of my alternate personae in the hopes of shifting it, but it even lingered when I was the fresh and perfect Benedetta. I decided to just live with it as DV.

Then again, maybe the smell was coming from Bounty.

If the Glorios blade was accurate, our friend Aolpho was moving around a lot. We tracked him through a purple forest, a series of pink valleys, and finally a frozen orange lake at the very tip of one of the spikier of the Skullcap peaks.

"We didn't consider this," I grumbled, huddled in my griffin-hair blanket for warmth. "We might be able to track him, fight him and capture him, but he still moves at godly speeds. We're never going to catch up to the bugger."

"Have faith," said Bounty, whose eyes were fixed on Xandra.

"A gold coin frock wouldn't suit you," I said firmly.

"Are you absolutely sure?"

"I'd stake my life on it."

A large salmon fell at our feet, flapping wildly. Bounty prodded it with her toe. "Supper? I'll cook."

"It's not supper," I said sharply, examining the sky. "It's rain." The clouds had that nasty pinkish-silver sheen which suggested that major seafood storms were on the way.

Bounty looked at me disbelievingly. "Oh, come on. We don't really get rains of fish. That's something we say to scare the tourists."

I rolled my eyes. "Don't tell me this is actually your first trip to the Skullcaps?"

"I climbed a mountain or two in my carefree youth, but I'm more of a city girl these days."

"Fabulous. Xandra!" I called out. "Do you know what a rain of fish means?"

Xandra was suitably alarmed. "We passed some caves a while back. Let's get to shelter."

"I can't believe you two are getting all hysterical about a few flying kippers!" Bounty laughed.

By the time we reached the shelter of the caves, Bounty had stopped laughing. Her bare arms were scratched and torn by the claws of falling lobsters, and she had a nasty head wound from a projectile perch. The trouble with rains of fish in the Skullcaps is, sometimes the fish come down frozen. The rain that blattered in with the fish was close to freezing. The other two shivered wildly when we crammed into the first cave we came to. I felt quite smug to be the only one in sensible clothes.

"Light a fire," Bounty commanded with blue lips. She had dragged a large lobster in with her, holding it at arm's length.

"I'm going to boil this sucker alive. See how he likes being bitten." One of its claws nipped her on the wrist and she yelped, throwing it back out into the storm. "Never mind. Light the fire so we can warm up!"

"No wood," I told her.

"Don't you have a woodcutter persona?" she suggested. "With a full bag of kindling as part of her costume?"

"Nope. No woodcutters, no pyromaniacs."

Xandra peered out through the cave opening. "It might be easing off. All I see is a light shower of guppies." There was a loud squelching sound from outside, and she moved rapidly back inside the cave. "Whale," she said shortly. "Messy. Let us never speak of it again."

I sighed. It can be exhausting, living in this magic-infested empire of ours. There must be places in the world where people wake up safe in the knowledge that they're not going to have to cope with a rain of sea-mammals and assorted crustaceans.

We rode out the storm without a fire, which meant we were all cold and grumpy for the next few hours. We took turns trying out the knife of Glorios the Backstabber, but it had taken to always pointing directly at whoever was working it, which was less than helpful.

"You said this would be easy," I accused Bounty. "You said you had inside information that would help us find him."

"Thing is," said Bounty. "I don't know if anyone can find a god who doesn't want to be found."

I looked at her incredulously. "You mention this *now*?"

"He has to want to find us. My information suggested that Aolpho has a thing for feisty women." She preened a little. "If we interest him enough, he'll come straight to us."

"That's your plan?" Xandra demanded.

"We're the bait," I sighed. "Bounty, you know I hate being bait. This is the stupidest plan you've ever come up with."

"I agree," said Aolpho the Apostate, appearing among us. He flicked his hazel eyes in my direction. "You must be really annoyed that it actually *worked*."

~

To be honest, we were all surprised. For a god who was clever and powerful enough to dodge the most cataclysmic religious event in history, Aolpho was underwhelming. He was small, with brown hair and a wiry body. Usually gods create impressive forms for themselves: height, beauty, intimidating muscles. This one dripped with ordinary.

He sat cross-legged, and patted the cave floor. A perfect campfire appeared, complete with marshmallows on sticks. He had done his research.

"We've been looking for you," Bounty said redundantly, sitting down in a hurry.

"I know that," said the stray god. He looked at Xandra. "You wanted a conversation with me?"

She cleared her throat. Not even the sight of a god put a dent in dignity. "Before the Decimalisation, Zibria was glorious. We were the gold-paved city, with hundreds of amazing gods at our beck and call. Khalali the Protector of Children, Iseus the Bronze, Xorban the Peacemaker…"

"Glorios the Backstabber, Michi the Sneak-thief, Yalora of the Gratuitous Violence…" added Bounty helpfully.

Xandra gave her a dirty look. "And when the Emperor's Decimalisation left us with only one god as our patron, who did we get? Not Llura the Lovable or Quixar the Magnanimous…"

"Zorbah the Drunken, Khisthmus the War-starter…" muttered Bounty.

"We got Raglah the Golden," Xandra snapped. "A useless waste of space who spends his time turning into different kinds of bird in order to chase after women. The sexual harassment suits alone are bankrupting the city!"

Bounty was furious. "You never intended to let us hand Aolpho over to the Emperor, did you? You wanted to swap him for your own useless deity!"

"You would have had a god to take back," Xandra flared. "The knife wasn't the only bargain I snapped up at the post-Decimalisation auctions. We've got Raglah parcelled up for you in the handcuffs of Llura the Formerly Lovable, ready to be transported to the imperial palace."

"You don't think maybe bringing back the wrong god might annoy the Emperor?"

"Bounty, Xandra," I said warningly. "Do we remember why we're here?"

Aolpho chuckled good-naturedly. "It's a nice offer, Officer Spydaughter. I'm ever so flattered. But I'm afraid I have greater ambitions than to be the pet god of the Gilded City." He raised an eyebrow slightly. "How needy do you think I am?"

He flicked his fingers in Xandra's direction and her whole body slammed back against the wall of the cave. She crumpled to the ground in a mess of jingling gold coins.

Bounty flung the net—or tried to. In the split second before she threw, she started screaming and fell to her knees, her hands curled in pain.

A curious smile passed over Aolpho's face, as if he was pleasantly surprised by this turn of events. He got to his feet and stood over Bounty, his hand outstretched as if to touch her.

Of course, I wasn't going to let that happen. I inserted myself between them. "No," I told him firmly. "You're not going to hurt her anymore."

He eyed me, not seeing anything beyond the mortal,

undeniably human body of Delta Void. "And what are you, to stand in my way? Some kind of hero?"

"I'm a lot of things," I grated between my teeth. "In about three seconds time, I'm going to be a goddess."

If I fail to exercise any of my personae for a year or two, they get rather forceful about the matter, pushing themselves forward. I hadn't let Constellation have control of my body since I was fourteen, when she took me over and rampaged through Mocklore, killing anything that crossed her path. I didn't realise how much pressure I had been exerting to keep her trapped in the back of my mind until I suddenly released it. She burst out of me in a rush, her all-powerful body replacing mine.

"I thought I was the only one," Aolpho said delightedly as my hair turned ice-white and the godly power spilled out of me.

While I still had some control over Constellation's actions, I blasted him against the cave wall, forcing him away from Bounty and Xandra.

But she was stronger than me, and it wasn't long before it was her thoughts, her desires in the driving seat. *Look out, world.*

The power engulfed me. It felt like sunshine and tasted of lime juice. I took a moment to relish my freedom. Delta Void would never again be my prison. Every other persona she controlled had limits of some kind. Even the maddest and baddest of them would sleep occasionally, returning control to her. But the loveliest thing about being a goddess is, we never sleep. There was no going back to mortal meat. I would be a goddess for eternity.

Aolpho's eyes drank me in. "How have I existed in this world without ever hearing about you?"

"I can't imagine," I at drawled him. "I make a splash wherever I go." Blood, mostly.

"Between us," said the other god, his eyes bright. "We could take this world back for our kind."

Who cares about the world? The mundanity of other deities astounds me. The only reason I let him continue to exist was because his costume complimented mine so nicely. "Don't talk," I said. "You're boring me."

"So what would interest you?"

I laughed trillingly. "Aren't we going to fight?" Fighting other gods is my favourite thing. It's so invigorating. Last time I was free, I killed three of them before the rest took an interest and forced me back into Delta's subconscious. It had taken forty of them to contain me. Thanks to their mad mortal Emperor, there were only a quarter of that number left in Mocklore now. No one would stop me this time.

"Why would I want to fight you?" he said with what he probably thought was a seductive smile.

I looked into his mind. The complex colours of it proved that he was a god, if a minor one. I can't even see human thoughts; they're too grey and tiny. I learned the thing he cared most about, a solitary mountain peak in the midst of the Skullcaps, home to a thousand different kind of wild-flower. With a thought, I obliterated it.

Now he was angry. "What have you done?"

"Shall I do it again? How much do you care about this messy little world anyway? We can design a new one to match our outfits."

Furious, he flung himself at me. Finally! I flexed my powers in his direction, shaped into claw-sharp fingernails. He slugged me in the jaw, an amusing thing from one with godly powers. It was a physical fight, limbs and light every-where. Delightful!

Then something was wrapping us, trapping us. Fronds of salty thread encased our bodies, binding us together. "It tastes of Oceandra," he snarled.

I tried to pull away, but the fronds held us together. "Netted," I said in amazement. I wanted to obliterate the mortal who had insulted me thus, but my powers could not reach beyond the net. Three minutes of freedom, and I had already found my way into another prison.

"It will rot," Aolpho snarled. "All things die, even possessions of the gods. We will be free one day, and take our revenge upon the bounty-hunter's descendants."

"And in the meantime?"

He shot a bolt of white-hot light into my stomach, hurting me. I laughed brilliantly and hurt him right back.

Our battle was endless. We existed only inside the net, two gods with infinite power in an infinitely small space. Mortals would have driven each other mad; I rather think we drove ourselves sane. We laughed, bit, kicked, punched, hated, tormented…we were lovers for a while, then mortal enemies again. For a while I think we became friends, the only two in the universe who understood each other. Then we went back to fighting and torturing each other—

Until I rolled free of the net like some mythical queen rolling out of a carpet, on expensive floor tiles in a pretty black and white pattern. I was DV again, which came as a shock after so long as Constellation. I stopped rolling when someone stuck out a boot to stop me. I stared at that boot. It was the reallest thing I had seen in—well, an eternity. It was made of sturdy grey leather, and paired with another. They were good boots.

Lying on my back, I stared up at the man who owned the boots. Mostly I saw grey, from his clothes all the way up to a piercing pair of cold grey eyes. "Can you stand?" he asked.

I wasn't sure. "Is it necessary?"

A hint of a smile passed briefly over his face. He leaned down, offering a comradely arm. We got me as far as sitting upright on the floor, then gave up. "Did you free me?" I asked. The room was huge and very grand, decorated with elaborate tapestries and ancient statues. It took another moment to realise what I had been freed from. I recalled pain and torture, insane giggles and ice-white hair.

I had a companion as crazy and all-powerful as myself. That must have been fun. Gods, how long was I in there?

"Did I get anyone killed?"

He approved of the question. "A mountain top vanished, which is upsetting some botanists. And cartographers. And a few mountain climbers who were very near at the time. That would seem to be the extent of the damage." He raised his voice, sounding chill and furious. "Constellation and Aolpho have both been banished from this realm. Are you satisfied enough to release your prisoner?"

I turned my head, still dazed. There were Bounty and Xandra, standing guard over a middle-aged, aristocratic man in fine golden pyjamas. He was bound to a fine mahogany chair with silken ropes. Bounty held a sword to his throat and Xandra stood over him from behind, an axe poised to do terrible things to his skull.

The prisoner in gold pyjamas looked annoyed, as did the man in grey.

It occurred to me that the only person who had the power to banish two gods from Mocklore was the person who had done it before, with significantly more gods. Emperor Timregis himself. "Oh, Bounty, you didn't," I breathed.

"She did," said the man in grey. He gave Bounty an exasperated look.

Something clicked. "You wouldn't be the Imperial Champion, by any chance?" Which made this the palace...

"Aragon Silversword, at your service." He offered me his arm again. "Want to try standing?"

"I'll give it a go." This time, we were successful at getting me on my feet. I grabbed hold of the discarded net of

Oceandra and tucked it in my belt. You never know when something like that is going to come in handy.

"If you wouldn't mind releasing the Emperor?" Aragon asked Bounty. His tone of voice suggested that his patience was about to explode into little explosive bits.

"I had to do it," she said defiantly, her voice breaking slightly. "It was so long before your Emperor would even deign to see us, and even then he said he was happy to leave them both in there until he could be *bothered* to banish them. Can you blame me for taking drastic measures?"

"Bounty," he growled. "My job is to protect the Emperor from harm and you are currently holding a sword to his throat. Did you expect me to be happy about this development?"

Sounded like their relationship was heading into rocky territory. A pity, really, he was one of the more sensible boyfriends she'd taken up with in recent years.

Bounty lowered the sword. Xandra did the same, backing away from the Emperor before she lowered the axe. "Are you okay, Delta?" Bounty asked me.

"I'll live," I said dryly.

Her face took on a strained expression that I realised was her trying not to show how worried she had been. "We didn't know if it would work. We figured there was a 50-50 chance you'd be left in the net after Constellation was banished. But you're here!"

I walked over and hugged her, carefully removing the sword from her grasp. "How long was I out?"

Bounty chewed her lip. "Time is relative…"

"Two months," said Aragon.

I liked him. Straight answers were exactly what I needed right now. "The Emperor's a busy man, I suppose?"

Aragon looked at Bounty. "Never too busy for blackmail and abduction."

"Twenty minutes head start to get away," she said in a small voice. "You *promised* me. Word of honour."

I nudged her. "I don't think a promise counts if it's given at sword-point, Bounts."

"I always keep my promises," said Aragon Silversword. He half-lifted an eyebrow at us. "You'd better start running."

Xandra grabbed one of Bounty's arms, and I grabbed the other. We headed out the double doors, skidded on the expensive tiling and then veered to our left.

"Do you realise how many corridors there are in this place?" Xandra complained. "You should have asked him for two hours head start!"

"Sorry things didn't work out with Aragon," I panted as we ran.

"This is actually the least messy break-up I've had in ages," Bounty grinned back at me. "Don't fret. Aolpho's gone and you never have to worry about Constellation ever again. I call that a happy ending."

"You won't get the bounty," Xandra reminded us as we burst out through a side door into the gardens and headed for the nearest wall. "And the people of Zibria have some serious explanations to make to our patron god. He must still be in the handcuffs."

Bounty and I boosted Xandra up the wall, then I lifted Bounty. She wriggled as I held her up. "Are you okay, DV? I know how losing a persona affects you, even a psycho like Constellation."

Once she was secure on the wall, they both leaned down to help me up and over. "I'm okay," I said when we hit the grass on the other side. "I'll be fine."

Bounty shook her head. "They were two of a kind, weren't they? Aolpho and Constellation."

No argument there. "A matching set."

"Maybe, wherever they are now, they're together."

I'm sure she meant it to be comforting. It wasn't.

Two garden walls later we were out of the palace grounds and into the city. When it seemed clear that Aragon Silversword had not, in fact, sent any guards after us (probably too busy grovelling to the Emperor for letting him get kidnapped in his own palace) we decided to go shopping instead of running for our lives.

At least, Bounty and Xandra decided to go shopping, ostensibly for disguises, but mainly for shoes. I trailed along behind them both, thinking my own thoughts.

I know how losing a persona affects you, Bounty had said. She knew me well. The death of one of my selves usually overwhelmed me with loss, depression, darkness. This time, I felt fine. The implications were obvious.

Whatever strange gift the Emperor had for banishing gods from the mortal realm, he was beastly careless about where they ended up. In Constellation's case, she had literally gone back where she came from. She was making herself comfortable again in the back of my mind with the rest of my personae, willing to be patient until the next time I lost control and unleashed her on the world.

It wasn't all bad. No one had gotten killed this time, and her brief run into the real world had bought me a few more years of control. Next time, I would be better prepared.

That wasn't what was worrying me. *Maybe,* Bounty had suggested, *wherever they are now, they're together.*

I had a sinking feeling that when Constellation had returned to her cozy home in the back of my head, she had brought a friend with her.

III

BONUS CONTENT

ESSAY - "BOOTS ARE PRETTY: FEMME FANTASY AND THE MOCKLORE STORIES"

I started writing *Splashdance Silver* on the day I started university. You know how it is, wandering around campus all inspired and feeling like a grown up, and there's a brand new blank notebook burning a hole in your pocket…

Brand new blank notebooks were the bane of my life, when I was seventeen.

(I remember that a boy I knew walked past and asked me what I was doing—I told him I was writing a novel and he said something along the lines of, "All right for some." Yes, this is the sort of thing you have time to do when you choose a humanities degree over science. Suck it up.)

I was thinking about the fantasy epic I'd been writing on and off since my fourteenth birthday, and how I was kind of over fantasy that took itself too seriously, so what if I made it funny and light-hearted and sarcastic instead?

The year was 1996—two and a half years later, that book made me a published author for the first time.

I was in love with my Mocklore stories, but they broke my heart a little over the years, too. They were responsible for some of the biggest successes and most gutting failures of my writing career. Eventually, I left them behind, moving on to other, different, successes and failures.

All the stories in this book were written a decade or more ago, including the previously unpublished two, though I took the editing pen to them to tidy up the worst and most glaring examples of 'sentences I would never write now'. Putting the collection together has been a fascinating glimpse into my teenage and early-twenty-something brain, and also to the era in which they were first imagined: when 'girl power' meant the Spice Girls and feminism meant everything Kat says in *Ten Things I Hate About You*.

Rereading the stories for the *Bounty* collection has been weirdly eye-opening about what I considered empowering back then. There's a femme sensibility to the Bounty and Delta stories that doesn't fit at all with the person I think I was in my teens or in my twenties—I never learned to wear lipstick, I never had more than one pair of boots at a time, I and the only thing I ever liked shopping for was books. Why are my stories so full of thin, pretty girls who like to decorate themselves with shiny things while they're saving the world? What was my obsession with elegance as a superpower? Why were the handsome men all so grumpy?

My only conclusion I can come to now, in retrospect, is that teenage me was so over the unrelenting masculinity of sword and sorcery—the male gaze, the male power fantasies, the male narrative, the valorisation of female characters who succeeded only on male terms—that I wanted to take the genre and wipe girl cooties all over it.

I wasn't the only one doing it back then, not by a long shot. The 90s were filled with women writing fantasy fiction, writing female heroes, and even sometimes (shock!) allowing their female heroes to be girly as well as capable. (Even Alanna of Trebond wore a dress sometimes.)

I read a lot of fantasy fiction in my teens. Like, a LOT. I

absorbed it all—old and new, crappy and awesome, serious and hilarious. While I liked the high epic tales of prophecy and wars, I had a particular taste for the sword and sorcery stories, usually featuring a duo or a small team of ratbag characters who had serial adventures. I loved Fritz Leiber's *Fafhrd and the Grey Mouser* in particular—there was something about 'grungy best friends having terrible adventures' tales that really clicked with me, even though the only women in those stories were a series of interchangeable sexy lamps wearing strips of leather and fur.

There were books that gave me female heroes, female generals, queens and sorceresses, but I also consumed a heap of books (not all of them written/published before I was born…though many of them were) presenting women as glamorous love interests who flitted in and out of the lives of the real heroes, and who were always, *always* defined by whether or not they were sexually alluring to the main character, the man writing the story about the main character, and the (imagined) men reading the books.

These days, I have filters to avoid that sort of thing. But it took me years as a teen reader to start building those filters. I had a lot of time on my hands, so I swallowed a tonne of books where the most active contribution a girl could make was to wear an armoured bikini on the front cover. (Even when the authors acknowledged or challenged the problematic tropes around women in fantasy fiction, the cover art often worked against them.)

There was a lot of comic fantasy around in the 90s—we hadn't yet settled on Terry Pratchett being the Only Funny One (though he remains entirely inimitable), so there was also Robert Aspirin, Esther Friesner, Robert Rankin, Piers Anthony, Diana Wynne Jones, among others. Most importantly, we had Xena and Buffy, tearing up our screens. Women could be tough and scary in these stories—even if the joke was how scary they were—but only while also being beautiful. In comic fantasy novels, the humour often came from the sexy lamps with swords not being sexually available for the male-but-not-macho hero—the question the narrative rarely asked was whether those women wanted the hero to be available for them. (The ongoing joke in *Xena*, of course, was that the heroines were much more interested in each other than in the men they crossed paths with, a narrative that became more and more explicit over the years, while still pretending on the surface, to the network and their more conservative critics, that it was subtext rather than, as is clear in retrospect, text.)

If I could sum up the Mocklore aesthetic, it is this: *girls in boots, saving the day, with their friends.* Those were the books I most wanted to read, and I am glad I added more of them to the world.

Girls saving the day with their friends still describes a lot of what I write now, though I don't tend to get as excited about descriptions of the boots they wear while they're doing it.

A big part of what I craved was the satisfying narratives I found in other, more female-oriented genres—teen romance, chick lit (this was the era of Bridget Jones and her sisters), friendship drama, family sagas—only I wanted that with swords and magic and flying sheep, too. I wanted stories where girls weren't just tolerated or allowed in via special circumstance; I wanted stories where girls were powerful and present, and able to take that for granted. The best way to create those stories in fantasy fiction seemed to be to borrow heavily from genres where that was the norm.

We talk more these days about women in fantasy: about female warriors and the princess archetype; about what is problematic and what needs to be worked on; and about the fantasy we want to read in this world.

We talk about practical armour, about challenging gender

essentialism as well as racist tropes, and colonialist values (Intersectionality! Always important). But still, the female characters who are most valued in the fantasy genres are those who succeed in traditionally masculine roles. We clap when women in fantasy wear trousers, pick up weapons, get muddy, get violent. We want our Furiosas and our Sarah Connors, our General Leias and our Ghostbusters. Arya Stark had a willing, enthusiastic fandom from the start; Sansa Stark's fandom had to fight to be heard.

I wouldn't create a character in chainmail lingerie today, I think—it's not a trope that needs to be be perpetuated or reclaimed. I'm quite happy for the practical armour movement to wash over our genre (hell, I was fighting for it then; I remember writing an earnest essay to the cover artist of *Liquid Gold*, justifying why Sparrow's armour needed to be sensible and cheesecake-free). But in the 90s, when I was discovering fantasy fiction for the first time and the fantasy bookshelves spilled over with cover art of women in fetish-wear so absurd as to be hilarious, you couldn't escape it. My favourite is still a *Dragonlance* cover that depicted women standing in the snow, wearing fur boots and fur bikinis. To keep out the cold, you know? Hell, at least they were allowed to wear boots.

Those boots clearly made an impact on me. When you saw sexy lamp glamour girls on the covers of fantasy fiction, boots were often the only practical item of clothing they were allowed. Sometimes a cloak, as long as it wasn't fastened properly. Is that why my Mocklore stories are undeniably boot-obsessed? It's as good a theory as any.

Bounty came about because I asked myself the question of what kind of character actually wear midriff-baring chainmail voluntarily. Those pulp fantasy covers—and the characters that inspired them, going back to the randomly beautiful glam-babes who wandered attractively through the

Robert E Howard and Fritz Leiber sword and sorcery stories, not to mention the very limited options for female characters in traditional RPG gaming modules—were always about the male gaze, not the person inside the chainmail cheesecake. What is she thinking? Why did she choose to put that outfit on that morning?

Xena was a major influence on me, and I can see that influence in these Bounty and Delta stories in particular, written years after the original Mocklore novels were published. *Xena* emphasised practicality, function, capability. Yes, the opening credits gave a slow pan up Lucy Lawless's curves cinched in tight by a black leather corset, but every single episode demonstrated her strength and competence. She didn't need to wear layers because she was better than anyone else—she regularly beat up warlords, and sometimes gods, without breathing hard. Likewise, Gabrielle walked around everywhere with her abs on display (a costume development that occurred gradually as the character grew up in age and confidence), the Amazons wore monstrous costumes over their casual 'tribal swimsuits with props' aesthetic and then there was terrifying Callisto in her shiny metal bikini.

I realised some time ago that my problem with the hypersexualised portrayal of women in fantasy art (and superhero comics too) is less the skimpy/skin-tight costumes and more the presentation of body language—when the women in those costumes are drawn as strong, confident and athletic instead of pouting, twisting and arching their backs, 80% of my objections melt away. *Xena* offered that—even when the women wore wildly impractical fantasy outfits, they walked around like they were wearing business suits or gym clothes. Ready for action. Taking no bullshit.

Also, the women were allowed to be funny, which I adored about that show. There has never been another action franchise like it. If the much-touted remake ever comes to be, I will be fascinated to see how the 21st century reshapes the *Xena* narrative for a new generation, and *super* fascinated to see how the characters are dressed.

These days, the fantasy stories I write are a lot more about what is inside people's heads, and less about what everyone is wearing, which might have something to do with the fact that since parenthood struck (especially since I had my second child), I'm barely able to assemble an outfit beyond jeans and a t-shirt. But feminine gender performance through touches of glamour is something I do enjoy, despite my lipstick ignorance. I wore nothing but skirts (mostly velvet) for most of my twenties, I use jewellery as armour when public speaking, and I'm fascinated by people who use fashion and other aesthetic choices to create a dramatic effect. (Nails, I can do nails)

Likewise, I've always loved what I call 'fantasy with frocks' and the use of costume in historical drama. One of my favourite things about the *Game of Thrones* TV show is the astounding costume design that reflects family loyalties, politics, plot points and history—the artist who designs and hand-stitches the embroidery for some of the most signifi-cant outfits is a genius. Clothes are important!

Women have always used clothes as social and political tools—look at how Elizabeth I cemented her image as an untouchable goddess figure through makeup and fashion.

When Julia Gillard became Prime Minister of Australia, I raged about how much the media called attention to her appearance, her hair, her shoes. But I also noticed that yes, she did change—she became more professionally styled, and we saw it happen, because how could it not?

All through her Presidential campaign, men told Hillary Clinton she should smile more.

In the years since I first picked up my Mocklore quill, there has sprung up a whole new Hollywood subgenre—the fairy tale romantic comedy. From *Shrek* and *Ella Enchanted* through to the more recent *Once Upon A Time, Enchanted* and *Mirror, Mirror,* we see the archetypes of fairy tales turned on their heads, but we also get to remind ourselves that there has always been a fantastic genre entirely revolving around girls having adventures, women being fierce villains, and kick-ass ballgowns.

Fairy tales are ~~always~~ often about clothes. The power of the right dress, to transform or disguise you, to change your destiny. It wasn't just Cinderella putting up with that bullshit (and repurposing it for her own needs), it was Donkeyskin's frocks and Rapunzel's hair and Snow White's lips. Fairy tales are about beauty and virtue, but they're also about how women are looked at and perceived by others.

These days, when filmmakers tell Snow White's story, they put her in trousers (or in the case of *Mirror, Mirror,* a fetching pair of culottes), they turn her into a willing bandit, and they make the prince work harder for his happy ending. Ever since Princess Fiona showed Shrek she had sick martial arts moves, 21st century princesses have been expected to kick butt WHILE looking fabulous. But fairy tales were always magical stories that revolved around girls, and their fantasies, even in the days when Snow White was wanly singing about wishing on a star, and Cinderella didn't want anything out of life but a new dress and a party.

Girls and magic and swords and banter are still pretty much what I want out of a story today, as long as they have good solid boots to rely on, and loyal friends at their backs. That's not too much to ask, is it?

ESSAY - "THE BOOBS, THE BAD AND THE BROOMSTICKS"

from *Pratchett's Women: unauthorised essays on the female characters of Discworld*

Terry Pratchett is one of those writers that you can see noticeably improving and honing his craft as he goes. One of the aspects of his writing that improved massively over the years was his treatment of female characters, and I always meant to stop at some point to figure out exactly how it was that his portrayal of women changed and developed over several decades.

I started reading the Discworld books in the early 90s, when *Small Gods* was the latest release. This meant that I read all the books before that in (mostly) the wrong order, and all of the books after that in (mostly) the right order. So it took me some time to figure out what was going on with Pratchett's women, and to wrap my head around the chronology.

The first ten books of the Discworld series are problematic in their portrayal of female characters, particularly the younger women. I certainly don't think this was intentional on Pratchett's part, but an unfortunate result of the fact that in these early books he was largely parodying fantasy worlds and tropes, and only just beginning to develop the Discworld into something more substantial and complex. You can certainly see from his novels that Pratchett was very much aware of some of the dreadful sexism in his source material, and that he was often writing female characters in direct response to problems he saw in the fantasy genre.

His apparent intentions to point out the silliness of the portrayal of women in fantasy, sadly, often backfired.

In these early Discworld books, we find Pratchett mocking the semi-clad, bosomy fantasy women who traditionally reward the handsome hero with their sexy selves. He did this at first by creating semi-clad, bosomy fantasy women who a) say bitchy things to the (not handsome) hero in the hopes that no one would notice they are still a cliché of the genre and/or b) amusingly fail to fall in love with the protagonist but instead choose to reward a less obvious male character with their sexy selves. Examples of this phenomenon include Bethan in *The Light Fantastic*, the glamorous priestess who is cross about being rescued from a temple but chooses to hook up with the aged Cohen the Barbarian instead of giving Rincewind a second look; Conina in *Sourcery*, the glamorous warrior woman who chooses to hook up with the nerdy Nijel instead of giving Rincewind a second look; Ptraci in *Pyramids*, who is totally hot for Teppic and vice versa, until they discover they are siblings and he promptly hands her an empire and his best friend; Princess Keli in *Mort* who goes for the dweeby wizard (finally a hot girl with a taste for wizards, as long as they're not the protagonist!) over Mort; and finally Ginger of *Moving Pictures* and Ysabell of *Mort*, who are constantly bitchy to their respective guys, but ultimately choose them.

I should admit at this point that when I was fourteen and

reading the Discworld novels for the first time, I adored Conina and Ptraci and Ginger and totally wanted to be just like them when I grew up. I look back on that now and shudder, just a bit. Teenage self, how about we aspire to be something other than a Josh Kirby cartoon character?

And oh, Josh Kirby. There's that, too. Even when the writing in the Discworld books challenged and questioned the roles of female characters in fantasy, the covers were reinforcing the clichés so hard that the boobs of the heroines could be classified as lethal weapons in their own right.

Pratchett writes a lovely paragraph in *The Light Fantastic* (1986), only his second Discworld novel, in which he describes Herrena the Henna-Haired Harridan, a barbarian warrior. He expands at length about how in other fantasy worlds she would be dressed in a lurid but impractical costume, but in fact she was wearing some quite sensible armour. Have a cold shower, chaps, the woman is appropriately attired.

This elegant and witty piece writing is completely sabotaged by the fact that the cover art, as with all Discworld covers for the first couple of decades, depicts Herrena bursting out of a tiny postage stamp bikini with enormous beach ball bosoms. This is a character who only appears for a page or two in the entire novel, and thus can only have been included on the cover in order to raise the number of scantily-clad breasts to four.

Sadly, that is what I see now when I look back on my favourite Discworld heroines of my teen years—good intentions that simply didn't go far enough. The girls got to look pretty and make the occasional witty line, but they didn't get personalities that ran deeper than their bra size. (Also, it has to be said, they all pretty much had the SAME personality, which was Difficult+Snarky+Beautiful.)

There were some exceptions. Lady Sybil, in *Guards*

Guards (1989), is an unusual romantic interest in that she has a fully defined personality, gets lots of witty lines that aren't particularly mean, and is an equal match for the protagonist, Commander Vimes. She's also a woman of mature years who is not lithe and pretty, and thus escapes much of the usual 'I am standing here in my fur bikini being ironic about the sexist portrayal of women' depictions of early Discworld women. She was developed more substantially later on, but this was a good start.

Then there were the witches. After two books which featured the same hapless wizard running away from trouble and occasionally colliding with astoundingly sexy women who didn't want to sleep with him, Pratchett turned his attention to feminist issues with *Equal Rites* (1987), a book which tackled one of the most problematic ideas with which he had saddled his world: that magic was segregated by gender, men becoming wizards and women becoming witches, both types of magic being almost entirely different from each other. In *Equal Rites,* a girl is born with the magic and destiny of a wizard, and with the help of her mentor witch Granny Weatherwax, has to fight the system to be allowed into the Unseen University instead of simply settling for being a witch.

My teenage self hated this book.

Which is bizarre, because it sounds exactly like my sort of thing. But I think we've already established that there is a big difference between my teenage self's reading tastes and my own.

The problem was that my teenage self was reading my way through the backlist of Discworld books in the wrong order, and having read the blurbs, I had completely fallen in love with the concept of that one. So I saved it for last. By the time I got to it, my expectations were through the roof, and I resented that it was not the book I thought it was going to be: it was about a child, not a teenage girl or adult woman (yep the fact that it wasn't Conina-Ptraci-Ginger in a wizard's hat seemed like a flaw to me at the time), and while the best thing about the book was indeed Granny Weatherwax, I had already read her being far more awesome elsewhere, and she seemed a pale shade of herself without Nanny Ogg or Magrat to grate against. I later revisited *Equal Rites* more than once, and came to terms with it, though I never really learned to love it. Still, it hardly matters now that it is the least interesting book that Pratchett ever wrote about witches. Given it comes third in a series of nearly 40 books, that's good news. He got better.

Despite my lack of love for *Equal Rites*, I was disappointed over the years that while the Discworld was legendary for cameo appearances and continuing characters, we never returned to Esk's story. No matter how many times we visited the Unseen University, she wasn't there. We never saw how she turned out, and never got to see her as an adult. Until, of course, the Tiffany Aching book, *I Shall Wear Midnight* (2010), which also features cameos from Nanny Ogg and Magrat. *I Shall Wear Midnight* felt very much like a satisfying line was being drawn under the saga of the Lancre witches, and having that unexpectedly delightful resolution about Esk made me want to go back and revisit the other witches stories, from the beginning.

Thanks to the wonder of unabridged audiobooks, I reintroduced myself to *Wyrd Sisters* (1988), and immersed myself utterly in what is still, I believe, one of Pratchett's most effective standalone books. You can praise *Reaper Man* and *Small Gods* all you like; I'll take a Witches book over those two every time. Finally, Pratchett stopped satirising fantasy and started looking further afield for material to poke sticks at. And he decided Shakespeare would be his first port of call! This glorious work amalgamates the best and worst aspects of the plots of *Hamlet* and *Macbeth*, producing one of my favourite fictional double acts of all time: Granny Weatherwax and Nanny Ogg. Also, for the first time, he created a young female character (Magrat) with the same ruthless, complicated comedic touch that he usually brought to Rincewind, Mort and his other male protagonists.

Magrat isn't a sexy treasure with which to reward the hero (or someone other than the hero). She's a real person, warts and all, and her voice is every bit as compelling and sympathetic as it is nasal and long-suffering.

The three Lancre Witches, maiden, mother and crone, (listen to them argue about which is which!) are a masterful creation. It doesn't matter what the plot is, any excuse to see them riff off each other, poke holes in the pomposity of the universe and then save it at the last minute, is a genuine pleasure. The surprise in coming back to *Wyrd Sisters* is just how good the plot is—how cleverly the Shakespearian elements weave together, into an elaborate comedy of errors. Indeed, all of the Lancre Witch novel plots tend to be about stories, and about the way stories work in a world of magic. This meta-element raises them into being far more than amusing romps with complicated sentences (which I think is a fair description of all the Discworld books before *Wyrd Sisters*).

These are stories about witches who know that fairy tales exist; witches who know about the dangers of cackling too much and getting a reputation for gingerbread houses. *Wyrd Sisters* is about what happens when the legends and stories about witches are used against them as a weapon; and how they fight back. It was fascinating to reread this one so soon after reading *I Shall Wear Midnight*, because there are huge parallels between the plots of the two books, another reason why I thought at the time that Pratchett had deliberately written it as his last witch book, tying up the last remaining threads of the characters.

But back to *Wyrd Sisters*! The female characters are absolutely in command here, on both sides of the story—the Duchess is a magnificently awful villain, one in a long line of marvellous female antagonists set against Granny Weatherwax, and she completely overshadows her husband, as is appropriate considering the parallels to Lady Macbeth.

I also want to mention that there are some fantastic male characters in this book. Pratchett writes very interesting and complex male characters who work against the traditions of masculine fantasy heroes, the most obvious early examples being Rincewind, Mort and Vimes. One who often gets forgotten about, however, is the Fool in *Wyrd Sisters*. Everyone else is taking part in a comedy, up to and including the ghost of the dead king, but the Fool walks in a tragedy, carrying an abusive past and a more recent emotional burden along with his unwavering, committed loyalty to Duke Felmet, the villain of the piece. Even when he's being funny—and he is very funny—he's utterly miserable. The romance between Magrat and the Fool, with its many wrong turns and awkward silences, is one of the most egalitarian and sincere love stories I have come across in fantasy fiction. On the other side of the scale, Tomjon is a great creation, and I like what Pratchett says about destiny and kings through his character—for all this story is mostly about Shakespeare's stories, it also nicely undercuts some of the sillier notions of fantasy fiction, notably the legend of the lost king turning out to be exactly what his kingdom needs despite no actual training, a trope that Pratchett also plays with to great effect in the City Watch books. The relationship between Tomjon and his sidekick, the playwriting dwarf Hwel, is a pleasure to read.

Ultimately, the best thing about this book is that triad of witches: Granny Weatherwax, Nanny Ogg and Magrat Garlick, each such vibrant characters that they leave the rest in the shade. The scene in which the three of them perform a huge feat of magic, recharging broomsticks and flying around the kingdom to transport it in time, is epic and breathtaking—though any scene with the three of them in it makes me happy, even if it's them talking about cups of tea and what kind of sandwiches they like best.

After my *Wyrd Sisters* reread, I moved straight on to *Witches Abroad* (1991), which has always been one of my favourites: this is the Discworld novel which most effectively deals with the role of the witch in stories and fairytales, and is pure Ogg-Weatherwax-Magrat hilarity from beginning to end.

Only when listening to Nigel Planer read the unabridged book did I realise something I had never entirely noticed before: this is a fantasy novel in which all the important characters are women. This is a fantasy novel by a bestselling male author in which all the important characters are women. We have the trio of Granny Weatherwax, Nanny Ogg and Magrat, travelling to foreign parts. We have the witches/cooks of Genua: Lilith, Mrs Pleasant, and Mrs Gogol. We have Emberella, the hub around which the story is constructed. But the only male characters of any note are a) a frog turned into a prince who rarely speaks and is basically a Maguffin, b) a cat-turned-human who has no agency, barely any voice, and no personal needs beyond a bowl of fish-heads, c) a zombie, and, d) a dwarf one-note-joke about Casanova, who arrives in the final act and provides some comic relief. (Casanunda becomes a far more important character in later books, but really if it wasn't for that I'd not have bothered to mention him at all.)

How rare is it to find a book that does this? How rare to have a story with so many women in it that you don't even need a romance because the women already have plenty to do? In the fantasy genre. This revelation completely did my head in, forcing me to re-evaluate a novel that I had already loved for half my life.

Despite the glamour girls and snarky wenches which mostly populate the first decade of Discworld, the witch books redeem this period for me as a feminist reader. They are packed with female protagonists who are allowed to be as three dimensional, complicated, flawed and fascinating as Pratchett's best male protagonists, and are also allowed to be more important than the men in their stories.

But that's not the good news. The good news is that after this, Terry Pratchett only got better at writing women—and in particular, at writing young women who had a soul as well as (or even instead of) a great rack. There was Angua, Cheery, Agnes/Perdita, Susan Sto Helit and Sacharissa Crip-slock. There was even another book that featured all female protagonists (and no witches)...but I'll get to that eventually.

WANT MORE? Read the rest of the essays in *Pratchett's Women*.

THE GREAT ABRIDGED MOCKLORE CHRONOLOGICAL TIMELINE

AUTHOR'S NOTE: this timeline is a monster. The full version is forty pages long. It began because the second Mocklore book, *Liquid Gold*, involved time travel, and I had to keep track of things. Then it got a little…out of control, and suddenly I had outlined over a century of Mocklore history including the geneology of every major character and quite a few minor characters.

This version is highly abridged, to cover the fifty or so year period most relevant to the published Mocklore works, and the Bounty/Delta stories in particular. But you can definitely see the shape of several dozen more stories that I meant to write, and almost certainly won't get around to now…maybe. Possibly. We'll see.

The numbering of the years are for my benefit; in Mocklore, numbers are never used except unofficially. Year 1 marks the beginning of the reign of Timregis.

- **31 The Year of the Scarlet Skull-shaped Omen —** Nellisand Witchdaughter marries Vicious Bigbeard

Daggersharp. They launch a new ship, the *Saltwitch*. Delta and Theta Void born.

- **32 The Year of the Vampyre Aelves** — The Faerie Quene and the Faerie Prinse are banished behind the Icewall. Bounty Fenetre born to Sukie Fenetre and Lord Nanneke of the Hobgoblins. Someone claiming to be the Faerie Quene contacts Zibria, demanding a tithe of seven young people every seven years.

- **33 The Year of the Meaningful Comet** — Luc Triclover born to Ma Fortuna and Old Ticker Triclover. Imago Void launches a clockwork comet into the sky which returns every thirteen and a half years; whatever shape you see when you gaze at it is incredibly meaningful.

- **34 The Year of the Unnamed Plague** — Princess Keela becomes Lord of Teatime. Demond Death-Iris is made Prime Minister of Mocklore.

- **35 The Year of the Underworld Strike** — Sparrow found as baby in the Troll Triangle. Princess Svenhilda is born to Jarl Erik and Wench Brunlinde. Mindette Masters leaves the *Saltwitch* and goes to work at the Polyhedrotechnical in Cluft, founding the Department of Certain Death.

- **36 The Year of the Sculpted Concubine** — Kassa born to Vicious Bigbeard Daggersharp and Black Nell Witchdaughter. Daggar, Sparrow and Tione visit from twenty-three years in the future. Lady Talle of Zibria is born to Princess Medusa. (*Liquid Gold*)

- **37 The Year of the Knight of Knights** — Baron Camelot of Eaglesbog rescues the Empress Ilia Rose from the last giant dragon in Mocklore and is named Legendary Knight of Knights. Prince

Randolf of Skullcap accidentally falls down six flights of poisoned stairs and is killed. The *Saltwitch* is scuppered, and at Black Nell's insistence, is replaced with two ships, Bigbeard's *Dread Redhead* and Nell's *Splashdance*. Tybalt Ramses III arrives to join the crew of the *Dread Redhead*, but Bigbeard and Black Nell duel to see who gets the new crewmember. Nell wins.

- **38 The Year Cluft Mysteriously Vanished —** Empress Ilia Rose runs away with Baron Eaglesbog. Timregis hires warlocks to extend the Skullcaps far enough to swallow Eaglesbog completely (Cluft vanishes as a possible side effect). The Baron and Empress assume new identities – Tedd and Leda Smith, who open a Smithy and Embroidered Tapestry shop in Skullcap.
- **39 The Year of the Touchstone —** Panthas the Heartless (god of nasty tricks) casts down a huge rock from the heavens and abducts five mortal females to sit on top of it: Princess Medusa of Zibria, Black Nell Daggersharp, Chief Profit-scoundrel Hermiona, Wench Brunhilde of Axgaard and Princess Svenhilda. Young pirate Tybalt Ramses III rescues them. This was a prime incident cited as justification for the Decimalisation. Tithe.
- **40 The Year of the Triangular Trews**
- **41 The Year of the Bountiful Goose —** Prince Freifried, first son of Jarl Erik, is disgraced when he marries one of his father's Wenches, Melinor.
- **42 The Year of the Shiny Stone —** Abridged from "The Year of the Shiny Stone which our beloved Emperor caught sight of in a fountain and knighted it on the spot, keeping it as his best friend, confidante and bodyguard until getting into

a long argument with it about politics and having it executed."

- **43 The Year of Profit** — Daggar joins the Profithood. Zelora Footcrusher marries Braided Bones of the Languid Isles.
- **44 The Year of the Inside-Out Outback** — Teenagers Delta and Theta Void (assisted by Bounty Fenetre) visit the Outback for their switcher initiation and end up turning the Outback inside out—both lose many personae in the process. Sean McHagrty born.
- **45 The Year of Several Less Meaningful Comets** — Braided Bones joins the crew of the *Dread Redhead*. Bounty Fenetre joins the Triclover household. (*Hobgoblin Boots*)
- **46 The Year of the Superflood** — Zelora joins Hidden Army. Aragon Silversword becomes Imperial Champion. Griffin born to Tedd and Leda Smith. Hermiona dies, and leaves Daggar the Royal Seal of Gazparta. He uses it as a bootscraper. Clio born to Dahla Wagstaff-Lamont and Bleyn Silversword. Egfried Friefriedsson born to Friefried Jarlsson and Melinor. Tithe.
- **47 The Year those Blighted Mazes came Back** — The second maze invasion. Dahla Wagstaff-Lamont is killed in a house fire.
- **48 The Year Cluft Mysteriously Returned** — Princess Ranoma of Skullcap and her entourage accidentally squished by returned city. Vice-Chancellor Bertie of Cluft publishes a thesis on large, destructive magical activities.
- **49 The Year of the Twenty Trolls** — Bounty and Luc leave home to Seek Their Fortune. A rumour spreads that a new hero in the land slew twenty

trolls in one day, without a sword. Bounty enters the OtherRealm. (*Hobgoblin Boots*)

- **50 The Year of the Glimmer** — Kassa Daggersharp turns fourteen. Bleyn Silversword arrested for treason against the Emperor and executed by the Imperial Champion, his brother Aragon.

- **51 The Year of the Decimalisation** — Emperor Timregis reduces the number of Mocklore's gods to ten. *Splashdance* scuppered by Bigbeard Daggersharp. Kassa sent to finishing school, meets Talle of Zibria.

- **52 Year of the Frightened Hedgehogs** — Prince Radcliff of Skullcap caught in a stampede of hedgehogs and killed. The three sons of the Sultan of Zibria go a questing—only Prince Marmaduc returns in human form. Prince Bartfried killed in an accidental axe-thowing incident. Princess Bjornhilde of Axgaard joins the Order of Sparkling Nuns. Lady Luck, Amorata and Destiny decide that the greatest hero in Mocklore should decide which of them is most beautiful. Luc Triclover starts running. Bounty Fenetre returns from the OtherRealm. (*Hobgoblin Boots*)

- **53 Year of the Purple Plague** — Marmaduc XV becomes Sultan after his father dies of Purple Plague. He immediately proposes marriage to his 'cousin' Talle (technically his niece, though they are the same age) who runs away to hide in the imperial harem of Dreadnought. Having run out of heirs, Lord Rynehart of Skullcap tracks down his illegitimate children, Rorey and Ranessa. Aragon Silversword meets Bounty Fenetre. Final tithe. (*Queen of Courtesans*)

- **54 Year of the Tidal Puddle** — Princess Ranessa of Skullcap imprisoned for two counts of murder. Delta Void contracts herself to work for the Silver Warlock. Jarl Erik of Axgaard dies of the Purple Plague. His last son, Prince Thorfried, dies of an overdose of celebratory beer. Princess Svenhilda of Axgaard becomes Jarl Lordling of Axgaard, having run out of brothers. (*Delta Void and the Unicorn Soup, Delta Void's Day Off, Delta Void and the Clockwork Man, Delta Void and the Stray God*)
- **55 Year of the Dead Timregis** — Lord Rynehart of Skullcap accidentally poisoned by his wife. Prince Rorey becomes Lordling of Skullcap. Aragon Silversword assassinates Emperor Timregis, and is arrested by Prime Minister Death-Iris. A replacement Emperor steps in "to keep the peace"—the Silver Warlock.
- **56 Year of Too Many Emperors** — Braided Bones cursed. Princess Ranessa, begins as Professor of Assassination at the Polyhedrotechnical, and is promptly assassinated by Gootch, a mature age student. The Silver Warlock is removed from imperial office—literally—by the Profithood. Also ruling Mocklore this year: Emperor Bjornfried, Emperor Iulius (forcibly removed from the throne by his daughters the Void sisters), Emperor McHagrty I (former Captain of the Blackguards), Emperor Barnard, Emperor Lazarus, Emperor Boris (who brings Cutlass Cooper as his bodyguard), and Emperor Cutlass.
- **57 Year of Even More Emperors** — In which Mocklore is ruled by Emperor Cutlass, Emperor McHagrty II (son of McHagrty I), Emperor Pookie, Emperor Bear-face, Emperor

Superhuman, Emperor Minstrels (a band of wandering minstrels named Ion, Pale, Jorge and Stud-nose, who were in the wrong place at the wrong time), Emperor Frey, Emperor Silver Warlock (again), Emperor Abulus, Emperor Blackheart V (real name: Berthold Winebutter), Emperor Mustenny, Emperor Dianthus, and Emperor Silver Warlock (yet again). Kassa Daggersharp takes a job at the Whet and Whistle tavern.

- **58 The Year of the Second Glimmer** — Emperor Silver Warlock is challenged by the warlock Maarstigan, who wins by right of combat. After two months on the throne, Emperor Maarstigan implodes during a nasty alchemical incident. Talle the courtesan becomes the Lady Emperor. (*Splashdance Silver*)
- **59 The Year of the Plentiful Dandelions** — History of this year sequestered by order of the Brewmistress due to time travel complications. (*Liquid Gold.*)
- **60 Year of the Beautiful Lady** — AKA "Year that the Astoundingly Beautiful and Talented Lady Emperor discovered she had the Power to name each Year, all Hail the Lady Emperor." Kassa Daggersharp joins the Polyhedrotechnical College of Higher Learning as a professor.
- **61 Year of the Mystical Lake** — AKA "Year that the Glorious Empire of Mocklore was enriched by the reappearance of the long-lost Mystical Lake, all hail the Magnanimous and Humble Lady Emperor." Third and final maze invasion.
- **62 Year of the Historians** — AKA "The Year that the Lady Emperor got bored with naming the

Years and Returned that Duty to the capable hands
of her Historians, thank all the Gods."

- **63 Year of Drak** — The first-year intake at the
Polyhedrotechnical includes Sean McHagrty
(again), Clio Wagstaff-Lamont and Egfried
Friefriedsson. (*Ink Black Magic*)
- **83 Year of the Greyest Winter** — (Alternate
Reality) (*Liquid Gold*)

MOCKLORE CHRONICLES

Want more Mocklore? Do I have the books for you! The two original Mocklore novels in one volume.

SPLASHDANCE SILVER (Mocklore Chronicles #1)

Kassa Daggersharp has been avoiding her legacy as the daughter of infamous parents for far too long. But the death of her father, Vicious Bigbeard, leaves her the heir of a precious treasure trove, the Splashdance silver.

All she has to do is form a pirate crew from scratch, dodge the minions of the new Lady Emperor, learn how to control her long-neglected magic, and win the loyalty of the worst traitor in the history of the Mocklore Empire.

No problem, right?

LIQUID GOLD (Mocklore Chronicles #2)

The most seductively dangerous substance in the world is invented by Mocklore alchemists... and promptly stolen by a beautiful troll. This golden goo with the power of time travel causes havok throughout the Mocklore Empire, causing damage to reality and even the Underworld.

It's a problem for everyone, but especially for Kassa, whose unexpected death by trinket leaves her in a prime position to investigate what's going wrong in the land of the dead... while her crew, left behind, have to decide what their futures hold.

Comedy pirates, saucy witches, magical explosions, gratuitous historical trivia and flying sheep... it's just another day in Mocklore.

BUY THE MOCKLORE OMNIBUS TODAY!

INK BLACK MAGIC (Mocklore Chronicles #3)

Kassa Daggersharp has been a pirate, a witch, a menace to public safety, a villain, a hero and a legend. These days, she lives the quiet life, lecturing college students on the dangers of magic.

Egg Friefriedsson is Kassa's young cousin, a lapsed Axgaard warrior who would rather stay in his room and draw comics all day than train to be a warrior. If only comics had been invented.

All the adventures are over. It's time to get on with being a grownup. But when Egg's drawings produce an evil dark city full of villains and monsters, everyone starts to lose their grip on reality. Even the flying sheep.

It's getting harder to tell the difference between heroes and villains, but someone has to step up to save Mocklore, one last time.

BUY INK BLACK MAGIC TODAY!

The Gathering Hall was an immense cavern with bright bunting and fairy lights looped all around the walls. A huge mirror ball hung in the centre of it all, reflecting light outwards in a thoroughly misleading way.

Kassa, with a recently-released Aragon trailing behind her, was stopped at the door by a woman with disturbingly black lips. "You will remove all weapons before entering," she pronounced. Many weapons, most flickering from hidden to visible, were already heaped by the entrance.

Aragon had no weapons because they had already been taken from him by the mercenaries.

Kassa removed two daggers and a long coil of sharp wire from her right boot and pulled eighteen glittering spikes out of her left boot. Then she peeled up the hem of her dragon-scale coat, revealing several tiny darts which she handled very carefully. From her belt she discarded two leather pouches full of sand, a pair of embroidery shears and a small mace. From her bodice, she produced a whip with metallic edging. A slender, icy knife had been braided under her hair.

Aragon watched this disarming process thoughtfully.

Kassa looked up once and met his gaze. "I would not have been your prisoner long, Silversword. I did not need Daggar's pet army to rescue me."

"I believe you," he replied.

Having unloaded most of her concealed weapons, Kassa noticed that it was quite warm in the Gathering Hall, and she began to remove her dragon-scale coat.

Remembering the invisible gauze just in time, Aragon's hand grasped her shoulder firmly. "Trust me. Keep the coat on."

Kassa looked as if she was about to argue, until she too remembered what she was wearing under the coat. She gave him a twisted smile.

"That sword is a weapon, I believe," said the black-lipped woman.

"Tough," said Kassa, and she walked unmolested into the hall, grasping Bigbeard's sword firmly in one hand. Aragon followed her.

The music was loud and intrusive. Various executive mercenaries were dancing, drinking and brawling, in no particular order. Just as a flicker of interest in the music crossed Kassa's face, Daggar and Zelora appeared on either side of her and walked her into a corner of the room. "That sword," said Zelora crisply. "I believe it can tell you the location of the silver."

"Oh," said Kassa, shooting a dark look at Daggar. "You know about that, do you?"

Daggar eyed Aragon suspiciously. "What did yer bring him for?" he complained.

"It was him or a handbag," said Kassa breezily. "A girl can't go to a party without accessories. Isn't anyone going to offer me a drink?"

"Read the sword now," Zelora commanded, infuriated by this small talk.

Kassa gave her a long, cool stare. "I was planning t√o." The rubies in the hilt glittered menacingly. She found the hidden clasp and opened the secret compartment. The message slid out, revealing the scratchy letters of a forgotten language. Kassa read it carefully, frowning.

"Well?" said Daggar greedily. "Where's our silver, then?"

"My silver," corrected Kassa absently. "And I have absolutely no idea where it is."

~

The goblins in these caves were just like any other. They squished together in the smallest holes, they smelled like dirt, they watched the interesting bits of the world when they chose to, particularly when the Smug Family was on. But these goblins differed from the rest of their kind in one respect. These goblins actually had a vague sort of purpose. They were guarding.

Every now and then these squirmy, dirty little creatures would come out of their holes to explore, stretch their legs, beat each other up or go for scampers. But mostly they came out of their holes to play with the silver.

~

Zelora Footcrusher remained quite calm under the circumstances. She took a deep breath and led them all to a little ante-cave full of empty buffet tables. Only then did she actually breathe out. A moment, later, she exploded. "You can't read it?"

"I didn't say that," said Kassa. "Of course I can read it. It's Old Troll. The most complicated and highly devious of dead dialects. Not even trolls know how that language works any more." She shook her head. "I really don't understand my father. He devotes ten years to learning an ancient long-lost language, and he still writes his letters in crayon."

"So if you can read it, what's the problem?" asked Daggar, sounding a bit desperate.

"Listen to this," said Kassa scornfully. "Where the strongest swimmer reaches, far beyond the hills and beaches, down into the goblin's space, hidden where the trolls give chase. Hah! It's a children's rhyme, or something equally stupid."

Zelora's eyes were distant for a moment. "It is gibberish," she said crisply, and then she stalked away at a steady, reasonable pace.

"She knows," said Kassa quietly. "Daggar, she knows something!"

When money was involved, Daggar could move surprisingly fast. He headed off Zelora's escape route. "We can do this the easy way," he said pleasantly. "Which means that you help us, and we give you a share of our silver."

"My silver," said Kassa firmly.

"Her silver," Daggar corrected himself without missing a beat. "Or we can do it the hard way, which means that no one gets happy. Which is it to be, Footcrusher?"

Zelora glared at all of them, her eyes glinting in a fetching shade of red. "You will relinquish your claims to the gargoyle?" she asked after a moment.

"You married him," said Kassa with a careless shrug. "We've got a few days until full moon. It's up to you what happens while he's in manform."

Zelora pondered in silence. "Very well," she said finally. "I will show you and Daggar what the riddle means, as long as you honour your deal with the Hidden Leader." She glared at Aragon. "But not him. This one is not to be trusted."

"Silversword comes," said Kassa in a hard voice.

Zelora looked surprised, but not as surprised as Aragon himself.

"Ey?" said Daggar in bewilderment. "Can I jump in here with the stupid question and ask why yer willing to give this blatant villain another chance?"

Kassa looked at Aragon and couldn't honestly think of a good reason. "Because," she said firmly.

A weakness, thought Aragon Silversword. *All the better to kill you with...*

PRAISE FOR SPLASHDANCE SILVER

"Magical. Such detail. A bloody blast."

— LISA GORMLEY

"A fun read!"

— ROWENA CORY DANIELLS

"Roberts throws a bunch of fantasy tropes into a blender, and the result is a high speed, joyous adventure."

— RENE SEARS

"Immensely enjoyable and hard to put down."

— RIVQA RAFAEL

SHORT FICTION:

Love and Romanpunk

Please Look After This Angel & other winged stories

NON-FICTION & ESSAYS

It's Raining Musketeers

Pratchett's Women

50 Roman Mistresses

CREATURE COURT

(rerelease coming in 2019)

Power & Majesty

The Shattered City

Reign of Beasts

Cabaret of Monsters

ABOUT THE AUTHOR

Tansy Rayner Roberts lives in a messy house with lots of bookshelves. Sometimes the Tasmanian landscape still looks like Mocklore to her, but she has yet to spot a flying sheep.

Tansy is the winner of Hugo, Washington Small Press, Aurealis and Ditmar Awards. She writes about pirates, witches, superheroes, fairy tale newspapers and magical share houses. When not writing, she runs a literary gift shop on Etsy: Alice & Austen.

You can listen to Tansy across three different podcasts: Galactic Suburbia, providing a feminist point-of-view of the SF publishing world; Verity! six smart women talking about Doctor Who; and Sheep Might Fly, where Tansy reads aloud her stories as audio serials.

Support Tansy's Patreon to receive all kinds of rewards, including ebooks, exclusive stories and more.

Follow TansyRR at:
tansyrr.com/
news@tansyrr.com